W9-AEU-411

CITADEL RUN

CITADEL RUN

by

PAUL BISHOP

ASBURY PARK PUBLIC LIBRARY
ASBURY PARK, NEW JERSEY

This is a work of fiction. All the characters and events
portrayed in this book are fictional, and any resemblance to
real people or incidents is purely coincidental.

CITADEL RUN

Copyright © 1987 by Paul Bishop

All rights reserved, including the right to reproduce this book or
portions thereof in any form.

First printing: January 1988

A TOR Book

Published by Tom Doherty Associates, Inc.
49 West 24th Street
New York, NY 10010

ISBN: 0-312-93047-X

Library of Congress Catalog Card Number: 87-50875

Printed in the United States of America

0   9   8   7   6   5   4   3   2   1

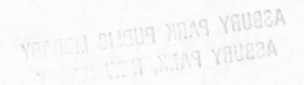

For my wife, Elaine,
who never doubted,
and always smoothed the road
with her infinite patience.

PART ONE

TORCHSONG

I hear the alarms at dead of night,
I hear the bells—shouts
I pass the crowd—I run.
The sight of the flames maddens me with pleasure.

—WALT WHITMAN,
"A Song of Joy"

ONE

CALICO

THE TALL MAN in the black-leather chaps smacked himself in the forehead with the callused palm of his right hand. He did it again with his left hand. Again with the right. Again with the left. He shook his shoulders left and right, stamped his boots into the dust, and breathed sharply, making *whoosh*ing sounds through his mouth. Stall walking was the same for every rodeo cowboy; a time alone in the midst of activity, a time to center your "try" before taking your wrap.

The noise of the crowded arena behind him had become one monotonous background roar, and the rich, heavy sweat smells of animal stock settled around him with the comfort of an old overcoat.

Sharp words cut into his concentration.

"Keegan's up, Calico!"

Closing his eyes, "Calico" Jack Walker heard the chunk of the chute gate opening, and the rising screams of the audience drowning out the noise of a passing jet. In his mind he watched a ton and a half of Brahma bull buck and twist Bill Keegan into a living bruise, his imagination so intense he could almost feel the pain.

The eight-second horn sounded and applause ex-

3

ploded. Shit! Calico thought to himself. He didn't bother to listen to the announcer's metallic voice spilling enthusiastically from the P.A. system.

Jazzbo Brenner poked Calico in the ribs with an elongated finger. "Great ride. It was a great ride. You're going to have to go some to beat him, Calico," he said, emphasizing a point already abundantly clear. "You ready?"

Calico opened his eyes and looked at Jazzbo's greasepaint-smeared face and bright, baggy clothing. You wouldn't believe to look at the animated rodeo clown that he was the most reserved of the rebel cops on the morning watch. "Yeah, I'm ready. You just be ready when Number 98 decides to have me for lunch."

"I've never let you down before."

Calico smiled at his friend and headed for the bucking chute. Why in the hell was he still playing cowboy at fifty plus years old, he wondered silently. It was obvious there would always be some young turk, like Keegan, trying to bring down the old guard. Somehow, though, it went against everything inside him to give up without a fight.

The International Police Rodeo Association held five rodeos a year around the country with one more in Canada. Calico had made all of them since the inception of the association, but this one, held just outside Los Angeles in Burbank, was the largest and the most important. For the past three years running he'd snatched up the all-round cowboy honors given for the best performance in the three riding events: saddle bronc, bareback, and bull.

Calico had been falling off stock ever since he was five years old, when his father sat him on a donkey backward and jumped him over a picket fence. Later he'd followed the professional "suicide circuit" until the Marines felt it was time to teach him how to be a man and sent him off to Korea.

He caught the tail end of the "police action" there. It was enough. He'd served under Lewis "Chesty" Puller at the frozen Chosan reservoir. Twenty thousand Marines surrounded on all sides by North Koreans. Puller had told them to go out and kick ass, and they did. All the way home. More scared of Puller than of any enemy.

When he got back stateside, he'd hired on with the police force in Los Angeles. It was a stopover until he had enough of a poke saved to head down the rodeo trail again. Somehow that set of circumstances never seemed to arrive. Police work infected him, and working the street became as much of an addiction as the rodeo. When the International Police Rodeo Association came into existence, though, Calico became a charter member. It gave him a chance to return to an old lover without having to leave his current mistress.

The first time he had captured the all-round title it had been nothing more than staying the distance on all his stock. The following year the competition had been a bit tougher, the young turks on the rise, and the previous year he had been lucky to win. This year he felt he'd be lucky just to walk away.

Keegan had taken second in the saddle-bronc competition, Calico third. In bareback the positions had been reversed, and now it was all down to the bull riding. Keegan's ride had been well executed, his animal performing better than expected. As a result the two judges scored him high with a combined total of 188. It was going to take a hell of a ride to beat it.

Under a rain-threatening sky the whitewashed boards of the bucking chute creaked and bulged from the inside as Number 98 declared his presence. Calico looked at the bull through the cracks in the boards, seeing him for what he was: a rogue man-hater.

He'd sweated the bull after drawing its number from an old coffee can, and learned he couldn't have a bet-

ter mount for what he needed to do. Number 98 had
never been ridden for the full eight before, so there
was no doubting the bull's performance. The responsibility for a high score rested on the rider.

"Fit?" asked Ray Perkins from the side of the chute
where he was ready to help cinch up the bucking rigging.

"Sure. No problem," Calico replied tensely. "Eight
seconds ain't any longer than eternity, is it?"

Perkins laughed as Calico pulled a rosin-soaked
leather glove from his rear pocket and slipped it on his
riding hand. The palm of the hand had a piece of skin
the size of a silver dollar missing from the middle, and
Calico saw Perkins looking at it with concern.

"Don't go worrying yourself, now, over something
nothing can be done about," he told his old squad-car
partner. "Tore it in the bareback, but it's gone as
numb as a dick full of novocaine."

"Come off it! How are you going to hang on with
your hand in that condition?" Perkins asked, using a
shoelace to tie the glove in place.

"Guess I don't have much choice, do I? I'm going to
use a finger wrap."

"Are you out of your mind? This bull spins toward
your riding hand! If you come off on the wrong side
you'll get hung up!" Perkins held onto Calico's wrist.

"It's the only chance I've got to ride this bastard."

"You're crazy!"

"Yeah, I know." Calico slipped his hand between
the boards and climbed up to the top of the chute,
swung his legs across it, and looked down at the most
repulsive chunk of animal he ever wanted to see.
Number 98 was 1,800 pounds of gristle and meanness,
more than a match for an old cop's 200 pounds of
aches and pains.

"Okay, hotshot," Perkins said from below him,

"just don't break up the ambulance crew's poker game."

Calico smiled briefly and lowered himself onto the hurricane deck of the bull's back. Number 98 snorted, giving him a faceful of fetid, steaming breath. Unlike broncs who are happy to just dump their rider and run, Brahma bulls tote a grudge, living for the chance to sink a horn into human flesh.

The flat, rosined braid of the bucking rigging slipped easily over Calico's riding hand, and Perkins pulled the rigging tight, like a man pulling a bucket out of a well, until Calico nodded his head. Taking the free end of the rope, Calico laid it across his palm. Then, instead of just wrapping it behind his hand and across the palm again, he brought the tail of the rope between his third and little fingers first. Ray Perkins shook his head sadly, but Calico ignored him. With the fist of his free hand, he pounded his riding hand shut around the rigging and pulled hard. There was no give in the rope, and the bell attached below the bull's brisket clanked loudly.

The voice from the P.A. system boomed out over the crowded arena. "Next up is IPRA's returning all-round champion, 'Calico' Jack Walker, on Number 98. He's going to have to turn in a tough ride this time out, folks, if he hopes to hang onto his title. Good luck, Calico!"

Hauling himself into shape, Calico dragged his thighs over the loose, wrinkled skin of the bull's hide until they were as close to his riding hand as possible. There was a second of time waiting for Number 98 to square himself, and then Calico nodded go; the fleece-lined strap around the bull's flanks was yanked tight, and the chute burst open.

One one-thousand. Number 98's first leap out of the chute was a spectacular aerial display worthy of the

Blue Angels, ending suddenly with straight-leg impact designed to jar every bone of its human cargo. Calico held his shape, body hunched close to his riding hand, free arm grabbing air and balance. He was grinning from ear to ear. The storm engulfed him, leaving nothing between life and the devil except his own skill and determination.

Two one-thousand. With incredible speed and power the Brahma twisted toward Calico's riding hand, throwing its horns over its own withers in an attempt to gore a human leg. Calico reacted immediately. Anticipating the beast's move, he dug a good hold with the blunt spur of his inside foot, and clawed the outside spur high over the bull's shoulder. Number 98 roared in pain and twisted back the other way, trying to gore anything on either side, or smash something with the hard poll on the top of its head.

Three one-thousand. Calico's neck snapped backward, hard, as Number 98 bucked and jerked in a rage, but he still got in several good-scoring licks with his spurs before the bull began twisting again.

Four one-thousand. There was no way to dummy the ride out, Number 98 was like a firecracker with dynamite in both ends. He bucked skyward and sunfished his belly, rolling it upward on either side toward the sun, like he knew his own reputation as a mankiller was on the line. His head fought left and right, his horns searching viciously for a target in the muscled form astride his back.

Five one-thousand. Vision blurred, head pounding, ears ringing, tailbone jammed halfway up the spinal column, riding hand tearing apart. No chance to change strategy as the bull twisted in instead of out like it had done in the past.

Six one-thousand. Calico's nose started to bleed, pouring red corpuscles down his chin and splattering the chest and arms of his white shirt as Number 98 twisted beneath him.

Seven one-thousand. The bull bucked, threw his belly up, hit the ground straight-legged, and spun toward Calico's riding hand. To compensate, Calico pushed out desperately with his riding hand. He was so, so close. Unwillingly his riding arm was fatally straightened, leaving no elasticity between himself and Number 98, who had the taste of victory in his mouth.

Eight . . . Calico lost his shape and started to slide, spurs clawing for any kind of purchase. His grip opened involuntarily, and the bucking rigging began to slip across his palm. *No way! No way!* Calico screamed internally, and then the rigging caught between his entwined fingers . . . one-thousand.

The time horn sung out like the coming of angels, but the Brahma didn't care. He bucked and twisted again as the burden on its back tried to jump clear. There was no grace in the dismount. Calico bounced off on the wrong side of the bull, nearest his riding hand, and found his fingers still trapped in the rigging strap. Like a rag doll in heat, he slammed into the bull's side and caught the flat of a horn across his ribs for the effort. There was no air in his lungs, and he was only vaguely aware of Jazzbo Brenner throwing himself with suicidal abandon on Number 98's back and pulling his riding hand loose. Free of the rigging, Calico dropped to the pulverized ground and instinctively rolled away from the Brahma's slashing hooves.

Jazzbo and Ed Martin, the other rodeo clown, drew the enraged bull away from its human quarry, and an army of helping hands dragged Calico from the arena.

"I got the ride . . . He never touched me!" Calico told the confusion around him.

"You're crazy as a loon! You're an idiot! Why did you have to hang on?" Ray Perkins yelled at him.

"I got the ride, damnit! I got the fucking ride!" Calico screamed back.

There was more confusion, more pain, especially in his ribs, as Calico was loaded on a stretcher and hustled to the first-aid room. The portable X-ray machine was wheeled in and radiation took a couple of steps closer to sterilizing the world. The doctor came, went, returned, and went again. Calico found himself pushed, poked, and bounced worse than a repeat ride on Number 98. Finally there was the bliss of silence and aloneness. He closed his eyes and gave over to the pain.

He didn't know how long he'd kept his eyes closed, but when he opened them there was a woman sitting beside him holding his hand in her lap. Her blond hair was thick and lustrous, cut in the page-boy style currently back in vogue. It framed a heart-shaped face with cool blue eyes and a Cupid's bow mouth. Her body was slipped into skintight jeans and a frilly blouse which emphasized the slimness of her hips and the swell of her large breasts.

Calico took one look at her and snapped his eyes closed again. "Oh, shit! I've died and gone to Hell!" He pulled his hand back.

"It's nice to see you too, Walker!" Her voice still carried the same whine which had grated on Calico for the entire ten years of their marriage.

"Marsha, don't you know ex-wives are supposed to leave their ex-husbands alone? That's why they call them ex-wives."

"When will you grow up and realize you're going to kill yourself if you keep playing these stupid, childish games?" Marsha's cheeks were filled with color, and her voice had risen quickly to a shriek. It made Calico smile.

"I became a policeman so I wouldn't have to grow up," he replied, and was suddenly aware again of the pain in his ribs. "What does the doctor say this time?" he asked.

Marsha stood up from beside the first-aid cot and straightened her designer jeans over her eel-skin boots. "Nothing serious, he claims. Half a dozen bruised ribs, couple of hairline cracks. There may be more but you'll have to wait for the swelling to go down before anyone can tell for sure. You were lucky, again."

Calico nodded his head and groaned. Lucky, right. "Have they announced the all-round champion yet?"

"Calico! You piss me off so much I can't stand it! You're laying there, all busted up inside, and all you're worried about is some stupid rodeo championship!"

"I love it when you talk dirty, Marsha. How come you never did that when we were married?"

"God, you're a bastard. I hate you." Marsha had her voice under control again, and just stood glaring at Walker.

He grinned. "So that's why you divorced me. I thought it was because I left the toilet seat up or something."

"Ooooh!" Color rushed back to her cheeks, and Marsha looked around for something to throw. Anticipating her, Calico sprung off the cot to grab her. He didn't make it, the pain in his ribs driving him flat again.

"Calico!" Marsha knelt down over him, anger replaced by concern.

"I'm all right, woman. I'm all right." He coughed and pushed himself gingerly to a sitting position. "Just what are you doing here anyway?"

"I came with Sal Fazio."

"Oh, come on! Not Sergeant Sally. Haven't you realized yet he only takes you out because he thinks it gets to me?"

"Did you ever stop to think maybe I only go out with him because I know it gets to you?"

"Yeah, well . . ." Calico paused to rub his ribs tenderly. "That still doesn't explain why you're dithering over me here. You told me once you'd had enough of that when we were married."

"I did and I'm not here for a booster dose. I came to give you this." Marsha picked up a voluminous carry-all bag from beside the cot and extracted a legal-size buff envelope. She dropped it in Calico's lap.

"What's this?"

"It's a subpoena. I'm taking you back to court. I want my share of your pension."

"What! You can't do that, Marsha. I bought you out of my pension when we got divorced eight years ago. You got a cash settlement. That's all you get." Calico's color was up now, and it was Marsha's turn to smile. She did it sweetly, like a cat twisting a barbecue stick into a canary.

"Sal says I can get more. He says there's been new legislation and if I take you back to court I can get half your pension for the ten years we lived together."

"And just where did Sweet Sally get his information?"

"Don't call him that! He's just passed his bar exam and was at a lawyer's business luncheon."

"A regular Conan the Rotarian, huh? Come on, Marsha, we don't need to do this. If you're hurting for spare change, I'll keep sending you the child-support money you'll lose when Ren turns eighteen next week."

"I just want what's mine, Calico. I don't need any handouts from you."

"Oh, right." Calico stood up in exasperation. "You

just want half of the pension it took me thirty years to earn, and which I paid a huge chunk of change to buy you out of. Is that what you mean by getting what's yours?"

"I earned ten years' worth of that pension as much as you did!" Marsha angrily shoved her face toward Calico's, the four-inch heels on her boots making up only part of the size difference. "I put up with all the bullshit you and your asshole partners pulled, like that time you and Wild John got drunk after work and you had him call me and tell me you were dead!"

Calico couldn't help but laugh at the memory.

"You bastard!" Marsha swung a closed fist and struck Calico on the arm. He backed away, fending her off while still laughing. "We'd only been married two months! I almost killed myself before you came home, I loved you that much!" Marsha struck out at him again, tears running down her face.

"And there was that time, when I was pregnant with Ren, and you and Wild John raced to Tijuana and back in the police car during morning watch. Had your pictures taken with the little Mexican man and his moth-eaten donkey. It was a stupid thing to do. You jeopardize your whole career, our life together, for what? A few laughs, a reputation? You never stopped doing those things. You and the rest of your Peter Pan buddies!" She hit him again and again in the arms until he grabbed her hands and forced them down.

"Okay. Okay." His ribs felt like they were being torn apart. "You're right, I've done some crazy things, but I don't regret one of them. And don't ever try to make out you didn't know what you were getting into. You loved the wildness. It was why you married me."

"People change, Calico."

"Only if they want to. I never have."

"No, you never have." Marsha had calmed down

somewhat, but she still pulled her hands forcefully out of Calico's grip before turning away to pick up her purse again. She took out a pack of Kools and a lighter.

"I'll see you in court." She followed the statement up with a puff of smoke, a turned back, and a scuffling of high-heeled boots.

"Do you know how much your ass wiggles when you stalk around in those boots?" Calico called after her before she got out the tent exit.

"Drop dead!"

"Then you'd never get my pension."

"Fuck you, asshole!" came the final note from outside.

Calico grunted and sat back on the cot, throwing the subpoena on the floor. The doctor came back in looking harried and disgruntled. He produced yards and yards of ace bandage and began wrapping it around Calico's torso.

"Ace bandages, the universal cure-all, huh, Doc?" Calico asked. "I understand you can get them in prescription strength now for acne and nose colds." He winced as the diminutive doctor pulled the bandages tight and then handed him a slip of paper.

"Here's a prescription for pain killers. You'll need them by morning." The doctor's bedside manner was terse to say the least.

"I've got to go to work in the morning. Eleven o'clock tonight, actually."

"There's no way you're going to be up to that. You'll be lucky if you can get up to go to the bathroom by tomorrow."

"Doc, I haven't taken a sick day off work since I got on the force, that'll be thirty years next Sunday, and I ain't about to take one now because of a few bruised ribs."

"You're crazy if . . ."

"Why does everybody keep telling me that?" Calico interrupted. "It's my body, I know what it can take."

The doctor shook his head and moved out of the tent without further comment. Cowboys and cops, there was no arguing with them. Calico followed the silent exit with his eyes and saw a familiar figure standing by the tent flap.

"Hey, Ren. How you doing, boy?" Calico threw the doctor's prescription on the tent floor next to the subpoena, and waved his son inside.

"Better 'n you by the looks of it," Ren Walker answered his father. "Berserko come by and give you a bad time?" He was as tall as his father, but graced with his mother's slimness. His fine brown hair was cut short, and businesslike glasses protected his washed-out blue eyes. Like his father, his face wasn't model handsome, but instead was made up of lines and angles, giving it a rugged appearance. Most women liked it.

"How many times I got to tell you not to call your mother that?" Calico reached for his shirt on the back of the cot and struggled to put it on. Ren didn't offer to help. He knew better.

"I've lived with her for eighteen years. That's seven more than you did. I think I've got a handle on what she's really like," Ren retorted sharply.

"It still don't make it right, you calling her names. She never let you want for anything."

"Let me tell you something, Pop. Most kids get all broken up inside when their parents get divorced. After ten years of seeing how Mom treated you, I couldn't have been happier when you two split."

"She loves you, Ren."

"Only when it suits her."

The two men were silent as Calico did up his shirt buttons and stood up to tuck it in.

"Anyway," Ren said eventually, "I've got another surprise for you." He handed his father a sheaf of papers.

"This is my day for surprises. What is it this time?"

"It's the charter license for King Harbor."

"You mean we got it?" Calico's face lit up with a huge grin.

"Yeah, we did. I found a boat too."

"No kidding. Where?

"Newport Beach. It's an Egg Harbor. A forty-six footer, high bow and low stern, supercharged Caterpillar twin diesels, and forward fly bridge. Draws three feet. Everything we've been looking for." Excitement danced behind Ren's glasses as he spoke.

"How much?"

"With full instrumentation, a hundred and ten thousand. You got to come down and have a look at it. It's beautiful."

"You got it. How about tomorrow after I get off work? About ten o'clock okay?" Affectionately, Calico reached out and grasped his son's arm. "Ren, are you sure this is what you want to do? Helping your old man get started in the charter fishing business ain't exactly riding in the fast lane. And what about your writing and the job with that fancy newspaper?"

"Pop"— Ren turned serious—"I can't wait for you to retire next week and get into something new. I've been planning it for as long as you have. It will finally give me the chance to catch up on all those years when you weren't there. I'm doing this for me, not you. I can still write, and the newspaper will always be there. I need to get some college behind me before they take me seriously anyway, and I can do that while we're working together."

The two men smiled at each other and then Calico's expression changed.

"Shit! Who won the all-round?"

Ren laughed. "Was there ever any doubt? Number 98's a beaten bull. You scored 191. Beat that young upstart, Keegan, all to death."

Calico smiled again. "Well, then. Let me get out of here and pick up my prize money. I need the cab fare home."

As they walked out of the tent, they both saw Sal Fazio entering one of the portable toilets. Calico looked at Ren who grinned mischievously back at him.

"No, we couldn't do a thing like that, could we?" Calico asked his son, both working on the same wavelength.

"No. It just wouldn't be right," Ren responded. Both men, though, had turned away from the rodeo arena and were sneaking up on the occupied convenience.

Giggling like naughty school boys, they silently slipped a discarded length of rope around the cubical and tied it securely with a couple of half hitches. They laughed louder.

"What's going on out there?" asked Fazio from inside. "Is that you, Walker? I'll have your ass if you do something stupid!"

Calico and Ren had tears of laughter flowing down their faces as they pushed the toilet over onto its door. Fazio screamed from inside. "Walker, I'll kill you, you asshole!"

Around the two men, other cowboys, tired from the day's events, stopped loading their horses and joined in the laughter. The police band in the background was playing "Good-bye, Old Paint" as the sun broke partially through the purple-gray sky. Ren and Calico saluted the now bouncing, overturned convenience as if it contained an admiral gone down with his ship.

Calico snapped off his salute and grabbed the exposed collection bag beneath the toilet and shook it vigorously. "Watch closely, boy. You have to make sure the contents get distributed evenly. It's a fine art, but, if you work hard, you too can become a professional asshole."

Ren couldn't stop laughing. "Where the hell did you get your mean streak, Pop?" he asked, gasping for breath.

"Mail-order catalog. Came free with a complete collection of Elvis records."

TWO

TAMIKO

―――――

TINA TAMIKO TRIED to slip unobtrusively into the roll-call room, but her briefcase clattered against the edge of the doorjamb, turning the heads of the twenty or so uniformed cops listening to the start of the nightly ritual.

"What happened, Blanche? Fingernail polish didn't dry in time to get here?" A tall, gangly cop with bad acne scars peppering his cheeks like a lunar landscape got a half-hearted laugh from the line. Tina didn't recognize him and ignored the jest. She put her briefcase down with the row of others along the back wall and slipped into an empty seat next to her partner in the back row. The fact she managed daily to get all the equipment on her Sam Browne belt—ammo pouch, radio holder, baton, handcuff case with a leg restrainer cord looped over it, mace, and holstered .38 Smith and Wesson stainless-steel four-inch—around her almost-nonexistent waist was something even Ripley didn't believe.

"I was under the impression morning-watch roll call started at 2300 hours, Tamiko. Have I been wrong for the last twenty-five years?" Lieutenant Heller loved giving probationers a bad time. Promptness was one of his pet peeves.

"No, sir. I'm sorry. It won't happen again," Tina answered quickly. She felt a burning blush rise up her neck. It made her angry. She was only six days away from the end of probation, yet she still felt intimidated by the old-timers. Thirty seconds late and they were making a big deal out of it. Hell, if it had been Calico or one of the others they would have had a smart comeback to make everyone laugh. She could never seem to get her tongue in gear fast enough.

"Okay with you if I take roll call now?" the lieutenant asked condescendingly. Without waiting for an answer he went back to reading off his deployment sheet.

"Brenner and Martin, nine-A-sixty-nine."

"Here!" Jazzbo Brenner and Ed Martin, sans clown makeup, both answered up from behind a litter pile of empty coffee cups and overflowing ashtrays which echoed the decor around them.

The two side walls of the room displayed pin maps of the area's reporting districts, each one kept up-to-date by a civilian volunteer to show the most recent crime stats. Most of the cops never looked twice at them. The back wall, festooned with suspect information and composites, fed them the type of information they were hungry for. If crime went down, fine. If it didn't, that was fine, too. But if you wanted to go home at the end of your shift, you better be damn sure you knew who the bad guys were.

"Walker and Tamiko, nine-A-twenty-one."

Calico and Tina answered up and accepted their regular car assignment.

"Perkins and . . ." the lieutenant continued to call roll from his raised desk at the front of the room, but Tina tuned him out.

"Who's the loudmouth with the crater face?" she asked Calico, swiveling the rotating seat of her floor-bolted chair toward her partner. "And who the hell is he calling Blanche?"

Calico laughed softly. "That's Guy Stack. You'll get used to him. You just have to remember he hates women, especially women cops. Calls all females Blanche. He thinks it's funny."

"It isn't."

"If you say so."

"Where did he and all these other guys come from anyway?"

"He and the black grizzly sitting next to him are part of the Metro task force brought in to help track down the idiot setting all the fires in the north end."

"You mean Torchsong?" Tina remembered catching snatches of something on the radio news reports over the past couple of weeks.

Calico scratched his right arm just under the two chevron strips identifying him as a P-3 training officer. "Yeah. The fire department has asked us to help out. They've sent one of their arson investigators over to fill us in."

Tina looked up to the front of the room and saw a sandy-haired man in a gray suit with a silver Fire Department badge hanging from his breast pocket. He was sitting in the first row next to two sergeants.

Heller finished up giving out car assignments. "Sergeant Zeloff will be nine-L-thirty, and Sergeant Mellor nine-L-forty. Sergeant Fazio is nine-L-twenty, but he's going to be a little late."

There was a spontaneous outburst of laughter from the back of the room by those in the know.

"Did I say something funny?" asked Heller, loosening off a heavy scowl directly at Calico who sat looking innocent and cherubic. Rembrandt would have found him irresistible. The laughter stopped immediately.

"Okay, listen up!" Heller continued, his voice dropping two octaves. He'd heard somewhere it was a good way of getting a group's attention. All it really did, though, was give the troops fodder for impolite impersonations. "We're going to skip reading the rotator announcements tonight since we've got a lot of other stuff to cover . . ." The assembled cops cheered briefly, rotator announcements being just about the most boring things in existence, especially as the manual stated they would be read three days in a row in case anybody who was on a day off missed them. Repetition, the Bible of the bureaucrat. "You can see we've got half a dozen Metro units working uniform in the division tonight on the Torchsong task force."

"The department loves task forces," Calico said sotto voce to Tina. "They always make it seem like something is being accomplished."

Heller carried on, "Since this is a problem all of you should be aware of, Investigator Shields from the fire department's arson squad is here to brief you."

Shields stood up from his chair, turned to face the officers, and then planted his spreading butt on the table behind him. An out-of-date pair of horn-rim glasses perched on his thin nose, but somehow he carried an air of competence.

"I'm sure you've read in the papers, or heard about the crackpot they're calling Torchsong," Shields started out and was reassured to see he had everyone's attention. "He's responsible for two warehouse and three apartment building fires here in Van Nuys division, and one just the other side of the border in North Hollywood division. Once the newsboys found out we had connected all the fires to the same 'torch,' they came up with the 'Torchsong' tag since the first fire burned down a building which had originally been a music emporium."

"Sounds like their editorial departments should be

writing for late-night television," said Ray Perkins. Like most of the other cops around him, he was wearing the short-sleeve summer uniform shirt which didn't require a tie. Unlike most of the other morning-watch coppers, except for the sprinkling of probationers, his badge was shiney and his combat boots spit-shined. He'd never really put Marine boot camp behind him.

Shields gave a half laugh of agreement before continuing. "Even though the journalists have managed to make the problem sound like a bad *Kojak* plot, the fires are occurring and we have to do something about them.

"There's little doubt the suspect lives somewhere in this division and has limited transportation, that's probably why the fires have been so close together locationwise." Shields paused to clear his throat and adjust his glasses.

"Do you think he's a gang member since most of the fires have been in the area of the Blythe Street barrio," Calico queried.

"No, definitely not. We're as sure as we can be in a situation like this that the firebug is a juvenile. We're also fairly certain he's of Latino descent because of the location of the fires, occurring in the barrio area as you pointed out. However, the traditional profile of a firebug like this makes him almost positively a loner with poor self-esteem, an extremely unstable home-life, and a substandard intelligence level. He probably has poor physical capabilities and could possibly even be deformed. There is a slim chance it could be two suspects working together, one acting in a passive capacity as an audience for the other, but it's unlikely."

"You keep saying 'he.' Is there any chance 'he' is a 'she'?" Tina spoke up for the first time.

"Equal rights for female firebugs? Huh, Blanche?"

Tina didn't need to look around the room to know who made the crack.

Shields waited for the small amount of laughter to pass. "Chances are slim the firebug is a female. Nine hundred and ninety-nine times out of a thousand a pyromaniac is a male. Once in a while a female pops up, but not often. Kind of like your indecent-exposure suspect.

"Our arson squad has investigated all of the fires, of course, but, to be blunt, there are no clues in the clues closet and things are getting scary. Our bug is becoming more and more sophisticated as he goes along. It appears, from the kind of incendiary devices he's using, he has access to a copy of *The Anarchist's Cookbook, The Poor Man's James Bond,* or some other similar publication. He isn't worried about human life either, the death toll is up to fifteen, most of them kids and mothers who were overcome by smoke before they could get out of the rat warrens they called homes." Shields' monotone had taken on the weary edge reflected in the serious faces of his audience.

"Where do we come in?" asked Calico, breaking the silence which had temporarily descended.

"The Torchsong task force will be out patrolling the barrio area, stopping all possible suspects. All the fires have gone down between 0200 hours and 0400. During that period we want all of you to be especially aware of any possible fire activity in your areas. If a fire is started and you respond to the scene, keep your eyes on the crowds. Chances are our suspect is going to be among them, getting his gratification from watching the flames and all the other activity. Any questions?"

When nobody took the opportunity to respond, Lt. Heller dismissed the assembly. "Let's get out there. Communications is backed up ten calls and they're threatening to hold P.M. watch over." Everyone groaned, but the older, more experienced training officers still took their time getting up. The scramble to check out cars and shotguns was left to their enthusiastic recruits, who swarmed around the kit room like so many blind pigglets searching for a tit.

"Who's your little slanty-eyed recruit? She a spinner?"

Calico looked over his shoulder at Guy Stack. Somewhere in the dim past he remembered having worked with Stack. The impression in his mind was of an egotistical jerk who never stopped talking and was given to overreaction. Competent, but a pain in the cajungas. "Stack, you've got about as much class as a wet fart at a ladies social. Next thing you'll ask me if her gash runs from side to side instead of back to front."

"Does it?" Stack sounded intrigued.

Calico shook his head in amazement. "Why don't you ask her yourself. I've got no idea."

"Sure you don't. You expect me to believe you're hitting the hole with her on morning watch every night and you're not knocking her off?"

Ray Perkins had walked up during the last exchange. "You're treading on thin ice, pal," he said to Stack. "How long has it been since you worked patrol Valley side?"

"About five years, why?"

Perkins stooped to pick up his briefcase. He also picked up Calico's, knowing his friend's ribs would make the simple task damn near impossible. "It isn't Sleepy Hollow out here anymore. You heard what the lieutenant said, Communications is backed up ten calls. We see everything the downtown divisions get, only we have to deal with it differently. You can't just bust heads and walk away when you're working a Valley division like you can downtown. If you're expecting to hit the hole and catch six hours' sleep because you're working the Valley, you're in for a big surprise."

Geographically L.A.P.D. was split into eighteen divisions, or areas as the current nomenclature had it. Five of those divisions spread across the San Fernando Valley, separated from the inner city divisions by the razor's slash of Mulholland Drive running across the top of the foothills.

Over the years the separation had become as much philosophical as it was physical, breeding two different styles of police work and an almost unfriendly rivalry between the cops on either side. Neither style of police work was better than the other, each designed to handle the serious crime problems in its area in the safest and most efficient manner possible, but neither style could be applied to the other area without disasterous results. Inner city demanded a more intimidating, physical approach; problems were solved by throwing manpower at them until they went away or moved into another division. The Valley, filled with middle- and upper-class bleeding hearts, had to be handled with much more of an eye toward public relations.

"If someone sticks up a liquor store out here in the Valley," Perkins told Stack, "we still get to thump him when we catch him, but we're expected to call him 'sir' while we're doing it."

Stack snorted his disbelief of Perkins' statements and walked away.

"One of these days someone is going to sew that asshole's lips together," Calico said, shaking his head and moving out to the parking lot where Tina was loading their car and checking the shotgun. She took Calico's briefcase from Perkins and put it in the cruiser's trunk.

She was the only female officer of Japanese descent in the department. Coupled with being a woman, her Oriental origins had smoothed the road for her in an age when city employment recruiters were only worried about federal employment quotas demanding minority representations. Brains mattered, but they weren't the main consideration. If you had a dark skin pigment, breasts, almond-shaped eyes, or a feathered headdress, you had a job.

She was fairly tall for a Japanese woman, thanks to the genes from her English mother, which had also provided her with high cheekbones sharp enough to cut diamonds. Her long, shining black hair was piled in a bun on top of her head, giving her another three inches of height and an almost regal bearing. Calico had often speculated that her slim waist could be encircled by a large man's two-handed span, and he found the slight protrudence of her front teeth somehow very attractive. That bothered him. Police work was changing. It was strange being attracted to your partner.

"You want to drive tonight, partner?" he asked Tina as she checked the car for new dents which might be blamed on them if they didn't report them first. "I still feel like I've got half a ton of Brahma bull shoved up my ass."

"No problem. I heard you did pretty good out there today." Tina finished checking the shotgun and locked it into the rack parallel with the leading edge of the front seat.

Calico slammed the trunk lid and slid stiffly into the car on the passenger side. He tossed his ticket book on the dashboard and took a plastic statue of Jesus out of his shirt pocket, hanging it by a short chain from the rearview mirror.

The first time Tina observed the ritual with the small statue she was amazed; Calico didn't fit in with her impression of a religious zealot. She asked him about it and immediately felt she'd screwed up when he stared at her intently without saying anything, as if she'd betrayed an unspoken trust. She let the subject drop, but later in the evening Calico broached it himself. He told her the statue had been given to him by his mother before his first rodeo ride. He'd kept it ever since, not so much as a good luck charm, but as a reminder to be careful and go home alive. The following day, Tina looped a small plastic Budda over the mirror next to Calico's Jesus. He stared at her sharply again, searching for any trace of mockery. Finding none he'd smiled hugely, and the first ties of a new partnership were cemented.

Since graduating from the police academy, Tina had worked with numerous training officers, but Calico was the first one she really felt comfortable with. Her training officers on day watch and P.M.s had run to type, either overtly suspicious of working with a female officer, or constantly hot to get in her shorts. Neither type thrilled her, but she'd been warned to expect those kinds of reactions when she applied for the job. If she paused to consider the situation objectively, her previous training officers hadn't been all bad. She'd learned a lot from many of them and was grateful, but she was never able to form any kind of equal-footing partnership with them.

Calico, however, was a different story. She'd put in almost a year on the street when she was partnered with him on the morning watch. Calico just expected her to know what she was doing. The first partner to treat her as competent until proven otherwise, instead of guilty until proven innocent. His offhand manner gave her a chance to breathe, and suddenly she found herself doing her job better and enjoying it more. She'd learned more in the last two months about actual police work than in all the rest of her time on the job.

The moment Calico logged on the CRT computer attached to the middle of the dash, a call was directed to them. "Nine-A-twenty-one, see the woman. Possible victim of an ADW. Suspect at scene. One five five three one Saticoy Street. Code two. Incident number seven fifty-four."

"We've been there before," Tina said as she pulled northbound out of the covered parking lot. "That's Hendredon's place, the moron who's always smashing up his mother's china."

"That's the one." Calico shifted in the passenger seat, trying to find room for his bulk amid all the equipment which had been added to the police cruiser in the name of progress. He also fought to cope with the seat being pulled almost all the way forward so Tina could reach the gas pedal. "You can always rely on Hendredon to supply a little excitement at least once a month when his mother forgets to give him his medicine."

Tina had spent a solid week of her off-duty time studying the street names and numbers in the division until she knew within a block where a location was and the quickest way to get there. One of her earliest training officers slumped over in the driving seat one night in a pitch-black residential area. The car had drifted into the curb and come to a jarring halt.

"I've just been shot," he'd told her in a calm voice. "Where are you going to tell the backup units to come?"

After the first split second of gut-wrenching panic it was clear her partner was okay and his little charade just a test. Tina had looked rapidly around her for a street sign or a familiar landmark. There was none. She was angry with herself, unaccountably ashamed for appearing so foolish, and vowed never to be caught out again.

Traffic was light and the trip across the division flew under the tires quickly. Tina drove confidently and pulled up two houses short of their destination. Ed Martin and Jazzbo Brenner were waiting for them.

The house at one five five three one was lit up like a museum display. The front bay window was smashed outward, the draperies torn away, and it was easy to see the floral-print couch which was standing on end and being used to barricade the front door. The night stillness was shattered at regular intervals by the crash of crystal smashing followed by almost inhuman wails of misery.

The four officers met on the front sidewalk. "Just like downtown Saturday night," said Jazzbo. "When is his mother going to learn to stop replacing the family china?"

"Probably when she remembers to give Ira his medicine on a regular basis," replied Calico. "You guys check around back yet?"

"No, we got here just before you did."

"Okay. Tina and I will check it out." Calico tore a page out of his officer's notebook and scribbled on it. "Tell communications to contact Dr. Nutting at this number. He's Ira's doctor and always comes out to take care of him when he gets like this." Calico handed the paper to Jazzbo.

"A doctor who makes house calls in this neighborhood?"

"Yeah. He's a sleezeball retained by the trust fund set up by Ira's father. There's also a lawyer who pays all the bills and picks up the tab for all the damages. Both of them make a bundle off the poor bastard."

Jazzbo turned to go back to his car. "We should all be as lucky as old Ira, somebody to take care of all life's little details."

"It should be easy for you. Your brains have already turned to mush. All you need to do now is stop taking your Librium," Calico said with mock seriousness.

Ed Martin laughed, and Jazzbo pulled a face. Tina led the way toward the back of the house.

A five-foot chainlink fence enclosed the backyard. Calico unlatched the gate and entered it carefully. He knew Ira's dogs would be out there, and they weren't to be trusted. Both he and Tina pulled out their batons as they picked their way carefully through the dog droppings spread everywhere.

They heard growling echo softly from the rear of the large yard, but couldn't see any threatening shapes. At the backdoor, Calico looked into the house's laundry room and then tried the doorknob. It twisted easily, the sounds of more smashing crockery covering any noise the two officers made.

Tina followed Calico's lead through the door, pulling it shut behind them to keep the dogs out, and both of them entered the battlefield of the kitchen.

"Howdy, Ira," Calico said, smiling at the huge bulk about to smash a crystal punch bowl. Ira's frail mother was huddled by the stove, whimpering.

Ira looked at Calico in incomprehension, but didn't let fly with the bowl.

"You remember me, don't you, Ira? I'm Officer Walker." Calico's voice was soft, soothing. He'd talked Ira down before. He could do it again.

Ira grunted and cocked his head like a confused ape.

"You better put him away this time, Walker! He's crazy. He's gonna kill me!" Ira's frail mother jumped up from the floor and began screaming. She lunged toward Calico, trying to grab onto his arm like a leech, but Tina intercepted her and pulled her away.

"Shut up, Edna," said Calico viciously. He kept his eyes on Ira. "This only happens because you like a little excitement once in a while. You stop giving Ira his Librium so he'll go a little nuts and we'll come out for a visit."

"That's not true!"

"It is too, Edna. We've been doing this same dance for too long and I'm getting tired of it. If it happens again I'm going to lock you up for child abuse."

"You can't do that, Walker! He's forty-three years old. He ain't a child." Edna struggled to get away, but Tina held her securely in a wrist lock. "You're hurting me, you fucking cunt! Tell your cunt partner to let me . . . ahhhh!!! She's killing me!" Edna screamed as Tina cranked down on her hold.

"I told you to shut up, Edna. If you don't, I'm going to let my partner break your fucking arm."

Edna shut up, going limp and dropping to the floor, almost pulling Tina down on top of her.

Calico held out his hand toward Ira. "Give me the bowl, Ira. It's too pretty to smash."

No reaction. Just a blank stare from the forty-three-year-old child. If they could get him calmed down the doctor would come and they could get out of there without any hassles.

"Where are your dogs, Ira?" Tina asked, using the same tones as Calico.

Ira's eyes flashed toward her, and Calico moved in a step. "The dogs is gone," Ira said in a muffled voice which seemed to well out of a sour spot in his stomach.

"Gone? What do you mean?" Tina asked. Calico took another step, his mace can hidden in his left hand.

"Men come and took them away, all of them. 'Cept for Bruno. He hid under the couch. They didn't find him." Ira had had twelve dogs by the last count, and their sign and smell was overwhelming in the small house. Dung covered everything from the floor to the couches. You couldn't take more than one or two steps without squishing in the muck. Animal Regulation must have paid a visit.

"Where's Bruno, then?"

"Out back."

Calico was close. He started to reach out with his hand for the bowl, slowly. Ira looked back at him and started to hand over the large hunk of crystal.

Suddenly, vicious barking and screaming erupting from the backyard shattered the moment. The backdoor of the house burst inward and Guy Stack hurdled through into the kitchen, gun drawn, pointed at Ira.

"Freeze, asshole!" he yelled.

THREE

STACK/THUMPER/FAZIO

CALICO TOOK AN involuntary glance toward the ruckus behind him, irreparably snapping the fragile tie he had developed with the childlike Ira. He couldn't believe his eyes. Guy Stack was scrunched in the kitchen doorway in a combat-shooting position, legs spread evenly, bent slightly at the knees like a bowlegged cowboy, stainless steel .38 fully extended in a two-handed grip, arms locked, weight forward, command presence leaking out of him like a faulty tap and splashing across the dirty linoleum floor.

Stack was the perfect picture of uniformed authority. At least he was until his partner, all six feet four inches, two hundred and fifty-eight pounds, ex-All-Pro cornerback, black as a coal miner's underwear, bald as baby's butt, Oliver "Thumper" Thurman, whacked him off at the knees. Not because he wanted to, but because, for the first time in his life, Thumper had his hands full with more than he could handle. Bruno, the last of Ira's collection of strays, a savage cross between a boxer and a great Dane with none of their redeeming values, was bound and determined to have Thumper's balls for a midnight snack.

Screaming useless commands and backing away frantically while trying to squirt tear gas into the eyes

34

of the near-rabid animal, Thumper was spewing chemical spray everywhere but where it was needed. A thin stream of the irritant splashed across the nose of Edna Hendredon. Thumper collided with Stack, bringing both men to the floor in a tangle of arms, legs, and snapping dog teeth. Wailing like a stuck banshee, Edna tore away from Tina and hurled herself on top of the pile like a kid playing king of the mountain.

Calico looked back at Ira just in time to throw up an arm and ward off the descending arc of the punch bowl. The heavy crystal shattered on impact, slivers exploding outward in rainbows of reflected light. Ira moaned in confused anger and charged, head down toward the kitchen door. In two steps he was up to full speed and in three he slammed his skull into Calico's sternum, tossing the already-bruised policeman aside like a bull goring a matador.

Reacting out of instinct, Tina leaped over the tangle of dog and humans blocking her path and landed in front of the kitchen doorway two physical steps and about a million mental ones ahead of Ira. As the giant charged toward her, she stepped sideways, grabbed his arm, shifted her weight to match his momentum, and threw him over her hip into the doorjamb. He hit with the flat splat of a water balloon exploding on a hot car roof.

Still holding onto Ira's hand, she lashed out her right leg, pivoted on the ball of her left foot, and connected her boot-shod right heel with the jutting line of the giant's jaw. Ira dropped to the floor like heavy Jell-O and Tina twisted his arms behind his back and slapped on the cuffs. It was only then she noticed the silence behind her.

She laughed at the look on their faces. Stack, Thumper, and Edna Hendredon looked like a ménage-à-trois caught in the act, Edna's dress pulled to

her waist, and the two cops' uniform shirts pulled out
of their pants in the tussle with Mother and dog. Their
faces were slack-jawed, their eyes disbelieving. Even
Bruno appeared shocked by the vision of the petite
little Japanese girl bringing down Goliath. Calico, too,
was stunned.

"What's the matter with you lot? You think judo
and karate only work in the movies?" Tina extended
her arm out, hand flat, palm down, and whistled in a
strange low singsong key. Bruno's tongue lolled out
and he scooted across the room to receive her affec-
tion. She rubbed his ears and then had him wiggling
his butt after her into the backyard.

"You're some kind of wonder, you are," Calico told
her, still full of amazement when she came back.
"That was a nice piece of work, partner."

"Hey, it's no big deal. How are the ribs?" Tina was
grinning from ear to ear and then started laughing
when she saw Thumper and Stack still trying to get the
cuffs on the ninety-eight pounds of wrath which was
Edna Hendredon. Jazzbo and Ed Martin had come in
through the front windows to help, but Edna still refused to cooperate.

Finally, Thurman grabbed the screaming woman by
the scruff of her neck and picked her up off the floor,
shaking her back and forth like a rag doll. Edna's head
flopped around and her eyes began to bug out like a
dying fish. Working together, Stack and Jazzbo twisted
her wrists up behind her back and cinched down a pair
of Peerless handcuffs. Without waiting to be told, Ed
Martin slipped a corded leg restrainer around her ankles, tightened it, and attached the snap lock to the
short chain separating Edna's new metal bracelets.

Hands secured behind her back, legs bent at the
knees, ankles secured and almost touching her wrists,
Edna looked as helpless as a paper suitcase at a bag-

gage handler's convention. It was an illusion. She still had one trick left up her sleeve, or in this case up her skirt. Letting loose a low moan which sounded closer to ecstasy than exhaustion, Edna began to urinate. The clear, yellow by-product of her nightly Coors' twelve-pack spurted from between her knees with Niagaran force, soaking Thumper's uniform pants, and puddling on the top of his shoes. When Guy Stack started to laugh at him, Thumper pointed Edna like a firehose and doused his partner from chest to toe before shoving the still dribbling woman into Stack's arms and storming out of the house.

Martin and Jazzbo pulled Edna away from the mortified Stack and gingerly began to carry her out to their police car.

"If you'll handle putting Ira on a seventy-two-hour observation hold over at Olive View Mental," Jazzbo called over his shoulder to Calico, "we'll book gorgeous here at the station for interfering and battery on a police officer."

Calico looked over at the still-sleeping giant who had almost been forgotten in the ensuing comedy of errors. "Sounds good. We'll have to get him M.T.'d first, though, make sure the karate kid here didn't break his jaw." Calico turned to face Stack who was wiping his uniform down with a dirty dish towel. "And what the hell were you trying to do, bustin' in here like that? This whole fiasco could have been avoided if you didn't think you were Wyatt Earp."

Stack looked up in disbelief. "What are you talking about? That idiot was going to bean you with that punch bowl . . ."

"He did bean me with the punch bowl! We know this character. We had things under control . . ."

"It sure didn't look that way! If you want to make something out of this, let's do it right now!"

Calico laughed. "Stack, you're about as threatening as a used condom. I'd love a chance to see Blanche here"—he jerked his thumb in Tina's direction as she let out a startled huff—"lay one upside your head. Personally, I'm not going to waste my energy on you. But if you're really feeling froggy, then go ahead and leap, Santana."

Stack's eyes tightened as he looked between the still-groggy Ira and the diminutive female rookie. Tension ran visibly through his body but seemed to dissipate into the floor. "Fuck you, Walker, and your Jap partner. Don't bother looking for me at your next backup call." He flipped Calico the bird and pushed his way out of the house.

"Blanche?" Tina asked in the pause after Stack's exit. "Blanche?"

Turning toward her, Calico looked sheepish and shrugged his shoulders. "What can I say? It seemed the right tag for the moment."

Outside, Stack collared his partner who was helping Jazzbo and Martin to load Edna into their patrol car.

"Let's get out of here. These assholes don't want our help."

Jazzbo and Martin both looked up, caught between amusement and puzzlement at this statement. Thumper finished guiding Edna, none too gently, into the rear seat of the black and white, and turned to face Stack straight on.

"Phew! Don't you white folks get to smelling funny?"

"Yeah, well, your pant legs look like some mutt mistook you for a fire hydrant. I'm going back to the station to change. You coming?"

Thumper followed his partner toward their car, "Shit, I'm not even breathing heavy."

*   *   *

Being the youngest child and only son in a family
with four daughters, a strong-willed mother, an invalid
maternal grandmother, and an absent father who
spent twenty-five years working double shifts at the
mill before drinking himself to death had not been
easy for Guy Stack. His youngest memories were of
hand-me-down girls' clothing tapered to fit his slender,
energy-burning frame. Even with his father working
double shifts there never seemed to be enough money
to buy the youngest Stack new clothes during the traditional period of back-to-school. His mother took
pains converting the blouses his sisters had grown out
of for him, even to the extent of switching sides with
the buttons and button holes, but the fabrics and the
colors were still feminine, and Stack hated them. In
turn, he hated his sisters as the indirect cause of them.

It wasn't so much that the kids at school noticed he
was wearing his sisters' clothes, there were many other
kids from the Pittsburgh steel town he grew up in who
had the same problems. But he knew. And the knowledge made him burn with shame every hour of every
school day.

By the time he was ten odd jobs and paper routes
occupied all his spare time. Half the money went into
the family budget, but the rest went toward heavy
jeans, good boots, and lumberjack shirts. By fifteen he
had adopted leather jackets and pointed boots. But,
even though he had the attitude and the eye for trouble, he also found himself drawn to the swagger and
authority of the heavy-handed cops who walked the
beats in his neighborhood, letting it be known there
was nothing that could bring them down.

When his father passed away, Stack blamed his
mother and his grandmother. He had watched daily as
the two women, who ruled the family roost, ran his

father into the ground. He blamed their constant nag-
ging and incessant chattering for keeping his father
away from home, and felt anger toward his father for
never having the courage to stand up to the shrew he
married and put her in her place. But his father hated
upheaval, and would do or say anything to avoid a
family confrontation. As a result, the man Stack
needed more than any other and looked up to more
than any other was driven first into a bottle and then
into the grave.

Stack was two days short of his eighteenth birthday
on the day of his father's funeral. At the graveside he
heard the self-pitying wailing of his mother, and saw
the disgruntled look on his grandmother's face, as if
the funeral was just another inconvenience caused by
a man she considered an incompetent fool, even
though he'd provided for her since the first day of his
marriage to her dowdy daughter. He saw his sisters,
two of them fat, ugly shrews, and two of them pompous, wraithlike shrews. God save any man who married them. He knew he would be expected to provide
for them now, so he decided to do what he always
wished his father would have done. He walked out of
the cemetery without looking back, and walked right
out of their lives forever. That afternoon he enlisted in
the Army, destined for Viet Nam, and later the police
force.

"You've got to learn to chill out a little, man."

Stack turned around in the locker-room aisle to face
Thumper Thurman. "What are you talking about?" he
asked aggressively.

"See, there you go again. Getting up on your high
horse the minute somebody says something you think
is criticism." Thumper stepped into fresh uniform
pants.

"I do not . . ."

"You do too. I've worked with you long enough to know, and long enough to earn the right to say so." Even though his words were somewhat harsh, they were delivered in the deep, even monotone which was Thumper's trademark.

The two men had been partners for four years in Metropolitan division, the department's hotshot squad which was assigned to any part of the city with a special need, or any particular problem which needed specialized attention. S.W.A.T., the Special Weapons And Tactics team, was a part of Metro. An elite core within the elite corps.

The hours demanded by Metro were horrendous, changed at will depending on the needs of the city. Constantly expected to step in and handle any situation and produce results, immediate results, was a gut-twisting pressure on every "element" member of the Metro team. A pressure which inevitably led to conflict and toe-stepping in any division to which they were assigned. To the media and the public, Metro officers were the flashy, exciting law enforcers television brought them to expect and believe in. To the regular street coppers doing the everyday routine of police work, however, they were also a curse, good only for breaking up warrant rings and sticking their noses where they were not wanted in an attempt to justify their existence during periods when all the maniacs, barricade suspects, and terrorists had taken the day off.

Metro was a tough row to hoe. A limited and uncertain social life made sustaining personal relationships, like marriage and family, an always stormy ritual. The stress of constantly being thrust into tense situations ran your adrenaline along a jagged edge. Flak from your departmental peers outside of Metro was confusing and hurtful. After all, weren't you just trying to do your job the same as they were? Weren't you both on the same side? It drove you closer to your partner, intensified the "us against them" focus of a cop's lifestyle. It made you hard, and, sometimes, it made you reckless.

Thumper Thurman had been reckless once, but that had been before he'd come on the job. College and football could have kept him out of Viet Nam, but he went anyway, for reasons established in his youth.

He had been seven years old when his parents and his six brothers and sisters had been killed in a car accident from which he, and the Oriental driver who had rammed them, were the only survivors. In the aftermath of the accident he was taken in by his favorite aunt and uncle, a childless couple who raised him willingly enough but were unable to provide the sense of the large, loving family which had been torn from him. The Marine Corps, however, had offered just that, a large family that loved him for the size, strength, and amazing reaction time which had made him the envy of rival high-school football teams, and the dream of every college scout and military recruitment officer.

The Marine Corps had also provided him with something else: the killing field of Viet Nam where Thumper could release his anger at a god who had left him alone in the world, who had not allowed him to die and follow his family into the eternity of oblivion. With reckless abandon, he took on any assignment which would throw him in the face of death, where he could bury himself in the carnage of his enemies, drink their blood, kill them all. He had come to Viet Nam with a hatred for Orientals which would have done any southern bigot proud, and what he learned there did nothing to change his attitude.

His eventual return to civilian life, like that for

many of his contemporaries, was not easy. His size and speed were still with him, however, and he found the Oakland Raiders football franchise, who were known for taking on offbeat prospects, willing to take a chance on a monster-size brute who could run the forty in four point four seconds, could bench press four hundred and fifty pounds and had hands which could gentle an egg tossed off the Empire State Building. It didn't matter to them that he had missed college ball, like it did to the other teams he'd approached. All he had to do was produce. He had found another family.

All-Pro in his rookie year as the Raiders' starting cornerback, eight interceptions, four touchdowns, and three opposing team receivers taken out for the season. And then disaster. A pileup during a fumble recovery had twisted Thurman's knee like a spaghetti strand. Surgery was routine and successful, but there would be no more midfield collisions or helmets pounded into exposed midsections. He no longer had the top-flight speed needed for the professional athlete. Thumper believed he could get it back, but the team's head office did not agree. Again he had been snatched from the bosom of a loving family and thrust into a world he could not cope with alone.

Families have a way, though, of seeking out and taking care of their own kind, and the police department found room for Thumper. It gave him a cross between the regimentation of the military and the freewheeling abandonment of the Raiders. It also gave him a purpose, a sense of right and wrong which had been missing in his other substitute families. It brought his rage under control, reflecting it only in the almost overly calm exterior which was his public face.

"You don't get to guys like Walker by getting physical or going for their throats with words. They've been around too long to be phased by that kind of action. It gets to them far more if you ignore them, treat them as if they don't exist, aren't worth your time."

"It's easy for you." Stack was still in a sulk. "Nobody wants to get in the face of a ten-foot nigger."

"Now, see how you are. I'm trying to help you out, and you want to call me names."

"You made that broad piss all over me!"

"Yeah, I know." Thumper started to laugh. "And you should have seen the look on your face. Man, it was priceless." He took a large can of deodorant out of his locker and sprayed it under the vast expanse of his left armpit. Instead of a fine spray, a thin stream of liquid blasted out of the can and ran down his side, rippled over his ribs, and soaked into his underwear. Thumper looked at it in disbelief.

Stack's smile was a mile wide. "Hey, chill out, man," he said, and then almost fell to the floor laughing.

Calico and Tina had also returned to the station after a side trip to the local contract hospital where X rays were taken of Ira's head to determine the extent of any injuries. The doctor had diagnosed bruising only and had given Tina an odd look and a wide berth. A second side trip had seen their charge dropped off at the mental facilities of Olive View Hospital. Ira's doctor had been waiting for them. All that remained to be done was the routine filling out of reports to send through to the department's mental evaluation unit who needed to be notified of the incident.

"You want coffee?" Tina asked her partner, digging into her pocket for change.

"Sure. Make it double sugar, okay."

Tina walked over to the vending machine in the

large coffee-cum-report-writing room which was
empty, except for the two of them, until the door
swung open to admit first an odor and then a scowling
presence.

"Walker, I want to see you in the Watch Com-
mander's office."

"Sure, Sarge. Right now?" Calico put on a beatific
smile as he looked up at Sal Fazio.

"Right now." Fazio turned smartly on his heel and
walked out of the room.

Calico took the cardboard cup of coffee from Tina's
outstretched hand, pinched his nose closed with his
free hand, and followed Fazio out the door leaving
Tina in a fit of giggles.

In the glass-surrounded booth of the Watch Com-
mander's office, conveniently emptied for the purpose
of this confrontation, the smell surrounding Sal Fazio
was even stronger than in the coffee room. Fazio was
a short man by police standards. He barely passed the
five-foot six-inch height requirement, which had only
been lowered to five feet in recent years to aid with
the recruiting of females. His frame was wiry, his fore-
arms corded with muscles, making his potbelly look
even more conspicuous. Thick, curly black hair covered his scalp like a fungus and could be seen sprout-
ing from the open collar of his uniform.

"I want you to know, Walker, I'm planning on making an official complaint about your actions at the
rodeo today."

"Is it against department policy now to win the all-
round event?"

"That's not what I'm talking about and you know
it!"

"Then what are you talking about?"

"I'm talking about you turning that Andy Gump
over with me inside!" Fazio was turning red in the face

and starting to sweat. The perspiration added to his stench. "I've taken twelve showers, used carbolic soap, and a half-dozen scrub brushes and I still can't get rid of the smell!"

"Do you have any witnesses to this incident you seem to think I'm involved in?"

"You know I don't. If I did I'd have you up on criminal charges. I know it was you, though, and you're not going to get away with it."

"I'm sorry that you're suffering from these delusions, Sal, but if you don't have any witnesses how do you expect to make even departmental charges stick?"

"I don't care if the charges stick or not, Walker. How long before you pull the pin and retire? What is it? A week from now?"

"That's about right. End of the week I've got thirty years on and it's going to be bye-bye to this shit-burg and hello to a life on the open ocean. What's the matter, Sal, you jealous?"

"Of you? Never. But I'm going to make this last week as miserable for you as I possibly can. I'm going to do everything I can to get your pension taken away from you. I'm going to file departmental charges and then I'm going to find somebody who's going to be willing to testify against you."

"Sal, what happened to us? We were partners, best friends. I don't even recognize this asshole you've become."

"You know what happened, Walker. Best friends don't fuck their partners' wives."

"Damnit! I've told you a hundred times, I never screwed Julie. That was just something she threw at you as she was storming out the door for the last time. It was the one thing she knew would hurt you the most, the one thing which would fester inside you and tear you apart. And you let her get away with it. I can't help it if she had to go elsewhere to get the physical satisfaction she needed."

"She didn't have to go elsewhere!" Fazio was screaming loud enough now for the record clerks in the next room to hear.

"Exactly!" Calico shouted back. "I've been telling you that for years, but you won't believe me. She left you because you were more married to this job than you were to her, not because you were lousy in bed.

"Not only that, but if she was throwing it about it wasn't with me. I was married to Marsha at the time and I didn't fuck around, not while I was married!"

Both men had squared off like wrestlers.

"You fucked her, Walker, and now I'm going to fuck you. If I can't get all your pension, then at least I'm going to make sure Marsha gets half of it."

Calico shook his head in frustration. "Take your best shot, pal," he said quietly. "I'm just so damn sorry you've let yourself become so bitter."

"You better get out of here, Walker, before you make me puke."

"Funny, you smell like you already have."

FOUR

ARLO'S

"**G**OOD NIGHT, HONEY. I love you."

"I love you too, kid. See you when I get home."

Helen Brenner hung up the phone in the dark of her bedroom. She had a small smile of satisfaction on her face as she swung her feet out of bed, making allowances for the swelling in her stomach which was getting close to its due date. She slid her feet into a scuffed, familiar pair of mules and padded first into the bathroom, and then down the short hall to the bedroom where the four-year-old twins, Billy and Kim, slept peacefully. She watched their faces in the glow of their night light and her smile widened.

She had been married to Jazzbo Brenner for almost ten years, most of which he had spent working morning watch at one division or another. It was a rare night, though, when he didn't call to tell her he loved her and to make sure everything was okay. She didn't mind being awakened in the middle of her night; in fact, it had become part of her sleep routine. Somehow his calls were a securing bond between them, something that kept them close through the periods when other police marriages fell apart from lack of communication.

Getting back into bed, still in the dark, she shifted her growing burden around until she found a halfway comfortable position, pulled the comforter over her slim shoulders, and dropped right back to sleep. She never worried about Jazzbo, if she did she knew she would end up worrying herself into a box. She knew he loved her and the children too much to take unnecessary chances, yet she also knew he believed in his job enough to never turn away from facing a danger he considered to be in the line of duty. Nor would she expect or want him to. She loved him, and a big part of him was being a policeman, so she loved that too.

Not that they never had any problems. Problems were as par for the course in marriage as they were in life in general. But they never raised their voices at each other, and strove to solve problems by working together. She had always believed marriage was something you had to work at constantly. You did not sit back and think a marriage would take care of itself. If you did, it would die like a plant without light or water. Every day you had to get up and really look at your partner, think about what problems they might be facing and what you could do to help make those problems easier. If both partners did that for each other it was amazing how troubles seemed to disappear quickly and without leaving scars. True, both Jazzbo and Helen felt theirs was a unique, special relationship. But, because they both felt that way, it worked.

At his end of the connection, Jazzbo hung up the pay phone and turned back toward Arlo's Burgers, where his partner and a couple of other morning-watch units were scarfing down free food. "Arsenic Arlo's" was a morning-watch institution. Located by the small private, commercial airport in the middle of the division's west side, it served the worst food and the best coffee in the world. During the day the fast-food restaurant catered to a strange blend of transport pilots, white-collar workers from the surrounding office buildings, kids, street people, and freaks. At night, though, it became the dominion of the local patrol cars, and even the freaks had enough sense to just buy their food and move on without cluttering up any of the four Formica tables in the small lobby.

Ray Perkins was holding court inside, recounting Calico's performance to several other officers who hadn't been at the rodeo. Jazzbo noticed again how, when Perkins was excited about something, he talked like his mouth was full of words waiting to be spat out by a demented auctioneer.

"Ithoughtthatfuckingbullwasgoingtodohimforsure . . ."

IhavetwohundredamIbidthreehundredIhavethreehundred, thought Jazzbo. Sitting down next to Ed Martin, he picked up his container of luke-warm coffee and noticed Stack and Thurman picking up an order of chili dogs from the service window. Stack did not look too pleased about Perkins singing Calico's praises.

Outside the restaurant there was a squeal of tires as two other morning-watch officers played high-speed bumper tag through the maze of surrounding side streets. It was obvious the call load was going through its normal three A.M. to four A.M. drop-off: most of the drunk drivers had been delivered to the drunk tank, family disputes had been settled, liquor stores had closed down and made their money drops, and the neighborhood had settled into a lull while trying to recharge its batteries for the day ahead.

Calico and Tina pulled into Arlo's driveway and parked in the lot conveniently placed behind the restaurant, away from the prying eyes of passing citizens who might call the station to complain about so many police cars being in one place at the same time. Laughing at something the others hadn't heard, the partners entered the restaurant a few moments later.

"Hey, Calico," Perkins called out. "I was just telling these jerk-offs about you riding Number 98."

"To hear him tell it," said one of the cops Perkins had been talking to, "you couldn't have done it without his help."

"Oh yeah. Well, let's drop our pants right now and compare bruises," Calico retorted, making a gesture to undo his gun belt.

"You don't want to do that," Stack called out. "You might get Blanche there all excited."

"In that case, Eggbert, why don't you drop your pants?" Tina shot back at Stack, surprised at her quick response. "Then only your partner will get excited."

The other cops laughed, but when Stack stood up like a high-school kid looking for a fight, Ed Martin stepped casually between the two antagonists and turned Tina away from the confrontation.

"You get Ira checked into the loony bin okay?" he asked as he sat Tina down next to Jazzbo.

"No problem. How did it go with his mother?"

"She was still ranting and raving when we got her to the station, but the jail doctor said she was okay to book. Last time we saw her she was being turned loose in the rubber room."

"Like mother, like son, huh?"

"I guess."

The smell of burned chili oozing over grilled onions and foot-long hot dogs preceded Calico to the table.

"Hey, do you know who I bumped into the other day?" asked Ray Perkins, coming over to join the group. "Wild John Elliot."

"No kidding?" asked Jazzbo, looking up from his

coffee. "Last I heard they'd taken away his gun and shipped him off to teach at the department's driving school on Terminal Island."

"He's still there," said Tina. "At least he was when I went through the school about a year ago."

"Where did you see him?" Calico asked Perkins.

"I was up at the Academy qualifying. Apparently he still has to qualify even though they say he's too crazy to be allowed to carry a gun anymore."

"That's what happens when you make a sergeant like Fazio crap his pants by firing six blank rounds at him in the roll-call room."

Everybody laughed at the memory. "Wild John was a good partner, but, damn, he was a crazy mother," Calico chuckled.

"We had lunch together in the cafeteria," Perkins continued. "He kept me in stitches telling me about the time you and he raced down to Tijuana and back in the police car."

"That was a long time ago," Calico said. "Back when Sal Fazio was a real person. In fact it was Sal who covered for us, picked up our calls while we were gone."

"That's a bunch of crap."

Everybody in Arlo's turned to look at Guy Stack who was standing by the door ready to follow Thurman out.

"What is it with you, boy?" Calico asked. "Why are you so anxious to get everybody upset with you?"

"I just get sick and tired of hearing you old-timers talk about all the things you used to do on this job. I've heard the rumors ever since I joined this department about you guys driving to Tijuana or Las Vegas and back during morning watch, but I've never seen any proof of it ever happening. It's all talk as far as I'm concerned."

Calico smiled. "Oh, I get it now. This whole attitude problem of yours is a setup to get some action; one of our units taking on one of your Metro teams in a flying run."

"Is that what you call your imaginary escapades?"

"You have to be able to fly, boy, or you ain't gonna beat the time clock back for change of watch."

"What do you say, old-timer?" Thurman asked, seeing that maybe his partner had inadvertently put them into a good thing. There was no way anybody could outdrive either one of them. Both Thurman and Stack were among the best of the department's pursuit drivers, and Stack held the current lap record at the department's driving school. "You fancy your chances on a Mexican side trip? Or don't you want to risk that precious pension waiting for you at the end of the week?"

Before Calico could answer there was a hellish revving of engines, a mad screeching of tires, a thump of bumper contact, and the police car which had just become "it" in the bumper-tag game slid sideways and wrapped its front quarter panel around a telephone pole in a symphony of crushing metal.

"*Shit! Son of a bitch!*" came a voice from inside the crumpled vehicle, punctuated by a stream of boiling water bursting out of the ruptured radiator.

The cops inside Arlo's flooded out into the street, but the driver of the smashed police car had exited his vehicle and was pounding on its hood before they got to him.

"*Shit! Shit! Shit! Shit! Shit!*"

"Hell of a vocabulary you got there, Richards."

"Fuck you, Calico."

"Take it easy, son, we're all here to help you."

"Sure. When Fazio finds out about this he's going to burn me good."

"Only if he thinks you were screwing around when it happened."

"But I was screwing around when it happened."

"Don't get your balls in an uproar. You don't think you're the first casualty of bumper tag, do you? Precedent for this situation was set back when you were sucking on your mama's tit." Calico turned toward Tina. "Come on, kid. Time for the tail to wag the dog."

Life for Junior Morales was a constant struggle with confusion and frustration. Every day Junior fought to overcome the misconnections in his brain which stopped him from being able to function as a normal sixteen-year-old. It wasn't that Junior was stupid. It wasn't that he could not understand what the teachers in school were explaining. It wasn't that he didn't have the same emotions and desires as anyone else in his peer group. Nor was it the poverty-level family, the drunken and abusive parents, or the six normal and spiteful siblings that kept Junior from being able to express himself, stopping the flow of words from his brain to his tongue. It was the misconnections. Teachers and school administrators had a term for Junior: "educationally handicapped." The other children in the Blythe Street barrio had a term for him too: *"payaso"*—clown. Junior's father also had a term for him: "fucking ass stupid *puta.*"

Junior couldn't remember a time when he had not been his father's "fucking ass stupid *puta.*" He carried the label with him wherever he went. Once he had tried to sign his name that way, Junior Fucking Ass Stupid *Puta* Morales, but he didn't know how to spell the words, so he just printed it as usual, Junir Morles. Junior often left letters out of words. Sometimes even dropped entire words out of sentences, but nobody had ever tried to help him with the problem. After all he was just another wetback supping at the public trough, too stupid to be able to take advantage of what America and all her bleeding-heart liberals had to offer. Fucking ass stupid *puta.*

Junior knew he liked girls, though. There were lots of girls at his school who he liked. He liked to look at them and wonder what they would look like with their clothes off. He knew that was a bad thing to think about. He'd been caught at school once, masturbating while trying to look into the girls' locker room. His mother had been called and had taken him straight to see Father Mesina at Our Lady of the Fields. Father Mesina had talked sternly to Junior about his sins. He told Junior it was a sin to even think about seeing women naked, and he would definitely go to hell if he continued "touching himself."

Junior tried to explain that he couldn't help those thoughts, but the words just wouldn't come out properly. Just like they wouldn't come out properly when he tried to talk to a girl, to make her not laugh at him or call him *"payaso."*

His father had beat him that night on the dirt lawn of their filthy apartment complex, in front of all his brothers and sisters and half of the other barrio residents. Junior tried to run, tried to use the strength in his wiry frame to get away, to strike back, to do anything but lie there and take the beating and the taunts. *"Payaso." "*Fucking ass stupid *puta."*

Finally they left him alone, curled up in a ball, whimpering like a cowed dog with its tail between its legs. Eventually he was able to crawl away to the place he always went when the beatings were over, a place where it was so dark there was nothing to think about, no confusion or frustration to struggle with. With the doors of the empty garage storage space, located over the parking spaces, closed, it was so dark that Junior found he could become completely nothing. And nothing could hurt nothing.

That was the night that Junior discovered fire.

He had known a little about fire before that night. He'd found fascination in watching the phosphorous heads of matches explode into flames. But it had never gone beyond that until that night. That night he didn't so much discover fire, as the power of fire.

Night in the dark storage space eventually gave way to day and a tiny crack of daylight seeped into Junior's world of nothing. Another day of frustration and confusion was beginning. Junior scratched a last match across the abrasive of the pack's strike pad. The flare was beautiful as always, deep in its center there was a place where nothing could be something and nobody would ever laugh again. Junior dropped the match when it burned the tip of his fingers, and then climbed out of his sanctuary.

In front of his building, two younger boys ran past him on their way to school. They shoved him aside and cat-called at him, sticking their middle fingers in the air at him in the traditional gesture. Junior screamed at them in mad frustration, making them laugh. Only suddenly the laughing stopped. The two boys ran back past Junior without touching him. Junior turned to follow them, seeing the smoke and the flames for the first time, but not connecting them yet to the beauty of the small flames from his tiny matches.

Before the fire department arrived the flames had destroyed the storage space which had been Junior's sanctuary, and had spread through to the first apartment. The flames were beautiful, Junior thought, and suddenly his mind realized it was the birth of the small flame of his last match, dropped still alight in the debris on the floor of the storage area, which had sparked this monster of heat and destruction that sent fear into all his enemies.

Staring into the smoke and flames, Junior felt all the connections in his brain suddenly flare into life. For the first time confusion and frustration was outside of him, experienced by those who had forever taunted him. Inside he was in control. Thanks to the flames. The fire. The power of destruction which he had spawned so easily. In his groin he felt a swelling, a tumultuous hardening followed by a sticky explosion of ecstasy, an orgasm like he had never experienced before. And it was all because of the fire. He'd had to do nothing but stare at it.

The aftermath of the sexual release seemed to short-circuit the connections in Junior's head again. But there were several which remained active: the experience of the clarity in his brain brought on by the fire, the knowledge of the fear in his enemies, the sexually demanding need to regain the release of the pure orgasm he had experienced. All the new connections combined in the one thought to see the flames again. The flames were the answer, and Junior must have them again, and again, and again.

The night of the beating, when Junior had discovered the power of fire, had been the beginning. Junior's lust for the flames consumed him. Soon there was another fire in an abandoned music emporium. This time the flames leaped far higher than they had at Junior's sanctuary, and his orgasm shook him to the core of his inner being.

The connections in his brain would all come into focus when Junior concentrated on the flames. He knew he had to make bigger and bigger fires, and hated the firemen and the policemen who came and took away the flames, leaving him alone in confusion again.

For the first time in his life, Junior turned to a book for an answer. Once he had seen some of the "Pac-13" gang members looking through a book they had taken from a survivalist store they had burglarized. They were all talking about the bombs and booby traps the book showed them how to make. They had planned to use it to help them get back at the Delano Street barrio for a turf infringement, but eventually settled for the traditional drive-by shooting instead. The book made things too complicated, there was no machismo unless you pulled the trigger yourself.

But the book was what Junior needed, and he stole it from the stealers. In his new sanctuary, an abandoned apartment in the rear of a condemned structure, Junior forced his brain to function, to retain the information which would help him bring back the flames. And each new fire was bigger than the one before. But each time the firemen and the policemen came and took the flames away again. Junior knew he would have to stop them.

On the night Calico and the others became the tail planning to wag the dog, Junior was in his sanctuary. Around him, scattered on the floor, were half a dozen pornographic magazines. Each one lay open to a display of debased female flesh penetrated from every angle and in every orifice by fingers, penises, and tongues.

Junior's pants were pulled down to his ankles, his flaccid penis a shriveled appendage protected by his fist. The connections in his brain were misfiring again and the sexual release he craved was crying out for fire. With the flame of a disposable lighter he touched the edge of one of the glossy magazines, the pornographic images curling away from the heat like forest creatures running in fear. The flame caught and held, burning the sex spread across the pages and leaping to the next magazine beside it. Junior looked down at the largeness of his manhood which was finally throbbing with power and desire. His plans had been laid for the flames to return, and this time nothing, not the police nor the firemen, would stop them.

At Arlo's everything was ready.

"Nine-A-sixty-nine, could I have a time check please?"

"Nine-A-sixty-nine, roger. Zero three forty-eight."

"Roger, thank you."

The prearranged signal that Jazzbo and Ed were in position sounded over the radio.

Calico waved at Hal Richards from the passenger seat of his squad car parked behind Arlo's. He watched as Richards slid back into his own crashed unit and picked up his microphone.

"Here we go," said Calico to Tina, who was seated beside him struggling to keep a check on her apprehensions. Nervously she tapped her long, blood-red nails against the steering wheel. Calico looked at those nails and again found himself attracted to the woman beside him. He shook his head and banished the thought.

Richards' voice broke into the quiet of the radio waves and the scam began in full. "Nine-L-nine, requesting nine-L-twenty, or any other available supervisor, to meet me at my location, Woodman and Burbank."

There was a short pause before the RTO came back. "Nine-L-nine, nine-L-twenty will meet you with a five-minute ETA from Ventura and Beverly Glen. Switch to rover five for nine-L-twenty."

"Nine-L-nine, roger."

It was a good break finding out what location Fazio was coming from. That way the phony pursuit, which was about to go down, would not inadvertently cross the sergeant's path.

After waiting as long as he dared, for Fazio to get closer to the Woodman and Burbank location, Richards switched his radio over to the requested tach frequency. "Nine-L-nine to nine-L-twenty on rover five."

"Nine-L-twenty to nine-L-nine." Sal Fazio's voice sounded pompous even over the tinny radio speakers. "What do you have over there?"

"I have a half-dozen reports from earlier in the evening which need approval, no big deal. Holy, Hanna. . . !"

"Richards! What is it?" Fazio's voice demanded.

Calico, listening to the exchange on his own radio, had to smile. Richards, who was sitting in his crashed vehicle at Sherman Way and Hayvenhurst, miles west and north of Woodman and Burbank, was playing things just right. The light bar over the crashed vehicle spun into life, and the unit's siren split the night. Richards started to broadcast again, the wail of his siren in the background behind his voice.

"Nine-L-nine, I am in pursuit of a yellow Ford Mustang, no plates, heading northbound Woodman from Burbank in excess of seventy miles an hour."

"All units on all frequencies stand by, nine-L-nine is in pursuit." The RTO's voice was professionally calm as she rebroadcast the vehicle information and directions Richards had supplied.

Jazzbo and Ed Martin knew their cue when they heard it and, from their waiting position actually at Woodman and Burbank, they hit their lights and siren and sped off toward Richards' crash site. Theirs was a critical part of the scam. Since Fazio had been drawn close to the starting point of the phony pursuit, where the only thing really moving was a mongrel dog poking through a trash can, he damn well better be able to hear a siren shattering the night air for blocks around, or he was sure to get suspicious.

The RTO sought more information from Richards: "Nine-L-nine, what is your position now?"

Calculating the speed he was supposed to be traveling at and the time since his last broadcast, Richards replied, "Nine-L-nine, I'm still northbound Woodman approaching Victory. There appears to be only one suspect in the pursuit vehicle, a male, Caucasian, black hair, wearing a red shirt. Vehicle wanted for speed only at this time."

The RTO relayed the information, and then Fazio tried to get in and screw up the scam. "Nine-L-twenty," he broadcast to the RTO, "see if you can raise an air unit and get them to intercept the pursuit."

"Nine-L-twenty, roger." Everyone involved in the scam held their breath while the RTO made contact with air support. If one of the department helicopters was in the area it would not be long before the phantom Ford Mustang was found to be nonexistent. Her voice finally returned, "Nine-L-twenty, Air sixteen is responding from downtown."

That meant things had to happen fast. It was better than having an air unit available immediately, but it still didn't give them much time.

"Nine-L-nine, I am now westbound Vanowen crossing Van Nuys Boulevard. Suspect vehicle is driving erratically and committing numerous traffic violations." Richards continued his broadcasting, forcing Jazzbo to increase his speed to keep up with the distances Richards claimed to be covering.

Calico hit the lights and siren switches on the dashboard of his unit, alternately bathing the parking lot of Arlo's in red and blue light. Arlo and the two members of his night crew were leaning in the passenger window of the stationary police vehicle as Calico started to broadcast.

"Nine-A-twenty-one, I am now the backup unit in the pursuit. We are still westbound on Vanowen approaching Sepulveda." A two-second pause. "Suspect has now turned northbound on Sepulveda."

"This is Air sixteen. We should be over the pursuit in approximately three minutes."

Shit!

Tina eased the police unit from the back parking lot to Arlo's street exit. Calico waved back at Arlo and his crew who were all grinning from ear to ear. Stack and Thurman had cleared the area and were running parallel to the phony pursuit in case they were needed to intercept any of the other sergeants who might come too close for comfort.

"Nine-L-nine, I'm now westbound onto Sherman Way." Richards was expertly bringing the phony pursuit toward the crash site.

Down the virtually empty main street, Tina could see the lights of Jazzbo's unit heading toward them. In the sky, the single spotlight of the police helicopter could be seen also speeding toward the location but still a good distance away.

"Come on, come on!" whispered Calico, looking from Jazzbo's unit to the air unit and back. If the air unit got too close they would see what was going on and there was no telling how they would play it.

As Jazzbo and Ed flew past Arlo's, Richards started the last part of his broadcast. "Nine-L-nine, I'm out of the pursuit. Repeat. I'm out of the pursuit. Suspect vehicle forced me into a telephone pole at Hayvenhurst and Sherman Way. Suspect vehicle is now headed northbound on Hayvenhurst. Please have a supervisor and a traffic unit meet me at this location."

Calico took over the broadcast. He had to do this last part quickly. Tina had floored their car and had pulled out onto Hayvenhurst. "Nine-A-twenty-one, we have taken over the pursuit northbound on Hayvenhurst approaching Saticoy. Suspect's vehicle now wanted for reckless driving and hit and run." The helicopter was going to be over them in less than a minute, and they would need that time for the phantom Ford to vanish until he was needed again. "Nine-A-twenty-one, the suspect has lost us westbound on Saticoy in the industrial area. Please inform the air unit and ask them to check the area."

The RTO repeated the information and all the available units in Van Nuys and from the neighboring West Valley division started to stake out, or patrol the area for the phantom.

"What happens now?" asked Tina, realizing she was sweating in the cool night air.

"We make a show of looking for the Mustang and eventually head back to the crash site. Tell our story to the unit assigned to take the report on Richards' accident, fill out some paperwork, and pity some poor bastard who takes his yellow Mustang down to a doughnut shop this morning for an early cup of coffee."

"It sounds too easy."

"It isn't. Fazio will bitch and moan about Richards' driving and ship him off for a refresher course at the driving school, but that will be the extent of it. Beats Richards taking three days off without pay for screwing up in a game of bumper tag."

"I guess so."

"Just remember that one day it might be you looking into the jaws of the department dog, and unless there's someone around willing to be the tail and wag the dog away from you, you're going to end up bit. Now you've earned some favors."

Calico and Tina were still driving around the industrial area where they had "lost" the Mustang when the radio cackled at them.

"Nine-A-twenty-one, unknown trouble, one four six eight one Blythe Street, no PR no call-back. Handle code-two. Incident eight twenty-four."

"The barrio," Tina said. "Torchsong?"

Calico rogered the call and looked at his watch. "It's the right time. Shit! I was hoping to go home on schedule for a change."

FIVE

TORCHSONG

"**W**HAT'S THAT SMELL?**"** Tina asked, stepping out of the black and white and crinkling her nose against the heavy cloying scent which invaded her nostrils.

"Ether," replied Calico. He took his baton from its holder on the door panel and slid it into the ring on the left side of his Sam Browne. Cautiously, he took a slow look around the sleeping barrio.

"Ether? The chemical they use to make PCP?"

"Yeah. Smells like somebody's cooking up a batch of dope in an apartment lab."

The two-story tenement they stood in front of was one of the most rundown along the three-block stretch of similar tenements and small, single-story residences which made up the Blythe Street barrio. The streets and yards were littered with garbage, broken bottles, rusting hulks of abandoned cars, and the debris of too many humans crammed into too little space. Every room in every apartment or house would be filled with two or more Latin families. No more than a half dozen would be in America legally.

Every wall within sight was covered with gang graffiti, the offensive scribbling itself vandalized by the bullet holes of drive-by shootings. At the east end of the street, just off the main drag of Van Nuys Boulevard, the owner of an auto-repair shop had tried to fight the graffiti by allowing the garish splash of an ethnic mural to be created across the expanse of the back wall of his garage. Within the portrait, the Madonna and Child dominated over dusky-skinned men in prison chains, and bone-skinny mothers feeding babies from shrunken teats while their other infants, with eyes as big as their whole face, clung to the ragtag ends of multicolored skirts. There was no hope in the mural, only a despair and rage which gave a raw and brutal beauty to the visage. The effect had been spoiled, though, by invaders from another turf who had spray-painted a huge penis hanging from the waist of the Madonna, and added horns to the head of the Child and hatred in his eyes.

Several other police units attached to the Torchsong task force pulled in behind Calico and Tina, spitting more uniforms into the deceptive quiet of the predawn morning hours.

"PCP lab," stated Shannon, a raw-boned redheaded cop, as he approached Calico. He scratched a thumbnail across his aggressive cleft chin.

Calico looked up at him and nodded his head toward the address they had been given for the unknown trouble call. "Seems strongest from over there. Perhaps one of the tenants became tired of being asphyxiated by the fumes and called in."

Shannon's partner, a neatly trimmed ex-narco cop who should have known better, tapped a cigarette out of a pack of Camels and stuck it in the corner of his mouth. As he brought out a lighter, Shannon reached over and restrained his hand.

"Think about what you're doing, man. You want this whole block to blow?"

"Wouldn't be any great loss."

"Except for the fact we're standing here, too."

"Like I said, wouldn't be any great loss." The ex-narco cop smiled disarmingly and then shrugged. "We aren't close enough to worry about blowing anything anyway."

"I know that. But what happens when you forget that cancer stick is sticking out of your gob hole and we go walking into that complex? One spark in there . . ." Shannon left the circumstances hanging.

The ex-narco cop didn't reply, but he slid his lighter back into his uniform pants pocket and returned the cigarette to the pack.

"What are you thinking?" Tina asked Calico as Jazzbo Brenner and Ed Martin pulled up along with another task-force unit. Unknown trouble calls could be anything from a ruse to an ambush, or anything in-between. Coupled with the proper timing for a Torchsong call, this one was bringing all available units out of the woodwork. The only notable exception was Stack and Thurman, who had left Arlo's in the opposite direction when Calico and Tina had been assigned the call.

"I don't think we have any choice in the matter," Calico stated, as much to the other cops gathering around him as to Tina. "We're going to have to evacuate the complex before whoever's cooking in the lab makes a mistake and sends this whole place up in flames."

"You want to wait for some fire units?" Jazzbo asked. "I've notified communications to send out a couple."

"We better not. Let's start waking the tenants up as quietly as possible and try to locate which apartment the lab is functioning in."

"What's the layout inside like?" Shannon inquired. Having only worked in Van Nuys division a few times before being assigned to the Torchsong task force, he wanted to know what he and his partner could expect.

"It's a typical barrio rat warren," Ed Martin told him, "enclosed hallways with fire doors, and a rickety elevator leading up to the second floor."

"Tell you what, Shannon," Calico suggested. "Why don't you and your partner wait out here and get the residents organized as we send them out. The other units can help keep the lookey-loos out of our hair when the fire units arrive."

"Sounds good to us." Shannon turned away with his partner and walked over to talk with the other arriving units.

"You want to take the second floor while Ed and I clear the first?" suggested Jazzbo to Calico.

"Okay with you, partner?" Calico deferred to Tina.

"Let's do it," she replied.

Across the street on the roof of the tenement Junior Morales watched the proceedings with the clarity which became a reality only when he knew the flames were near. It was almost time. Soon the flames he desired would consume all around them, and this time they would never end, bringing the punishment of hellfire down on everyone who had sought to douse them in the past.

Junior had no idea why the policemen were talking about a lab, he had no idea ether was used to make PCP. He only knew the copy of *The Anarchist's Cookbook* he had stolen told him where to get ether and how to make it explode, taught him how to bring back the flames and kill those who would smother them.

To begin with he had worried that the police cars hadn't come to the barrio as a result of the call he had placed from the pay phone at the corner. Perhaps they had come because of the lab they kept talking about. But it didn't matter. He heard them talking about the smell of the ether, which the book explained would cover the smell of the gasoline he had spilled in the elevator and hallways, and he knew they were going to investigate.

The book had made things so easy for him. It was the first time in his life a book had made anything easy. When he was planning for the return of the flames the misconnections in his brain didn't exist. Sparks of energy jumped over them like the sparks of a brushfire jumping a firebreak. The burning in his brain was pleasant and it was easy to do as the book said and buy the five-gallon containers of ether from a chemical company which was only a short bus ride away. The salesman had never questioned him about what he wanted it for, and had actually seemed only too happy to help him bring back the flames.

Soon now the other things the book had taught him would stop the police and the firemen from saving the people in the apartments, and he wouldn't ever be anyone's "fucking ass stupid *puta*" again. He felt his penis start to harden and throb as he watched the policemen walk toward the apartment entrance.

Calico and Tina walked through the entrance of the tenement followed not too closely by Ed Martin and Jazzbo. Policemen have many paranoid habits, some as obvious as always sitting with their backs to a wall in a restaurant where they can watch the entrance. Calico always felt like Wild Bill Hickok when he did that, but it didn't stop him from doing it. Policemen also try to never put all their eggs in one basket. It was a cliché, but it was also common sense. It was stupid to tromp up to a location like British redcoats all in a line. If there were two routes to the same place it made far more sense to split up and use both of them. As a result Calico thumbed the elevator button while

Jazzbo and Ed Martin pulled open the heavy fire door
which led to the first-floor hallway and the stairwell.

The fumes of the ether were almost overwhelming
in the closeness of the tenement, overriding all the
typical smells of urine and decay. Junior had hidden
the containers with care, puncturing their tops to let
the liquid evaporate and, being the same weight as air,
to find its own deadly level.

The elevator doors opened almost immediately, and
Calico and Tina stepped in. A sudden impression
made Calico turn sharply in time to watch the heavy
fire door swinging closed on the backs of Ed and Jazzbo. The image he saw was crystal clear, the two police
officers starting up the short, narrow length of hall to
the next fire door and the apartments full of innocent
people they hoped to evacuate. He also saw the
painstakingly rigged half-match attached to the bottom
of the first fire door which, as the door closed, would
strike across the strip of sandpaper glued to the doorjamb, turning the fume-filled hallway into an inferno.

"No!" Calico yelled, trying to leap through the mi-
nuscule crack left in the closing elevator door and, as
if through sheer willpower, hold the fire door back.

He was far too late.

The fire door and the elevator door closed together,
and the explosion of flash fire which ripped through
the now-enclosed hallway sent two good cops straight
to hell.

As the ether exploded around them, igniting the
gasoline–liquid soap mixture Junior had smeared on
the walls, Jazzbo and Ed had one thought each before
the flames seared their lungs and bowed their bodies
like the fire doors at either end of the hallway. Jazzbo
thought of Helen and the twins. Ed Martin discovered
there was no God.

Junior heard the explosion and smiled. Orgasm be-

gan to build throughout his body and he began to light
the packs of matches scattered around him. Quickly,
because he must be at the elevator doors when they
opened, he ran, dropping the now burning packs of
matches down heating and air-condition shafts, knowing they would trigger the pools of ether and gasoline,
which he had poured down earlier, into the flames of
redemption.

"What is it?" Tina yelled at Calico in the confined
space of the painfully slow-moving elevator.

"It's all a trap . . ." Calico crouched down and ran
his hand across the floor of the elevator. It came away
soaking wet. He sniffed his fingers. Gasoline. Above
him he used his baton to knock out the tiles which led
to the escape hatch. One of the five-gallon drums of
ether crashed down with them. Tina screamed.

"Calm down!" Calico yelled at her.

"I am calm, damnit," she yelled back. "If I wasn't
calm I'd have shit my britches!"

The elevator shuddered as it slowly continued its
rise to the second level.

Calico swore when he realized the escape hatch had
been jammed, his mind racing for an alternate solution to being fried alive. "When the door opens dive
out and roll as far to your right as you can," he yelled
at Tina. "I'll go to the left." Calico didn't have time to
explain anything else as the elevator jerked to a halt
and the doors began to open with a hiss.

In the second-level hallway, Junior jumped awk-
wardly from the ladder which led up to the roof access. Smoke tendrils weaved around him as he picked
up his carefully prepared torch and lit its gasoline-
soaked head with another pack of matches. His eyes
hurt, burning from sexual desire and smoke. His stomach hurt and lurched around in his body cavity up to
where his heart should be. He heard the elevator ar-

riving, and held back his orgasm until he could watch the policemen inside it explode into flames.

"Now!" Calico yelled as the elevator doors cracked open. Tina was ahead of him, though, diving through the doors before the opening seemed even near to big enough. Calico followed her, his left shoulder smashing into the elevator door as he dove out, sending beelines of pain across his bull-bruised ribs.

The flaming torch, launched into the opening elevator from Junior's javelinlike throw, sparked the ether gathered inside into a gutting explosion. Heat and flames belched out, knocking Junior off his feet and singeing eyebrows and eyelashes from his face. He didn't understand what had happened. How had the two policemen gotten out of the elevator so fast? He dragged himself to his feet and ran for the roof-access ladder. Passing Calico, he hit the large policeman in the back of the neck with both fists. Calico slumped and fell into the line of flame which was starting to spread through the hallway.

Tina's roll had shot her across the hallway and slammed her into one of the rotting apartment doors which burst open, the lock splintering. Inside the apartment uncertain faces, full of slumber and fear, stared silently at the young police officer.

"The apartments are on fire," Tina told them in her night-school Spanish. It didn't seem to get any response. She repeated herself more loudly and grabbed the man lying closest to the door and told him to help get the others outside. She pushed him away and ran back into the hallway.

At the top of the roof-access ladder, the legs of the confused maniac the police had come to call Torchsong, but who felt he was nothing more than a "fucking ass stupid *puta*," caught Tina's eye as they disappeared upward. She ran to Calico's side and dragged him to a sitting position.

"I'm okay, okay . . ." he babbled, putting a hand to his head and trying to get his eyes to focus. "Get after the prick! He's gone up to the roof."

"Are you sure you're okay?"

"Yeah! Go on get going. I'm right behind you." Calico came unsteadily to his feet with the determination which had kept him on the back of old Number 98. Tina watched him for a second and then, as the flames in the hallway began to lick at their feet, she ran for the access ladder.

The fire door at the left end of the hallway sprang open, and a fireman lumbered down with breathing equipment, looking like an enraged alien from the mind of H. G. Wells, made his way past the flames to help evacuate the panicking residents. Calico saw two other firemen follow in the wake of the first before he turned to chase after Tina. I wouldn't have their job for anything, he thought. They were thinking the exact same thing about him.

On the roof Tina sucked in great lungfuls of fresh air. She could see flames licking up out of the air vents and saw the tar paper on the roof beginning to smolder in spots and fold in on itself. A great geyser of water from a fire hose splattered heavily in front of her. Shoving her revolver, which had been in her hand as she emerged onto the roof, back into her breakfront holster, she began to give chase after the blurred figure of Junior Morales who had already leaped across to the next rooftop.

The space between the roof of the burning building and the next tenement on the block was only about five feet, less than two car widths, and Tina went across as easily as the fire would if it got that far. The gum soles of her highly polished combat boots bit deeply into the gravel on the next roof as she sped after Morales. Behind her, Calico emerged onto the roof of the first building. He ran to the edge but didn't even attempt to jump the intervening space.

"Nine-A-twenty-one, my partner is in foot pursuit of arson suspect westbound across the rooftops from one four six eight one Blythe Street . . ." Calico spoke rapidly into the microphone of his rover. "Request backup units to respond to the west end of the barrio to intercept." He was out of breath, his lungs filled with choking smoke, and his ribs hurt like hell.

He waited only for the RTO to roger him and relay the information before he ran along the edge of the roof to the ladder which vanished over the edge and down to ground level. Hypes, looking for a private place to geeze, had long ago removed the board placed across the bottom story of the ladder to keep kids from climbing up, so his descent was fairly rapid and easy. Once again on terra firma, he began to jog along the back alley which ran parallel to Blythe Street but behind the apartments. Farther along and above him he could hear the pounding progress of hunter and quarry.

Tina was getting closer. "Give it up, you asshole," she yelled at the fleeing figure in front of her. "You're going to run out of build . . ." Her order was cut short as an antenna wire sliced in under her throat and bit deeply into her skin. Her feet continued to run until they were swept from under her and she bounced down onto her backside.

"Shit!" she swore. It came out closer to "Shyth!" through the sudden rawness of her throat. The palms of her hands had been grazed bloody on the rooftop gravel, and pain shot through them as she pushed herself to her feet again. Junior had gained ground, but he was still catchable. She began to run, harder, faster, ignoring the pain as wind was sucked down through the rawness of her throat. Her thighs began to tremble from the effort. There was no pain, she told herself, only a job which had to be done, by her, before others died.

The misconnections were all back and misfiring with a vengeance. Junior ran, with only the direction of blind panic. It wasn't supposed to be like this. The flames were supposed to wipe clear the misconnections, consume everything that was bad, firemen, policemen, his father and brothers and sisters. But they hadn't. The two policemen had gotten out of the elevator. They had started to save the people in the building, and the firemen were there too soon. It wasn't supposed to be like this. Semen soaked through his gray khaki work pants on the side where his now-shriveled penis was dressed. He didn't remember ejaculating, the orgasm overridden by confusion and fear.

Behind him he could hear one of the policemen pursuing him, calling out to him in his mother's voice. My brain is not right, he thought to himself desperately, my mother's voice in broken Spanish from the mouth of a policeman. The only word he understood was asshole.

Two more rooftops passed under his feet, but more slowly than before as with each step his feet became heavier. He raced to the end of the building he was on and realized there was nowhere else to go. Below him two squad cars converged, the occupants pointing shotguns and pistols up at him, yelling instructions at him which were only a blurred mass of sound. He turned to face his pursuer, the policeman with his mother's voice, and saw the face of a young woman framed by a fall of solid black hair which had become unpinned and fell almost to her waist.

Tina broke her gun out of its holster as Junior turned to face her. "Freeze!" she yelled at him, searing her throat with pain again. She brought the gun up into a two-handed grip and evenly distributed her weight on her straddled legs, her knees slightly bent, torso straight. Junior cocked his head at her like a confused puppy.

"Put your hands over your head!" No reaction. *"Arriba su manos,"* she repeated in Spanish. No reaction. She heard a noise behind her and glanced back to see Calico climbing over the edge of the coping where the ladder to the ground ended. She turned back to face Junior who had started to giggle. "Put your hands up! *Arriba su manos!"*

With the fingers of one hand, Junior twisted a match away from the others in the pack he held, and struck it across the abrasive. It flared singularly. With a flick of practiced fingers he twisted the match back into the pack, the phosphorus heads of the other matches flaring in chain reaction, burning the skin from his fingers. He began to walk forward.

"Goddamnit! I told you to freeze, mother fucker!"

Calico was onto the roof but still a good distance away from being able to help.

"Fucking ass stupid *puta!"* Junior screamed. Tina thought he was talking to her. She held her ground. Calico started to run toward them.

The flaming pack of matches moved, almost of their own accord, across Junior's chest and down to the tails of his disheveled shirt. Smoke tendrils started to rise as the cheap cotton began to smolder, and then the purity of flames engulfed Junior's torso as the gas-soaked material ignited.

The flaming maniac began to run toward Tina.

Her .38 bucked in her hand. Once. Twice. Three times. And still the monster ran at her. She had to kill it. Four times. Five. She saw the body of flame stagger back on impact but then continue forward, slower but relentless.

She waited a split second then fired her sixth shot where she new the monster's brain must be. In one smooth movement, fear coursing through her body, she ejected her empty shells and slid six fresh into the cylinder with a speedy loader. As the cylinder snapped shut, she looked up to see the arms of the fire reach out to embrace her, felt the lure of the fire draw her in almost willingly. She dropped to one knee, the flaming body falling from above her, determined to take her to its special version of hell.

"Tina!" Calico threw himself at the burning body of Junior like a cornerback taking out a receiver in the Super Bowl. His shoulders connected with the burning youth, and Calico felt the impact down to the soles of his undarned socks. He rolled away, came up on his knees, his ribs tearing. He saw Tina scramble clear and fire six more shots into the still-standing human torch. The bullets drove the hellish apparition to the edge of the roof and over. All the way down Junior never screamed once. The sickening noise of the splat he made on impact traveled up to roof level and filled Tina's ears.

Calico dragged himself across the roof to where Tina had again dropped to her knees, her empty revolver still held in two hands in front of her, now pointed at the ground. Her hair was tangled around her face, tears mingling with grime and smoke. He wrapped his arms around her and held her tighter than he'd ever held anyone in his life.

The aftermath of the shooting seemed, as far as Tina was concerned, to drag on forever. Most of it was spent in a blur of waiting, punctuated by flurries of activity which preluded other stretches of hurry-up-and-wait.

The first stop after climbing slowly down from the roof where the shooting had taken place was the paramedics van. Two youngish-looking paramedics had cleaned and bandaged her hands and took a cursory look at the wire cut under her throat. They pronounced it nonserious but advised her to see a doctor anyway.

Calico, while receiving a fresh dose of ace bandages around his battered ribs, advised Tina to wrap her throat with one since it seemed a universal cure-all. The paramedic wrapping Calico's ribs gave the bandage a disapproving tug which brought a "wufff" from Calico and cut him off from giving further medical opinions. Junior received a burst from a fire extinguisher and a covering of clean sheets.

Cops seemed everywhere, surrounded by a solid cordon of citizens all wanting a glimpse of the gore. Thin strips of yellow plastic with the words "POLICE LINE—DO NOT CROSS" emblazoned in black were strung higgledy-piggledy to keep the crowds back. News cameras and reporters, however, figured they weren't included as part of the unwashed masses the lines were established for and ignored them, unconcernedly trampling evidence and emotions wherever they went.

A portable spotlight on top of a mini-cam clicked on and blinded Tina as she sat on the bumper of the paramedics van waiting for Calico. A microphone was thrust in her face.

"I'm Byron Murphy, Channel 8 There Now News. Can you tell us your reaction to what happened here, Officer?"

"What. . . ?" Tina looked up in confusion, using a bandaged hand to shield her eyes against the glare of the camera lights.

"Is this the first time you've ever killed a man?" the disembodied voice behind the microphone insisted.

Tina looked around, unsure of herself for the first

time that evening. Help came from an unexpected source.

"What the hell is going on here?" Sal Fazio stepped in front of the camera with an angry glare. "If you want the official police statement, we have established a press area over to your left with a press-relations officer who will answer all your questions. This officer is in the process of receiving medical aid and does not need you sticking lights and microphones down her throat."

The camera light stayed on. "The public has a right to know what happened here, Sergeant."

"They certainly do, but they're going to find it out from the official source, not from an injured officer who only has half the story. Now, if you would care to turn that blinding light off, perhaps I can get back to my job and transport this officer to the station where she can be debriefed." Fazio folded his arms in front of him as if daring the newsman to ask another question. The interviewer was undaunted, but a sudden wailing distracted his attention. Junior's mother had burst through the police barricade and thrown herself across the charred mess which had once been her son. The mini-cam light swung away, and the reporter raced off in pursuit of a better feature.

"Thanks, Sarge, but I could have handled it. They just caught me off guard."

"Yeah, they specialize in that. Fucking jackals. If you're done here I've got to get you back to the station. The shooting team is waiting to interview you."

"What about Calico?"

"He's already on the way with Sergeant Zeloff."

Back at the station Tina sat alone in an interview room for an hour and a half until the shooting investigation team, made up of a captain and two sergeants charged with investigating all police-related shootings where a suspect was hit, finished interviewing Calico. Finally the door to the interrogation room opened and the small room became crowded as it bulged to accommodate three more bodies.

Captain Bob Napier was a dapper man with a close-cropped, pointed beard. How he got away with the beard, in a department which had strict rules against anyone not undercover growing them, was a mystery. He came in with four cups of fresh coffee and a half-dozen jelly doughnuts picked up from the local Winchells by one of the desk officers.

"Hi, how are you holding up?" he asked to open.

The shooting investigation team was polite, supportive, understanding, low key, and, most of all, thorough. They led Tina through her story of the evening's events, her feelings that led up to the shooting, the beliefs in her mind about the situation at the time she pulled the trigger, time and time again until they had sucked her dry of every scrap of information and emotion she had to offer.

Tina answered all their questions in a calm voice which, toward the end of the session, gradually became raspy and exhausted. They never had to badger her as she understood they were doing their job just like she had done hers earlier in the evening. Finally they were satisfied.

"Do you have enough overtime built up to take a couple of days off?" Napier asked.

"I've got plenty of time on the books, but I don't think there are any specials available, manpower is low this month."

"I'll take care of that. Take two or three days off, until the shooting review board returns with a verdict. It will help. Don't worry about the review board either. I don't see any problem about this coming back in policy."

"Thanks." Tina smiled at the three men in the room with her, their jackets off now, ties loosened, dough-nut crumbs scattered across slim laps.

"How are you with this?" one of the sergeants asked her.

"Fine, I think. I know I had to do what I did."

"That's good, but if you get to feeling hinky give one of the department's peer counselors a call. You don't have to suffer this thing alone."

The shooting team finally took their leave and Tina made her way down to the locker room after filling out an overtime slip and checking out with the day-watch supervisors who were now on shift.

In jeans and a T-shirt she left the station and started up her three-year-old Honda Accord. Surprisingly, though she was tired, she didn't feel like going home. The adrenaline was still throbbing through her brain and she knew she wouldn't be able to sleep. She looked at the note in her hand which she had found taped to her locker door. It was from Calico, telling her he would be over at The Orphan's Home if she wanted company. She decided a drink, even if it was eight o'clock in the morning, didn't sound like a bad idea.

The Orphan's Home had been a cop bar ever since it had been established twenty years earlier. It opened at six in the morning when Harry Orphan, the retired C.H.P. officer who owned it, tossed out the cat, and closed officially at two A.M. when Harry locked the doors and went to his bed in the apartment complex next door. Anyone who happened to be inside when Harry locked the doors stayed there until he opened them again. At Harry's it was always Happy Hour somewhere in the world.

Calico slid off his bar stool when he saw Tina enter,

and guided her over to a booth already occupied by
Ray Perkins and Hal Zeloff.

"What happened to Jazzbo and Ed?" Tina asked
before sitting down. "Nobody was able to tell me anything at the station."

Calico cast his eyes downward. "It's bad. Jazzbo's
still alive, but hanging by a thread. He's got third-de-
gree burns over about half his body. Ed's dead."

"Shit!" Tina pounded both palms down on the
table, tears leaked down her cheeks. Calico put his
arm around her and Ray Perkins covered one of her
hands with his.

"Typical. Put 'em under a little pressure and these
goddamn females fall apart. What's the matter,
Blanche? Feeling sorry for the little dirtbag you had to
off tonight?"

Tina wheeled away from the booth table she had
been leaning on and became aware for the first time of
Guy Stack's presence in the bar. Thumper Thurman,
sitting on the stool next to him, put a restraining hand
on Stack's shoulders as his partner slid off his seat.
Harry Orphan started down the walkway behind the
bar, reaching for his nightstick. He wasn't fast enough.

Stack had a goodly amount of booze in him and,
like always when he drank, he was brooding about the
women in his life. He hated all of them, including his
ex-wife, a Vietnamese war bride who had come to
America, discovered liberation, and dumped the
spoiled and moody Stack for a stockbroker with a
mansion and a Ferrari.

"You fucking broads should know better than to try
and do a man's job," Stack slurred. "And you a gook
to boot. Shame, shame."

Calico stepped toward Stack angrily, but Tina was
too fast for him. All the emotion of the evening, all
the frustrations of fighting female prejudice from her

own family, citizens, many male officers, and all their wives and girlfriends, who believed women couldn't handle a cop's job, welled up inside her, and she launched herself across the room. One second she had been standing beside the booth and the next she took two steps and was hurtling through the air, one leg tucked tightly underneath her, the other stretched out to smash into Stack's jutting jaw.

Stack was nowhere near as shocked as everyone else in the bar, he didn't have time to be. The instant Tina's foot connected with his face he went down for the count, the power of the blow knocking him to the ground and the alcohol in his blood doing the rest. Tina landed in a crouch like a cat and turned with rage in her eyes.

"Don't do it!" Calico yelled at her as he could see her focus on Thurman who had stepped over the inert body of his partner and turned to face her. "They're not worth it."

Harry reached across the bar and touched his night-stick to Tina's shoulder. She whipped around out of her crouch to face him, more animal now than human, and tore it from his grasp. Screaming, she threw it viciously away from her, smashing the mirror behind the bar. Harry backed away and Tina turned to face Calico and Thurman again.

Calico had stepped in front of Thurman, his palms out toward Tina, who amazingly stayed put.

"Get your partner out of here, asshole," he said over his shoulder to Thurman. "Do it. Now!" he yelled when Thurman didn't move.

Slowly, Thurman rolled Stack over and then bent down to pick him up, throwing him over his shoulder like a sack of potatoes. When he got to the door of the bar Calico's voice stopped him.

"You tell your partner when he comes round that if

he wants a race he's got one. Next Sunday morning the clocks go back an hour, right?"

"Yeah, so?" Thurman easily adjusted Stack's weight.

"So, that means morning watch is extended an extra hour to cover the time shift. Enough time for a morning-watch run to Vegas and back. Turn around point will be the Citadel Casino. Get your picture taken in front of the Wheel of Fortune. Winner rakes in all the action he can handle. I'm putting five grand in the kitty, you two better find a way to match it."

"You got it, old man. We'll be here. You just see to it that you and the cunt show up." Thurman pushed out through the door with his burden. Calico didn't bother to watch him go.

"You okay?" he asked Tina gently. No one else in the bar had moved since the start of the action.

Tina sank down to the floor, her legs crossing underneath her, tears again leaking from the corners of her eyes. Calico moved over to crouch beside her and gather her into his arms.

"God, I'm sorry . . ." she mumbled in sobs against his chest. Calico was crying too, as was Ray Perkins. "It was just hearing about Ed and Jazzbo . . . final straw . . . ah, shit, poor Ed."

INTERLUDE

Citadel Casino—Las Vegas, Nevada
Monday—0200 Hrs

Deception is a game
won through
innocence

—ANONYMOUS MACHIAVELLI PROTÉGÉ, 1581

SIX

THE LAST BUCCANEER

M ORGAN WALES WAS a buccaneer in search of a
crew and a galleon to plunder. He was very tall
for an Englishman and moved across the floor of the
casino's private club with the lithe grace of a dancer.
His high, slanted cheekbones and long, pointed nose
gave his facial features a sharpness akin to that of an
ax head, blunt in profile, but riveting and dangerous
full on.

The thirteenth floor of the Citadel Casino didn't exist as far as its regular customers were concerned, as
evidenced by the hotel's elevators which, as in most
high-rise buildings, skipped directly from the twelfth
to the fourteenth floor. However, the private elevator
to the rear of the hotel's main floor whisked special
patrons from the noise and hubbub of the leisure suits
and polyester crowd gambling on the casino floor, to
the evening-dress splendor of the Citadel's private
club.

Entrance to the private club, nicknamed The Lucky
Thirteen by those who frequented it, was by invitation
which could be revoked at any time. Only the highest
of the high rollers were admitted, and cash was laid
squarely on the betting tables instead of chips. Morgan
had been on a streak in the ground-floor casino when
he had been invited "upstairs."

He'd come to Vegas three days previously, determined to have a good time, lose all his money, and then get back to what he did best—stealing more money. But like a gambler so desperate to win that if he bet on the only horse in a one-horse race the horse would get disqualified at the finish, Morgan was so desperate to lose he couldn't stop winning. His original stake of twenty-five thousand dollars had doubled in his first hours in the casino and now, three days later, he'd built it up to two hundred thousand dollars.

He'd become disgusted with himself. How the hell could he plan and pull another caper if he still had money in his pocket? It was his only superstition. He never pulled a job unless he was flat broke. But, like a hype looking for his next fix, Morgan needed to caper, needed the danger and the challenge. Without it he was dead inside. When the floor boss extended an invitation from the casino manager, Ollie Sebastian, nephew of casino owner Augustus Sebastian, to enter the sanctuary of The Lucky Thirteen, Morgan jumped at the chance. After all, his luck had to get worse sometime.

"Good evening, Mr. Wales. I'm Ollie Sebastian. Welcome to Citadel's private club." Morgan placed the man walking toward him with an outstretched palm to be somewhere on the cusp of forty. "I hope your luck holds."

Insincere sod, thought Morgan. He knew the only reason he'd been invited to the club was because he was walking around with over a hundred and seventy-five grand of the casino's money in his pocket. They wanted some of it back. As far as Morgan was concerned, though, they could have the lot. Only Lady Luck was refusing to get off his shoulders. "I guess having a big winner once in a while always convinces the other punters they have a chance, yes?" Morgan took Ollie Sebastian's hand and shook it briefly. It was like fondling a dead fish.

"Certainly, certainly," Sebastian replied. Morgan could recognize the predator instincts in the man. He was probably an even bigger thief than Morgan was, only Sebastian was getting away with doing it legally, and there was no challenge or thrill in that.

"Mr. Sebastian." A small, weedy man in a tuxedo which hung on him like an out-of-shape overcoat had appeared at Sebastian's elbow. "A phone call from Ellis in accounting."

"Yes, all right." Sebastian seemed to become suddenly preoccupied. "Please enjoy yourself, Mr. Wales," he said, dismissing Morgan almost brusquely before walking away, the weedy-looking man following in his wake.

Morgan smiled to himself. Phone calls from accounting at two o'clock on a Monday morning. Perhaps Sebastian wasn't stealing all his money legally. It was food for thought.

Entering his office at the rear of The Lucky Thirteen, Sebastian picked up the receiver from the white phone on his desk.

"Ellis?"

"Yes. I've just received a request from your uncle to audit the figures from the last quarter." The deep voice on the other end of the line betrayed a hint of worry.

"They'll hold up, won't they?"

"Yes. As long as he doesn't dig too deep."

"Do I need to remind you it's your job to see he doesn't."

"It'll look better if I can give him something."

"Yes, you're probably right. He'll expect a certain

amount of skimming, it's only natural. Give him the first level, but don't make it too easy."

"I don't think we should take your uncle lightly. If he finds out the extent to which we're ripping him off, he'll have our ears sliced off."

"You're always overly melodramatic, Ellis. My uncle is an old man. Ear slicing went out with cement overshoes and machine gun-stitched vests. I'll handle my uncle when the time comes."

"Yes, sir."

When Sebastian hung up the phone he noticed his hands were trembling and a red flush had worked up from his shoulders to burn the tips of his ears. He was still afraid of his uncle's power even if he refused to admit it to himself.

The extra Y chromosome that many scientists believe separate honest men from their criminal counterparts had been a part of Morgan's genealogy for generations.

He placed five thousand dollars down on top of an empty blackjack table. A gorgeous blond with long, tapering fingers dealt him two aces. "Split them," he said, doubling his bet.

The first ace was hit with a queen. Blackjack. The second ace with a third.

"Split them again." His bet was now tripled.

Another queen and a ten came out of the deck to cover their respective aces. Blackjack again. And again.

The dealer beat the rest of the table with a forced stay on a hard seventeen. "Must be your lucky night, sir," said the blond dealer with a sparkle in her eye as the pit boss moved up behind her.

"Yes, must be," said Morgan with a sigh. Shit, he thought to himself, God save me from dealers who love to see the house taken. He picked up his winnings and moved away. He'd only win more if he stayed.

Like his father before him, and his father's father before that, ad infinitum, Morgan had learned to be a thief through family tradition.

At six he was an expert at nicking candy from the shop on the corner of the street where he lived in a middle-class, downwardly mobile south London neighborhood. By eight he was an accomplished "dipper," able to lift a wallet from any suit in Heathrow Airport, or "Thiefrow" as it was known to the criminal fraternity. Because of his size and athletic prowess, intimidation came easy and the allowances of his classmates quickly made their way into his pockets.

When he was sixteen, Morgan's mother died in a car accident. His father immediately stepped up his son's criminal education, as if devoting himself to that would help him over the pain of losing his spouse. On his seventeenth birthday, Morgan celebrated by pulling his first solo "blag," a second-story job on the Mayfair flat of the Duchess of Malbury. The jewels garnered him ten thousand pounds sterling from a fence who only paid ten percent of their worth before shipping them off to Holland to be recut and reset. He gave the money to his father who was astounded, it was the largest haul in modern memory for a member of the Wales family. Daddy Wales was proud. Daddy Wales also spent every penny of it before the filth felt his collar on a minor shoplifting charge.

More out to cause aggro than from any basis of solid suspicion, the coppers turned over the Wales family "drum" and came across one of the duchess' diamonds which had been salted away against hard times. Daddy Wales was sent away for a seven stretch in Wormwood Scrubs behind it. He died of pneumonia two months short of early release.

Morgan learned two things from the experience: never caper while you still have money in your pockets, and never, never, do a small crime when there's a big one waiting for you right around the corner. Why shoplift when you can rob a bank? Why rip-off one car when you can steal enough jewels to buy twenty cars? Why masturbate when there's a whole world of women out there just begging to be taken?

At the craps table he noticed the stickman spoke with an English accent which was straight out of the same south London area where Morgan had grown up. There were several men and women gathered around the table, all in evening dress, the women dripping with jewels. Morgan took up a position along the rails at the opposite end of the current shooter and waited for the dice to come to him. It didn't take long, the table was pretty cold. A good sign. Perhaps Lady Luck would scramble off his shoulders to get her wrap.

"Mitcham," he said to the stickman, naming the neighborhood he had called home during his formative years.

The stickman smiled and replied, "Brixton, although I wouldn't want to claim it now."

"Complexion of the neighborhood darkened?"

"Perceptibly."

"Please place your bet and roll your 'come out,'" the boxman supervising the table spoke sternly. The stickman, whose nametag read "Merric," smiled and rolled his eyes at Morgan. Morgan dropped the thirty thousand he had picked up at blackjack on the pass line and proceeded to roll a natural seven. Shit, he thought.

During the time his father was in prison, Morgan had progressed through London's underworld. He'd had enough sense to connect with the organized mobsters who controlled the usual array of vice activities. He'd also had enough sense to stay independent from them while always kicking back a percentage from a job as a residual for being allowed to work their turf. Second-story work gave way to bank break-ins and eventually payroll robberies. He preferred to stay away from the heavy stuff with shooters, though, whenever possible. It was too messy and there wasn't the satisfaction of completing the job under the noses of the filth, all the time them never suspecting a thing.

The extra Y chromosome in his genes made him thrive on the fear and suspense generated while planning and pulling a big blag. Panic and daring fighting each other to the death in the darkness of his heart for possession of his soul. The feeling, just before a job went down, of being totally aware of his existence, even of the blood coursing through his veins. Knowing he was entering a rare, higher level of consciousness, getting a glimpse behind the veil of what it was like to be a god. Soldiers in battle sometimes reached it. Policemen sometimes did. And so did the true professionals of the thieves' trade. Once his taste for high risk had been piqued, he could never settle for anything less.

Morgan let his bet ride on the pass line. A natural eleven rolled out of his hand. Merric raked in the dice with his curved stick. His eyes locked with Morgan's and there was no doubt the younger Englishman could feel the tension Morgan was beginning to emanate. Merric began the verbal patter designed to let the other punters know there was a hot table starting, drawing them in like moths to a gypsy campfire.

Morgan picked up the red dice.

"Do you want me to blow them for you, for luck?" asked a redhead with sculptured eyebrows and a red-sequined gown cut down to her navel as she leaned against the railing next to Morgan.

Morgan frowned. "What an extraordinary idea." He threw the dice as the redhead pouted. The last thing he needed was more luck.

"The shooter's point is eight," Merric stated evenly as the croupiers at either end of the table began placing bets for the observers and raking in the bills from losers for the boxman to stuff in the drop box. Morgan let his bet ride on the pass line and dropped ten thousand dollars on an "all day" hard eight.

"Six," sung out Merric as the dice bounced to a stop. "The point is still eight."

Morgan threw twice more. Four the first time and then another six. The croupiers were getting busy as the table began to fill with money.

Morgan took the dice off Merric's wicker stick. They were hot in his hands. In fact he could feel the heat emanating all the way up his arm. He took another ten thousand and doubled his bet on the hard eight and changed it to a one-roll bet. On a whim he doubled the money on the pass line, bringing it up to one hundred and eighteen thousand.

He felt the boxcars roll out even before they left his hand. Merric frowned and several of the women around the table clapped their hands in delight. Across from him, Morgan saw Ollie Sebastian and several large men move across the room to stand at the other end of the table. He raked in the winnings from his hard eight bet and placed them down on the pass line, letting the money already there ride along.

"The point is ten," Merric called after the "come out" roll.

Turning to the pouting redhead next to him, Morgan extended the dice to her on the palm of his hand. He was playing a hunch. Delightedly, the redhead blew in earnest on the dice, her hot breath tickling the skin of his hand. As a final lucky gesture she licked the tip of Morgan's middle finger and then sucked the digit into the red "O" of her lips. The crowd around the table "ahhed" and "oohed" in appreciation. Morgan threw the dice, held his breath, closed his eyes as the dice bounced, opened them as he heard the crowd moan, and smiled when he saw the riveting digits of snake eyes. He'd crapped out.

"Too bad, sir," Merric said as a croupier pulled in all of Morgan's money from the pass line. Morgan saw Ollie Sebastian smirk and walk away.

Morgan peeled off two hundred-dollar bills from the still healthy remainder of his stash and stuffed them in between the redhead's cleavage. She squealed. "Need any help getting rid of the rest of your wad?" she asked. Morgan was sure she was referring to more than his money.

"Not tonight, ducky. I don't think I'll have any more problems." The redhead pouted, but moved away quickly when a roar came up from another craps table farther down the room. Morgan smiled to himself and tipped both croupiers at his table and the boxman. They were too busy with a new shooter to do more than nod. For Merric he folded up a thousand dollars and passed it over while shaking the stickman's hand.

"Best of British luck to you, sir, for the rest of your evening." The bills, now in Merric's hand, disappeared quicker than the eye could follow.

Morgan didn't know quite why he'd tipped the stickman so heavily, but he knew somewhere in the back of his mind a plan was forming. He moved away with a wave, and made his way over to the roulette table.

The rest of the morning passed quickly for Morgan. His luck was running again, but this time it was all bad. He dropped fifty thousand at the roulette table, moved back to the blackjack table and dropped another eighty thousand between it and the baccarat table next door. He was in high rollers' heaven, each losing hand bringing him closer to the bottom of his wallet, closer to a new caper.

At eight o'clock on that Monday morning, while Calico Jack Walker and Tina Tamiko were finishing up with the shooting investigation team and mopping up The Orphan's Home with Guy Stack, Morgan laid his last thousand dollars on the pass line of the craps table. Merric, who was finishing up the last tour of a double shift, passed him the dice.

He crapped out on his first roll.

A huge weight was suddenly lifted from Morgan's shoulders. He knew anyone else would be shattered by losing every dime they had. But he was different from everyone else and reveled in that fact. He was the best at what he did. Stealing money.

Visions of capers flashed through his head like a computer operating at full speed. Excitement flowed through him. He looked around at all the beautiful people throwing good money after bad into the Citadel Casino's coffers. He looked at the several obvious hardmen standing at strategic points around the private club, bulges under their arms giving evidence of badly cut suits and firearms. Above him he knew were cameras over every table and bird's-eye lenses which took in the whole room. There would be alarms which tied in directly to the Las Vegas Police Department, and a whole army of other security.

Morgan suddenly beamed from ear to ear. The plan which had been starting to formulate in the back of his mind had now jumped full-blown to the forefront.

Since the Citadel Casino had taken all his money it was only fair that he take all of theirs.

PART TWO

PREPARATIONS

"Be Prepared."
—THE BOY SCOUT MOTTO

SEVEN

LOVERS & SONS

A THIN SHAFT OF afternoon sunlight spurted through
a crack in the large bamboo shade and lanced
across Calico's closed eyes. The warmth and light penetrated his eyelids and projected psychedelic explosions across his sleeping retinas. He groaned and
rolled over. His elbow hit something hard and his eyes
snapped open.

"Where. . . ?" His heart leaped up into his throat
for a moment as he urgently pushed himself up and
gazed fuzzily at the unfamiliar surroundings. Reality
flooded in and he fell back onto the thin, covered mattress he was laying on. He closed his eyes, his head
supported by the rectangular pillow at the top of the
bed, and tried to control his breathing. His elbow
throbbed from where he had smacked it on the polished hardwood floor which the Japanese-style bed
was spread on. A thin yellow sheet with a hand-dyed
batik print tangled around his legs.

He was alone in the bed, only the lingering, warm
scent of a female body remained to confirm he hadn't
spent the whole night that way.

As his breathing and nerves returned to normal,
Calico opened his eyes and focused on the collection
of wind chimes suspended from the ceiling above him.

They were silent, moving slightly in the still air of the room, but not touching. Gradually he took physical stock of his body and was surprised to find a definite lack of aches and pains. His ribs still throbbed somewhat within their cocoon of ace bandages, but his back and shoulder muscles felt surprisingly supple.

The memory of making love to Tina flashed behind his eyes; him deep inside her as she straddled across his waist, her hands pushing against his shoulders, her small, upturned breasts bouncing in rhythm with her pelvic thrusts . . . There was suddenly a bottomless pit in his stomach and he shook his head to dispel the vision. "I'm too old for this shit," he mumbled to himself.

Rolling over, he crawled out of the bed and stood up. He stretched till his ribs hurt and then bent over and touched his toes, twice. He did it a third time when he realized he hadn't been able to do that in recent memory. "Damn," he said, feeling pretty good. Then he noticed a strange, unpleasant smell tickling the inside of his nose where it merged with the roof of his mouth. It was almost, but not quite, a taste. His euphoric physical mood was shattered when he realized it was the smell of charred human flesh. He thought immediately of Ed Martin and Jazzbo Brenner and felt guilty.

He looked around the simply furnished room for his clothes but couldn't see them. Aside from the bed there were several Oriental throw rugs spread across the floor and, in one corner, a huge, lacquered armoire with the fine design of a Japanese legend etched in gold filigree. The walls of the room were painted a light, almost undefinable color which hinted at both yellow and pink depending on the light filtering through the bamboo window screen. The screen itself was pulled almost closed, blocking out the view of the ocean behind a huge picture window.

He moved down a short hall and into the living room, stopping only briefly to visit the bathroom. He had refused to look in the mirror. His pants were folded and laying over the back of a low couch, his shorts underneath them, and his shirt on a hanger suspended from the entryway into the small kitchen. As he picked up his pants he saw the T-shirt, jeans, and silk underwear Tina had been wearing. They were crumpled up on the couch cushions looking like small sleeping animals. He put his pants back down and ran his thick, rough fingers over the silk underwear as if he were stroking a cat.

The scene at The Orphan's Home had left both of them emotionally drained. He'd only had one beer before Tina arrived, and even that he hadn't finished. He'd been too tired to get drunk. After he'd issued his challenge to Thurman, he had rocked Tina in his arms, both of them crying over what had happened to Ed and Jazzbo, and what they themselves had been forced to do. Neither had wanted to be alone but had needed to get away. They had taken her Honda. He had driven, and she had leaned across the hand brake to rest her head on his shoulder. She gave directions in a soft voice as they drove through the canyons toward her home in Santa Monica.

Once there, he carried her into the house, feeling slightly foolish, like a new groom. They had made love, immediately, on a pile of cushions in the living room, and then again later on her strange floor bed.

The crash of the surf brought his attention back to the present. He looked out through the living room's open sliding glass door, the wind billowing the champagne-colored sheers draped across it. On the large, enclosed terrace which faced the sea not fifty yards away, Tina moved naked through the determined, ritual movements of a martial-arts *kata*. Sweat rolled down from the hollow of her throat, snaking a path between her breasts, across the tautness of her stomach, overflowing the indention of her navel, and disappeared into the lightly thatched vee between her legs.

The progression of the *kata* floated Tina's lithe form across the terrace in a series of smooth, circular kicks, blocks, and punches. Muscles in calves and thighs quivered with effort. Others rippled across back and shoulders.

Calico watched her in silence, transfixed by the intense concentration which deepened the angles and shadows of his partner's face, her long hair swirling around her like a dark mist. He suddenly felt the stirrings of desire begin to betray his physical emotions. He wasn't the first police officer to have ever made love to his female counterpart, and he certainly wouldn't be the last, but he was an old-time hard-liner who wasn't supposed to be vulnerable to letting the little head do the thinking. Still, he couldn't tear his eyes away from the woman in front of him.

Across the terrace and back again, and again, and again, Tina moved almost silently, her pelvic center of gravity never varying its level as her kicks and punches snapped out to crack the wall of air around her. Each kick, each punch, became progressively more filled with the energy of anger, confusion, fear, pain, and emotion which purged itself in short explosions of breath from her mouth. Finally she stopped, her body slick with sweat. She turned to face Calico, staring at him through the veil of the window sheer as if she had somehow been aware of his presence all along. She moved through into the living room.

"Tina . . ." Calico started and then stopped. She moved across to him, aware of the excitement and need in him. "I . . ." he tried again, but she held a small hand up to his lips. With her hair down the top of her head was barely level with his heavy pectoral muscles.

"Don't talk. Don't think. I killed a man last night."

"You had to . . ." She stopped him again by pressing her hand tighter against his lips.

"I needed you last night. And I need you now. I need the affirmation that there is some good in the world, some pleasure."

She brought one of his hands up to her lips and buried her face in its callused palm, her small, sharp teeth nipping dangerously close to pain. She took her hand from his lips and brought his other palm up to caress a breast. One sleek leg and then the other wrapped around him as she tried to pull herself through him. Without a word he slid his hands down her back to the curves of her bottom. He hoisted her higher, easily supporting her negligible weight, and turned to carry her back into the bedroom.

On the thin mattress, laid randomly on the polished hardwood floor, in the airy room with the light, color-changing walls, their breathing quickened. Above them, the now-tinkling wind chimes.

"How are you?"

"Starved."

Calico laughed at her answer. It was much later. Night had fallen across the beach outside. They had made love and then slept, awakening in each other's arms, bodies satiated, emotions drained, yet also renewed.

Tina scrambled eggs and poured them out in a mound over toasted muffins and bacon strips while Calico took a quick shower. While Tina rewound the ace bandage around his ribs, Calico had called his son Ren, whom he had talked to from The Orphan's Home the night before, and agreed to meet him the next morning in Newport Beach to look their prospective boat over. He also called the hospital for an update on Jazzbo.

"How is he?" Tina asked when Calico hung up, her mouth full of eggs and muffin.

"Stable. Doctor says it's still touch and go, but the fact he's lasted this long is a good sign."

They were silent for a moment, acting busy with their food to cover their racing thoughts.

"Are you off tonight?" Tina asked Calico finally.

"Yeah. I have a stretch of three off. I go back Friday."

"They told me to take a few days until the review board comes back. I'd rather be at work. I wouldn't keep thinking about things then." Tina set her fork down with a sigh and pushed her empty plate away from her. "Have you ever shot anyone?"

"Twice, other than in the war. The first time I had about six years on the job. Wild John Elliot was my partner. We rolled on a bank robbery in progress and caught the assholes as they were coming out the front door. One had a sawed-off shotgun and peppered the police car with a round. Wild John and I both emptied our guns at the bastard. We were crack shots in those days," he said sarcastically. "We hit the shooter once, in the foot. It was enough to stop him, though. The incident scared both Wild John and me shitless. We were running around and screaming like fags with our dicks stuck in a glory hole." Tina laughed at the image. "The shooter's partner thought we were a pair of madmen. He threw down the cash and surrendered without a fight, figuring we were going to execute him on the spot. He never realized that neither of us had remembered to reload."

"What about the second time?"

Calico chased a remnant of bacon around his plate before answering. His eyes were downcast when he did. "The second time was different. It was a little more than eight years ago, right before Marsha and I got divorced. I was responding to a four-five-nine there-now call at a residence. I was working a P.M. watch L-car and was the first unit on the scene. When backup arrived I led the way into the house when the neighbors told us they had seen two men break-in through the rear door but hadn't seen them come out.

"I caught one of the burglars in the bedroom tearing apart the closet. The only light was from a street lamp coming in through a window from outside. When I told the guy to freeze, he turned toward me. He had a gun in his hand, and I blew him away." Calico went quiet and then sighed, ran a hand over his features, and continued in a lower voice. "It was a thirteen-year-old boy. The gun had come from the top shelf of the closet. It wasn't even loaded."

"There's no way you could have known that," Tina said with concern, reaching out to cover one of his hands with hers. "Nobody could ever say that wasn't a good shooting."

"Damnit." Calico jerked his hand off the table. "I'm not looking for sympathy. I know it was a good shooting. But that doesn't negate the fact that once or twice a year I still have to go out to the cemetary and visit the ghost of that thirteen-year-old asshole and wonder 'what if.' What if I had missed him, would he have changed or just grown into an adult asshole. What if I had hesitated, and it had been someone with a loaded gun with no qualms about shooting."

"You can 'if' yourself into a box," Tina told him.

"Yeah, that's my point. I don't want you to 'if' yourself to death because you had to blow away a demented scumbag last night who was trying to take you to hell with him.

"If I found myself in that same situation again on another burglary call, I'd still pull the trigger because it was the best option I had. If I shot another thirteen-year-old, then the only difference would be I'd have to visit two graves instead of one.

"You have to make up your mind you'd do the same thing again if you had last night to live over." Calico riveted Tina's eyes with his own. "You're a cop, and part of your job is making tough, split-second decisions in shooting situations. Decisions you're going to have to live with the rest of your life. Decisions other people who, with the comfort of hindsight, are going to be able to take all the time in the world to second-guess. If you can't handle that then don't strap on your gun and expect to work with me because you'll get one of us killed."

Tina stood up from the table, anger rising in her voice. "I don't plan on having any problems. After what that bastard did to Ed and Jazzbo, he deserved to die. It was just the first time I'd ever been forced to make that decision. Well, I made it. And I'll make it again when and if I have to."

Calico relaxed back in his chair and smiled. "Okay, then." His voice was soft and there was something akin to amusement in his eyes. "Come on, get dressed. We have to go and pick up my car before Harry thinks I've left it as a contribution to The Orphan's Home."

Later that evening they returned to Tina's house in separate cars after stopping by Calico's apartment. They were sitting on the deserted beach, wrapped in heavy sweaters as the waves rushed at them with the monotonous determination of spawning salmon.

Each of them had been wrapped in their own thoughts for a time, side by side, touching mentally but not physically, Calico almost dozing.

"What time are you going to meet Ren tomorrow?"

Calico replied from the edge of sleep. "About eleven."

"Are you really sure about leaving the department to go fishing?"

"I have to leave sometime whether or not I'm sure about it. At least with Ren's help I now have somewhere to go and something to do. I won't be like those poor bastards who retire from the department, spend all their time coming back to the station to try and talk over old times with someone who's too busy to talk to them, and then die from boredom in two years." Calico shifted his butt to a more comfortable position in the sand and hunched down in his sweater. "How about you? You have plans for tomorrow?"

"Yes. I'm going to visit my father."

"You don't sound thrilled."

"He can be difficult."

"Yeah?"

"Yes. He doesn't think I should be doing this job. It doesn't fit in with his image of how women should conduct themselves."

Calico chuckled softly. "Sounds like he and Stack would get along famously."

"Like two fleas on a dog's tail."

"Old Oriental saying?"

"No, bad dialogue from old Charlie Chan movie."

They went back to their ocean contemplations. The wind had picked up slightly and another couple of lovers walked by them obliviously along the water's edge.

"What you said to Thurman last night, did you mean it?" Tina asked after the pair had passed and they were alone again.

Calico opened his eyes but did not move otherwise. "You mean about the race?"

"Yes."

"Damn near half of the morning watch was in Orphan's when I issued that challenge. By now the whole division will have heard about it, and by the end of tonight Rumor Control will have spread it across the entire department. There hasn't been a race like this in years, and chances are there's already someone taking action on the outcome. I can't not race. I won't not race."

"What's this 'I' stuff? Don't you mean 'we' can't not race? After all, Thurman did say to make sure the 'cunt' was there. I assumed 'cunt' was his version of 'Blanche.'"

"You're not even off of probation yet. You can't even think about doing the run."

Tina turned to face him in the sand. "Oh, it's okay for you to risk thirty years and a pension, but it's not okay for me to risk eighteen months of time on the job. I'll be off probation by the race date, and anyway, I'm a woman, they would have a hell of a time firing me. That might not be right, but it's the way it is. If we got caught, you on the other hand would be out on your butt as quick as Fazio could set up the trial board. Perhaps you should stay and let me run the race."

Calico laughed and rolled over to take her into his arms. He kissed her as they fell backward onto the sand.

"Don't think this is going to make me change my mind," she said, laughingly moving her lips under his. "You're not that good."

In the harsh light of the post-morning fog the boat looked fairly miserable.

"Believe me it isn't as bad as it looks," Ren told his father as the two men walked along the dock finger and up to the gangplank. "She's structurally sound. They had her out of the water a month ago to scrape the hull and I had a good look at her then. We can repaint her, give her a new name, polish up the rails, revarnish everything. It'll be great, you'll see." Ren was almost bubbling over with excitement.

"You've known about this boat a month and you didn't say anything?" Calico asked his son. He was wearing a black crew-neck sweater over blue jeans and deck shoes. The creases in his face gave him a weathered look, as if he'd been out on the sea all his life instead of on and off for the last ten seasons.

"I waited for the price to come down. When the owner first put her on the market it was way too high."

"Why is the owner selling?"

"He isn't now, the bank is. Ted Burnly, the original skipper, gave over command of the charter business to Ted Jr. a couple of years ago, but Ted Jr. was more interested in catching broads instead of fish. The business went to hell and the bank foreclosed when Ted Jr. couldn't make his payments or sell the boat himself. Now the bank's stuck with a white elephant which they're willing to get rid of for the price of their investment."

"How'd you learn so much about it?" Calico asked as he followed Ren aboard. He ran his hand over the pitted railing and flaking paint in disgust. At the stern he looked over and down at the name: SHIRLEY—NEWPORT BEACH. He wondered who the hell Shirley was and if she had deteriorated as much as the boat which had been named after her.

"I was down here doing a lifestyles piece for the newspaper." Ren's enthusiasm was almost contagious. "I was keeping my eyes open, as always, for the main chance when I came across her. The story isn't an unusual one, charter fishing isn't exactly top of the exchange as far as being a solid business investment."

Calico leaned back against the stern rail. "Knowing that, do you still want to get involved in this?"

"Hey, you were the one who taught me to never be afraid of taking a chance if you believe in yourself. Well, I believe in myself and I believe in you. Between the two of us we can make this work."

"It won't be easy."

"You also taught me that nothing worth achieving is. What's the matter, Pop? Are you having second thoughts? Are you sure this is what you want to do?" Ren's voice was concerned, only an inflection away from hurt.

"Do you have the cabin key?" When Ren nodded, Calico motioned for him to open up so they could go inside and get out of the cold breeze coming in from the sea. Calico took a seat at the controls and looked out through the wide window in front of him. "I told you on the phone about shooting that Torchsong idiot, right?"

"Yeah, I read about it in the paper too. Why? What's this about?"

"You know perhaps your mother is right. Perhaps it's time I grew up. This is ridiculous."

"What is, Pop? Come on give."

"You've heard your mother yell at me before about the run I did in the police car to Tijuana and back with Wild John when she was pregnant?"

"Every time she gets mad at you she brings it up. It's one of her favorite pieces of ammunition. She usually mentions it if she's losing an argument and has to resort to fighting dirty by bringing up past sins."

Calico chuckled. "That was one of her favorite tactics, taking the focus away from a losing argument point by bringing up a winning point from the past."

"So what does that have to do with going into the charter fishing business? We already have several potential contracts lined up. We've been planning this for ages."

"I know, I know. The fact of the matter is I'm going to do another run."

"To Tijuana?" Ren looked startled.

"No, Las Vegas."

"Holy shit."

"Yeah."

"What happens if you get caught?"

"Probably only a suspension. But with Fazio after my ass he could get me fired if he pushed it, and then there goes the pension."

"We don't need your pension to run this operation."

"It sure would be nice, though, to have a certain amount of guaranteed income."

"The solution then is not to do the run."

"I guess so."

Ren looked at his father. "You'd never be happy with that solution, would you? It wouldn't be right for you. It wouldn't be the decision you would make for yourself alone."

Calico just shrugged and turned back to look out the window again. Ren turned to see what his father was looking at and had the same vision—the two of them working the boat together during endless days of satisfying labor, learning the ocean together better and better each day, father and son failing or succeeding together. The operating word through it all—together.

"No, it wouldn't be right," Ren said after a while. "There's only one right thing to do."

"You're sure?"

Ren extended his hand palm up toward his father, a smile on his face. Calico's face lit up in a beam of a smile that creased either side of his mouth with deep dimples and sparkled in his eyes. He slapped his own palm down across his son's.

"Go for it, Pop."

"Why can't you ever make an effort to understand my position, Daughter?"

"Your position, Papa? Just what is your position? Why can't you ever try to understand what it is I am trying to do? I had to shoot a man last night, and all you can think of to ask me is why I never think of you." Tina was frustrated by the same argument she went through every time she visited with her father.

"It is not my place to understand you. You are the daughter; it is your place to respect me." Her father was a small man, smaller even than she was. His features were fine but definite, eyes with a slight downward pull at the back of the sockets, nose straight and sharp, cheekbones angled downward from front to back heightening his regal Oriental looks. His short black hair was peppered with gray the same color of his British-cut, pinstripe suit. The shirt was ivory in color, offset by a black silk tie and a sterling silver collar bar.

"Papa, I do respect you, but this isn't feudal Japan. You've lived in America for twenty-five years, when will you begin to understand that?"

"You are my daughter, not my son. You should be at home taking care of a husband and children, not out killing innocent boys!"

"Father!" Tina couldn't believe her ears, she refused to let tears spring from her eyes. "That animal I killed last night was no more an innocent child than the spawn of Satan would be. I did what I had to do last night to protect the innocent, and I'm proud of it."

"If your mother was alive she would be as shamed as I am."

"That's not true, and you know it! She was the one who helped me to understand that I can be who I want to be, and not a little geisha with bound feet and a bound mind. It was her independence that made you fall in love with her, and it was your inability to control her will that continued to make you love her. Now it is you who shames her memory by denying her in death the traits which she held so dear in life."

"Do not talk to your father that way!" Sochi Tamiko turned away from his daughter in his swivel chair as if by turning his back on her she would disappear.

Sochi had been thirty-five years old when the electronics company he worked for in Japan had sent him to England on a special project. There he had met Tina's mother and had fallen in love. It had surprised him. He had been married before, in Japan, an arranged marriage between two families of high-powered industrialists. He had followed his duty and bred two sons, but when his wife died giving birth to a third son, his only emotion was gladness that the baby had survived. He felt not the merest loss for the woman who had borne his sons. She was a nonentity. He didn't know he was capable of love.

Tina's mother, Maureen, was different, though. She had been an executive with the English corporation he had been sent to work with, and Sochi had been enraptured by her boldness, intelligence, and her passion. He was a lost man.

They had prospered as a family, Maureen leaving her career to raise her stepsons while Sochi continued to fight the corporate wars. In 1960 they had immigrated to America and settled in Los Angeles where Sochi, with Maureen's capable help, had established his own electronics firm which now prospered. Their one regret was their inability to produce children of their own union. And then Tamiko was born, a joy no father could deny. Now Sochi had a wife who inspired him and still inflamed his passions, three strong sons to run his business, and a daughter to help his wife care for the home and brighten his later years. The only problem was that number one daughter wasn't having any of it.

Even as a child Tamiko had competed with her older brothers. Her grades in school were always better. Athletically she could, by comparison, run faster, jump higher, and think quicker than any of them. She refused to be domesticated, her will bending only after severe chastisements, but even then never breaking completely.

Maureen contracted cancer when Tina was eighteen. She died two years later. Sochi mourned for the loss of the English rose his headstrong daughter so reminded him of and, as if in an effort to block the pain of seeing the mother continually in the daughter, he redoubled his efforts to force Tina's ever-changing modern form into traditional domestic roles.

Tina knew one day, when his mourning was done, he would change and accept her, as he had accepted the same traits in her mother. But until then the battle raged.

"Papa, I love you. Why do you treat me this way?" Tina walked around in front of her father, forcing him to look at her. "I want you to be proud of me and what I'm doing." Sochi was stoic.

Tina reached out a hand and ran it down her father's cheek. "We shouldn't fight. It isn't right for a daughter and father. You will come to the house soon, yes? I will cook for you." Her father looked at her sharply but did not say anything. "Don't look so surprised. I can do those things, but I need to do much more as well."

Sochi touched his own hand to his daughter's as she crouched in front of him.

"I love you, Papa," Tina said, standing. She smoothed her simple dress across her knees and bent forward to kiss Sochi on the forehead. "I'll see you soon." Turning away she left the office, refusing to let her father see the tears in her eyes.

Sochi Tamiko sat motionless for a long minute and then suddenly raised his right arm and brought it down violently onto the padded chair arm.

EIGHT

DAWN RAIDERS

T HE QUARTER PLINKED into the tollbooth's metal
depository, and Calico wheeled his battered Jeep
Cherokee onto the tail end of the Vincent Thomas
Bridge which connected San Pedro to Terminal Island.

If anyone needed proof God is a woman, Calico
thought, all they had to do was visit Terminal Island, a
disgusting blob of land she created while she had
cramps. He'd been concentrating a lot on trivial
thoughts like that, trying to avoid thinking about Tina.
They had made love again the night before, and her
soft scent now lingered teasingly around him, a taunt-
ing reminder of the radical change in their relationship. Instead of seeing a blue uniform when he
thought of her, he saw her ebony hair fanned out
across the pink silk of a pillowcase. Beside her he felt
like an ancient warthog. He remembered her passion
from the night before and his chest ached. He growled
deep in his throat and forced himself to concentrate on
his driving.

Terminal Island was little more than a glorified
sandbar, expanded by manual labor into a filthy
hodgepodge of railroad yards, docks, wharves, slips,
factories, oil plants, and rundown offices. In the early
nineteen-hundreds the island had sported the fashion-

116

able Brighton Beach resort along its elongated and protected north shore. But the rich and famous had quickly become disenchanted with the industrial growth and dredging rapidly encroaching on their playground. Almost in a mass exodus, the wealthy fled the island, taking with them the fascinating bohemian contingent of gamblers, writers, artists, and drifters who congregate around the rich like small fish following a shark.

In place of the rich came the advanced elements of the multiracial community of fishermen, abalone harvesters, and cannery workers who would become permanent residents as the ugliness of the docks completely took over. Terminal Island was suddenly an industrial blight on the landscape, much like its connection to the mainland, San Pedro.

In the quiet of the predawn Wednesday morning, Calico drove quickly down the bridge off-ramp and through the ill-maintained streets toward the police department's pursuit-driving school. Along the way he passed closed stores whose darkened windows displayed every kind of nautical gear with monotonous regularity. The gaudy patterns advertising tattoo parlors added a splash of garish color to the area which was countered by dingy "wing-ding" joints; semisecret gambling dives where sailors indulged in cheap whiskey, fixed roulette, fan-tan, and whores. Union halls and posters were everywhere, giving testament to the organization of the waterfront workers and their knowledge of that strength.

Calico rarely entered this part of the city and the grimy sight of the docks quickly reminded him why. He turned off Seaside Avenue onto Mormon, deadended at New Dock Street, and followed his nose to Reeves Field. The Navy had taken over this portion of the island in 1937 about the same time the federal

prison was being built on Reservation Point at the opposite end. It had originally been a training facility,
and later a storage area for naval air power. At the
city's request, however, the Navy had loaned the police department a couple of deserted hangars and had
sanctioned the building of a driving course.

When Calico had become a policeman, pursuit driving was something picked up on the street after twelve
weeks of academy training and two years of suffering
through traffic duty. They didn't let rookies drive in
those days. But times changed rapidly in L.A., and
the police department was forced to keep up. With the
rapid influx of population, the advent of freeways, and
a larger, more complex system of streets and traffic
controls, pursuit driving became part of the academy
curriculum in the spirit of public safety.

Since its inception, Calico had been through the
course twice and had even held the lap record at one
time. There had been a lot of clear-eyed rookies
through the course since then, though, and his old record had been shattered long ago by the likes of Guy
Stack and the hordes of other young turks.

The main gate to the facility was open and Calico
drove through. The Navy still used part of the facility
for storage, but they only kept a minimum of personnel in the area, none of which were in sight. Calico
drove to the far end of the field, where the hangars
were, and parked.

The stress which was constantly applied at the
Academy was somewhat foregone during the three
days each group of recruits spent at the driving course.
The traditional spit-and-polish recruit uniforms were
replaced with jeans and casual shirts. Recruit morale
was always pretty high during the course, since pursuit
training came during the sixth and final month of the
Academy. Six months now instead of twelve weeks,

Calico mused, and still the majority of rookies hit the streets not knowing their ass from a hole in the ground about police work. They did know how to drive fast, though, he'd give them that much.

As he walked across the deserted tarmac the noise of a hangar door being pulled open reached Calico's ears, and he paused for a second to watch the day's preliminaries. The scene had always conjured up a fantasy for him which was like a scene out of a British war film: the ragged police cars, looking like tired gray Spitfires, being pushed out of their hangars into the dawn light; the recruits, stamping their feet in impatience like pilots awaiting the order to scramble, silhouetted by the orange rays of the rising sun, the steam of their breath enough to fuel a locomotive. There was the crisp snap of determination in the air as the metaphysical dawn raiders prepared to fight or die, not giving a damn either way.

"All right, listen up, you maggots!" A coarse voice Calico knew well snapped him out of the fantasy. He grinned as he focused on Wild John Elliot beginning to work the recruits like a tough dog herding a flock of woolly pigs.

"Push these bitches out to the start of the pursuit course and fire 'em up," Wild John told them. "And God save the first one I hear revvin' an engine like a maniac."

"Howdy, Wild John."

Wild John turned at the sound of his name. "Well, I'll be damned and gone to hell! Calico Jack Walker. You're a sight for sore eyes, boy. Come down here to see where you end up when they figure it ain't safe for you to carry a gun anymore?"

The two men shook hands fiercely.

"Somehow it doesn't make sense to me," Calico said to his friend. "I always figured you could do more damage with a ton of steel moving at seventy miles an hour than with some tiny hunk of pea-spitting metal."

Wild John laughed. "Yeah, well, the brass on this department always did have shit for brains."

"You always figure anybody who disagrees with you has shit for brains."

"Are you disagreeing with me now?"

"Do I look like I have shit for brains?"

"No, you just look like shit period."

"I'd have stayed married if I wanted to take that kind of abuse."

Wild John laughed again. He was a stocky muscle of a man, his large arms bulging out from the tight sleeves of his T-shirt. He wore heavy work jeans over worn cowboy boots. On the front of his T-shirt was the death's head logo of the special forces accompanied by the words: FUCK IT—KILL 'EM ALL AND LET GOD SORT 'EM OUT. His baseball cap had a patch with a bastardization of the department's motto: TO PROTECT AND SERVE—AFTER COFFEE AND DOUGHNUTS. He took the cap off to run stubby fingers through his blond crewcut, and then pulled it firmly into place again.

"How is your ex these days?"

"Getting porked by Sgt. Sally, and sniping away at my pension and my sanity."

"I didn't know Sal Fazio could still get it up."

"Up but not off."

"Rumor Control or personal experience?"

"No, word of mouth from the RTO with the big tits and the birthmark half the damn department's seen."

"You mean the one with the biblical fetish?"

"Biblical fetish?"

"Yeah, likes to play 'seek and ye shall find' in the backseat of a patrol unit during her lunch breaks."

"That's the lady."

A heavy revving noise reached them from across the field.

"Shit!" spat Wild John. "Come on. Somebody is gonna have to help me wipe the asses of these babies before I go insane."

"I thought you were insane. Isn't that why the department sent you down here in the first place?"

"Yeah, it's their version of a fucking catch-22. If I apply for a stress pension, I'm sane enough to realize I need out and therefore can't be stressed enough to qualify. If I don't apply for a pension, because I'm too insane to know I need one, the department takes away my gun and transfers me to where the runny-nosed idiots they're hiring these days can chip away at what's left of my mind."

"You have to have one wheel in the sand to become a cop in the first place. So maybe you are insane, but you aren't crazy."

"Yet."

The two men crossed the field to where the recruits were warming up the police cars, and Wild John leaned his malevolent face into the driver's window of the car occupied by the heavy-footed recruit. "This ain't your daddy's fucking highly tuned stock car, Stillwell. These bitches are held together by chewing gum and knuckle skin. My knuckle skin. And if you crack a rod or throw a piston because you overrevved the engine before it's properly warm, then it's going to be your knuckle skin, on your own time, which is going to go into fixing the bitch. You got that?"

"Yes, sir," Stillwell replied, backing off the accelerator. Calico caught the trace of arrogance in the voice.

While Calico stood back and watched, each of the ten recruits in the class took several laps in a police car with Wild John riding shotgun and explaining the various procedures to follow in a pursuit. They were then turned loose, two to a car, to have a go at what they had learned, fulfilling everyone's childhood fantasy of tearing around in a police car with the lights going and the siren wailing. Two of the three women in the group did exceptionally well, and Calico commented on it.

"I was surprised by the women, too, when I started teaching here," Wild John agreed in reply. "With the guys the first thing you have to do is break all the bad habits they developed racing around town as teen-agers. The girls have rarely developed those habits and it's easier to train them. They have a nice light touch and, if they have the guts to match, they do well out here."

Wild John waved the cars in and was confronted by ten grinning faces. "Okay, hotshots. Now we'll show you how a real cop does it." He threw a set of keys to a surprised Calico. "You were one of the best. You still got the touch?"

Calico shrugged. "I guess we'll find out." He walked over to one of the black and white units and climbed in. Wild John followed him over and spoke to him through the window.

"Do you remember what your time was last time you were out here a few years ago?"

"Somewhere around one minute twenty."

"It was one twenty point six, partner."

"You got all those figures running around in that little pointy head of yours?"

Wild John loosed one of his famous big-teethed grins. "The current record is one fourteen point five. You aren't even in the top ten anymore."

"Times change."

"People don't. You never like to be anything but number one."

Calico put his palm over Wild John's laughing face

and pushed him away from the window. He pulled a crash helmet over his head, adjusted the chin strap, checked his "cross your heart bra" seat belt, and pulled onto the track.

He took the first couple of laps easy, getting the feel for the ragged, asphalt–concrete pursuit course, designed to give the impression of the changing surfaces of city roads. Lap distance was somewhere between three-quarters and one mile, actually 4875 feet, a bastardized distance set by the limitations of the field area on which the track was built. There were numerous unbanked curves, bordered with orange cones, several hairpin turns, and one long straightaway. In the middle of the semi-oval course were two large mountains of dirt which often caused a chase vehicle to lose sight of its quarry for a few precious seconds.

As Calico approached the start/finish line for the second time, he slowed to a stop and waited for Wild John to give him a go. Wild John raised his arm and then dropped it dramatically, starting his stopwatch at the same precise moment. Calico put his foot onto the accelerator, but took off smoothly without laying rubber.

Braking hard before entering the first curve, he picked his line and accelerated through the turn. A series of three "S" curves flashed toward the police car, but Calico beelined them. He picked up speed down a short straightaway and then was forced to brake hard for a hairpin. He cursed himself, knowing he'd lost time, and pushed into a power slide through the next smooth turn, his traction dangerously close to breaking free. The orange cones along the border waffled in the vehicle's draft.

He was faster through the next hairpin, and even faster through the reverse curve which followed. He steered like a rally driver, his hands never leaving the wheel, never crossing over while making a turn. Concentration was deeply lined into his face.

Another series of "S" curves were straightened out under the wheels of the police vehicle, and the wide curve which led to the final straightaway loomed ahead. Calico judged his speed well and accelerated all the way through the final curve, coming out just short of the vehicle's top speed, and then jumped on every last rev the engine had to give as he screamed for home.

As Calico roared past the finish, Wild John tripped the stopwatch. He looked at it, chuckled, then showed it to Stillwell who was standing next to him. Calico saw the two of them conversing and gesturing as he turned and drove back toward them.

"So?" Calico asked as he pulled up next to Wild John.

"Well, partner, I'll tell you. I've got some good news and some bad news. The good news is you set a new track record of one minute fourteen even. The bad news is my man Stillwell, whose daddy is a pro stock-car racer and taught this little maniac everything he knows, says he can beat that standing on his prick."

Calico scowled and then shoved his helmet at the recruit. "Knock yourself out, kid," he told the recruit. "Watch out for that second hairpin, though, there's some loose gravel as you go into it."

"That's the oldest psych-out trick in the book, sir," Stillwell told Calico with disdain. "If there was loose gravel going into the second hairpin, you'd still be spinning through the cones."

Wild John almost doubled over with laughter. "Hee-hee. The kid's sharp, partner. He put you away with that one." He slapped Calico hard on the back. Calico just scowled.

"Action talks and bullshit walks, kid. If you think

you've got the stuff to go balls to the wall out there, then let's see it."

Stillwell strapped on the helmet and slid into the black and white's driving seat. "See you again in under one fourteen."

"Sure, kid." Calico slapped the top of the police car with his hand.

"You want to take a couple of warm-up laps?" Wild John asked.

"No need. I got this baby wired."

Stillwell pulled up to the start line and flashed away at Wild John's signal. From the sidelines Calico watched as Stillwell dug into the first turn and tore into the "S" curves which spat him out slicker than whale snot on a doorknob.

Through the short straight and the first hairpin, Stillwell was almost perfect. A powerful surge of the engine brought him smoothly through the next curve and lined him up for the second "S" set. Calico shook his head in wonder at the kid's skills.

The loose gravel Calico had tried to warn him about on the second hairpin almost proved Stillwell's undoing, but his powerful wrists, built up from lap after lap of racing on stock-car tracks with his father, fought the G-forces which threatened to tear the steering wheel out of his hands. Somehow the car maintained traction and was suddenly flowing like a flash flood through the following reverse curve without losing a millisecond.

Into the last wide curve, Stillwell pushed the police vehicle to the limit and, entering the final straightaway, he activated the car's lights and siren. Wild John clicked the stopwatch.

"No good news this time, partner."

"How fast?"

"One minute thirteen point six seconds."

"Shit!"

The other recruits cheered and yelled their congratulations as Stillwell drove back and climbed out. Calico walked over and shook the kid's hand.

"Nice job, kid," Wild John told his trainee, "but the show's not over yet." He turned to face all the recruits. "When you're out on the street driving in a pursuit, it isn't good enough to just be faster than the guy you're chasing. You have to be safe as well, and also be able to outthink the suspect. I'll show you what I mean." He turned to Stillwell. "Get back in the car and pull up to the start line. I'll be your copilot so don't leave without me. When Officer Walker drives past you, I want you to hit the lights and siren and chase him down. Once you've got him to stop—and remember ramming isn't within the policy of this department—I want you to go through the routine of a vehicle stop like you would if you had a suspect on the street. Okay?"

Stillwell nodded and hopped back in his car to get set.

"The rest of you watch what happens." Wild John winked at Calico and threw him another set of car keys. "Do your thing, partner. Make sure you check the glove box," he finished cryptically.

Calico drove his black and white to the start of the track's long straightaway and then raced toward the finish line. As Calico blew past, Stillwell hit his emergency equipment and set off in pursuit, Wild John strapped in beside him.

Through the first turn, the "S" curves, the short straight, and the first hairpin, Stillwell began to close the gap between the two vehicles, losing sight of Calico only once as he flashed behind the first dirt mountain. Distance remained constant through the power slide of the next turn, the second "S" set, and into the reverse curve.

Suddenly, halfway through the wide curve which led back to the long straightaway, Calico's vehicle was out of sight again behind the second mountain of dirt. As Stillwell came sliding into the turn, he had the shock of his life. Calico had slammed on the brakes, broken his vehicle's rear end loose, brought it around, and was headed straight back at the pursuit vehicle. Stillwell panicked, pulled the wheel to the right to avoid a collision, and flew off the track. Orange border cones bounced away in all directions and clouds of dust enveloped the pursuit vehicle as it rocked to a conked-out stop.

"What's the matter, kid?" Wild John yelled at the recruit. "Your suspect is getting away. Wasn't that move in your daddy's book of stock-car tricks?"

Stillwell was silent.

Wild John slapped the back of the recruit's helmet. "Get back on the track and get after him!"

It took three tries for the shaken Stillwell to get the car's engine started again. Slowly he pulled back onto the track, sweat soaking his underarms and beading across his forehead. Driving clockwise now, he set off after Calico. He picked up speed as the track unwound beneath him, but, filled with anticipation, he didn't come close to the speeds he had originally been traveling at.

Calico's car was nowhere in sight until Stillwell almost ran into it. The cruiser was stopped in the middle of the track, hidden by the first dirt mountain. Calico appeared to have deserted the vehicle. Stillwell screeched to a stop a foot short of the back bumper of Calico's vehicle.

"What are you going to do now?" Wild John asked when Stillwell didn't move.

"I don't know."

"How about getting out and taking a look at the car you've been chasing like a maniac."

Stillwell nodded and started to get out of the car.

"Wait a minute! Wait a minute!" Wild John yelled. "How about letting communications know what's going on?"

The other recruits, who were involved in the session, had come over to where the vehicles were stopped and were listening with interest to the lesson Wild John was giving Stillwell.

"You want me to do it now?"

"Kid, if you neglect to do it now when it's not for real, you're going to forget to do it when it is for real, when your life may depend on it. You might think the suspect you've been chasing is just a traffic violator, but he could also be the biggest asshole in the world who's just itchin' to blow your brains out if you make a mistake."

"You're right."

"Of course I am. So get on with it."

Stillwell picked up the car's dead mike and relayed his position and activity to a nonexistent RTO. He then looked over at Wild John who shooed him out of the car.

Approaching the empty car cautiously, Stillwell stuck his head in the driver's window, giving Calico the chance to slide unseen from under the far side of the car and sneak around behind the recruit. The cold steel muzzle of the gun Calico had removed from his vehicle's glove box found a home at the back of Stillwell's neck.

"Say your prayers, cowboy." Calico's voice was low and gruff. He pulled the gun away and fired one of its blank loads into the ground.

Wadding chewed up the dirt, and Stillwell fainted dead away.

Calico and Wild John were still laughing when they entered the training facility's office. The roach coach had pulled in a few minutes earlier and the recruits were being given a break.

"That little trick never fails to give 'em a shock," said Wild John as he took a seat behind a battered metal desk.

"It's a lesson that'll stay with them the rest of their careers, though. It has with me," Calico stated, becoming a bit more serious.

"I know Stillwell will never forget it."

Calico snorted. "He's probably not a bad kid. A little salty perhaps, but that'll be knocked out of him when he hits the street."

"I've a feeling he's going to be a whole lot more humble starting right now."

The office they were in was at the rear of the larger of the two hangars used by the driving school. Thin makeshift dividers had been set up as walls, but did little to subdue the noise from another group of recruits receiving instruction in the classroom area on the other side. Department memorandums, covered over with cartoons clipped from newspapers and men's magazines, and a huge poster of a gleaming Japanese rocketcycle being straddled by a pair of stocking-clad, extra long female legs made up the office decor. Some enthusiastic soul had graffitied the poster with the sage words: RIDING A JAPANESE MOTORCYCLE IS LIKE FUCKING A PIG—A LOT OF FUN UNTIL SOMEBODY SEES YOU.

Wild John pulled a prison bulletin off of the wall. "You seen this?" He handed it over his shoulder to Calico who scanned it briefly.

"What is it?"

"A listing of all the federal cons at the Terminal

Island Penitentiary coming up for parole hearings this month. Take a look about a quarter of the way down the list, under 'C' for Carradine. King Carradine."

"Shit, I don't believe it. His time can't be up yet. The bastard tried to kill us." Calico looked at the list in disbelief.

"He's served seven years of his twenty-year sentence for interstate transportation of firearms and assault on federal officers. If you remember, they plea bargained away the attempted murder charges we filed on him."

"Anything we can do about this?"

"Put in an appearance at the hearing to protest his parole."

"You think it would do any good?"

"Hard to say. If King gets out he's going to come looking for us."

"Every big-time con I've ever put away has sworn to come back and get me, it's the biggest cliché in the book. King is the only one I've ever believed."

"I know what you mean. He's a crazy bastard, and from what I hear, he's set himself up as a sort of demigod among the prison population. He might have established enough sway to get himself released."

Calico stared somberly at the list in his hands while his old partner sauntered over and took a seat in a swivel chair behind a battered desk.

Throwing his feet up on the desktop, Wild John pulled out a stump of cigar and began to chew on it. "Well, when are you going to get down to what this visit is all about?"

"You don't think I just dropped in to see an old friend, huh?" Calico asked wearily as he slumped into an old easy chair with stuffing shooting out of all its cushions. He balled up the paper in his hands and swished it into a half-full trash can for two points.

"Not a chance, partner. The word is you're set to do a morning-watch run to Vegas against that asshole Stack and his partner. Now you suddenly turn up here looking like a virgin about to break her duck. What's up?"

"I need a mechanic to help me get a car in shape. You're the best one I know."

Wild John swung his feet to the floor and rummaged through his desk drawer. "You haven't changed, have you? Still the same crazy bastard you were when we worked together. I like that about you. You're a throwback to the days when policemen could still have fun on this job." He took a photo from the drawer and extended it to Calico. "Remember this?"

Calico looked at the photo and laughed. It showed Wild John astride a moth-eaten donkey, a ragged sombrero cocked at a jaunty angle over his rumpled police uniform. Next to Wild John stood the small Mexican man who owned the donkey. Behind them, but visible, was a Tijuana signpost and Calico sitting in a black and white unit. Both policemen were grinning like a pair of idiots. "Where did you find this?"

"I keep it around for when I write my memoirs."

"You can't even spell memoirs, and you can't remember past last night, let alone nineteen years ago when this was taken."

Wild John feigned looking hurt. "And you expect a favor?"

"How about it? Help me get a car ready?"

A glint, like that of a child with a secret, crept over Wild John's face. "I'll do even better. Follow me. And bring that along." He indicated the photo in Calico's hand.

Wild John led the way to a small building the size of a three-car garage. Taking out a fistful of keys, he opened a rusty padlock and moved inside to where a large shape was shrouded by a heavy tarp. Without ceremony, he swept the tarp off to reveal an old police car. The roof sported a large metal siren speaker flanked on either side by small, round emergency lights, red to the front and amber to the rear, making it look like a dinosaur in the current age of futuristic solid light bars.

Calico looked at the shop number stenciled on the car roof. One eight eight. He looked at the shop number of the police car in the photo he was holding. One eight eight. Every aspect of the vehicle shone in the overhead light. Calico ran his hands over the peppering of shotgun pellet holes which pitted the driver's door. He knew, intimately, how they had gotten there. He also knew how the rear bumper had received the dent on its left side. The bumper had been rechromed but not straightened. The bullet holes had been smoothed over and repainted but not plugged.

"I'm astounded," said Calico in an almost reverent voice. "Where did you get your hands on this beauty?"

"The 1965 Plymouth Fury. Three hundred and eighty-three cubic inches of the meanest pursuit vehicle ever to come off the production line. A far cry from today's Chevys and Fords which fall apart at anything over eighty-five miles per hour. This baby tops out at around one hundred and thirty-five miles per hour, and will cruise forever at a hundred plus."

"I know, I know. I drove this bitch around the city for five years. But where did you get it from?"

"The police auction. They put her out to pasture when the odometer approached the one hundred thousand-mile mark for the second time."

"That's a mighty tired engine when you consider the mileage was put on driving around and around the city for three eight-hour shifts each day, every day. Not to mention the occasional side trip to Mexico."

"Don't kid yourself, partner. She'll still run the tires off of anything on patrol today." Wild John lifted the engine hood. "I've been working on her ever since they sent me down to this cesspool. The body might look the same, but there are a few improvements under here: high-lift competition Crane cam shaft, eleven to one high compression pistons, dual quad cross ram intake manifold, tubed headers, torc flight B&M high-performance transmission. And the heads have all been milled, poured, and polished."

"You sound like a proud parent. What about the rear end and the suspension?"

"Front and rear sways have been beefed up to one and an eighth inch with KYB gas shocks all around. The rear end will need to be changed for what you have in mind, but I've got a three oh eight with positraction which should do the job nicely. I've also got a heavy-duty, four-core truck radiator I can hook up in case you need it."

"Whew! That's a lot of car." Calico opened the door and slid into the familiar comfort of the driver's seat. "Ahh," he sighed, closing his eyes and resting his head on the backrest. "Nothing like the front seat of a sixty-five Plymouth for sawing a few z's on morning watch."

Wild John climbed in on the passenger side, excitement glowing in his face. "What do you think?"

"I think you're a maniac." Calico sat up straight and put his hands lovingly on the wide steering wheel. "How about gas mileage?"

"The most you can expect is about ten miles to the gallon." Wild John bit his lip in concentration. "But I'll get hold of a fifty-gallon cell and install it in the trunk. You'll be running leaded gas of course, but we can throw in a bathtub full of octane booster which should see you right. If you're lucky you'll run dry about two blocks before you get back to the station. You'll have to coast in from there."

"Funny boy."

"This is going to be great. You're going to be a legend in your own time."

"At least I'll be better off than Guy Stack. He's only a legend in his own mind."

Calico's head was spinning as he drove away from Reeves Field. Wild John's restoration project would definitely prove a run for the money for whatever Stack and Thurman schemed up, and there was no doubt in Calico's mind that they would have some kind of monster police machine to race with. In a game with no rules it was the kind of thing to be expected.

Thoughts of King Carradine also weaved their way through Calico's consciousness. Perhaps there was something that could be done to stop Carradine's parole. One last gesture Calico could make before retiring. Sometimes you had to forget the rules where justice was concerned, too. It would necessitate one more stop before he left the island, but it could prove worth the effort.

After all, King Carradine was the most dangerous man Calico had ever known.

NINE

KING T.I.

THE FIRST BULLET took Calico high in the left shoulder and knocked him head over heels into the oncoming traffic lane. The stink and noise of tortured brakes shattered the night as an overloaded flatbed swerved to avoid the uniformed body which had suddenly sprawled into its path.

A second bullet thumped dead center into Calico's chest. *Mother fucking son of a bitch! It hurts! It hurts! I can't fucking breathe,* Calico's thoughts screamed inside the cavern of his brain. *Kill the fucker! Kill the fucker,* John! Calico tried to get the screaming thoughts from his head to Wild John who had approached the crashed van on the passenger side. He wanted to scream, but his throat felt cut and the words slid back down his vocal cords and soured in his stomach.

It had happened nine years earlier. A simple traffic accident exploding into street warfare. Rain had been coming down in torrents for three days solid, regurgitating the innards of L.A.'s sewer system within the first three hours. Gutters were invisible beneath the flood which had crested the sidewalk and swept over doorsteps with a wash of winter tide.

The myriad of traffic-accident calls, which sprayed

out of the police radio during the first part of the storm, had reduced to a trickle, the public abandoning the streets to huddle in their homes. In place had come calls for help from nouveau riche residents whose cliffside dwellings were sliding down to mingle with the more secure foundations on the middle-class roads below. Horses were sinking into the quicksand of their corrals, and children and adults alike were becoming buried as they tried to rescue their pets. In the middle of the confusion, like a blazing cherry atop the cake left out in MacArthur Park, the five-story building of a local chemical corporation had somehow managed to turn itself into a five-alarm fire.

The police department had gone to "tac alert" with all officers working twelve- to fourteen-hour shifts. Bundled in yellow slickers and ratty rain hats, Calico and Wild John had been in the middle of the midnight to noon shift when they spotted the late model Chevy van lose traction as it forced too much speed around a flooded corner. The rolling monolith slid with wavering aim toward a choice of targets—a bus bench, a stop sign, or a fire hydrant. In his infinite wisdom, God, deciding to add a little slapstick to his night, slammed the van into the fire hydrant, knocking the yellow plug from its base to create a geyser which tried to throw water back at the night sky. Continuing its momentum, the front end of the van clipped the concrete bus bench and then spun through the plate-glass window of a sporting goods shop.

"I don't believe it," Calico mumbled in amazement through a mouth full of a Cupid's double chili dog. He'd just witnessed the three main rules of police work go down the drain. He was going to be forced to go hungry, get wet, and work overtime.

Wild John picked the transmitting mike up from the dashboard. "Nine-A-twenty-one requesting tow at

Ventura and Sepulveda on a blue Chevy van, license number One-Boy-Two-Eight-Eight-Seven, city property involved, a fire hydrant and a bus bench. We need Water and Power to respond."

"Roger, nine-A-twenty-one. There is a forty-minute delay on tow and an hour and a half on Water and Power," the RTO responded in a voice which was far too cheerful for the situation.

"She sounds like she's enjoying herself. What does she think we're doing out here, singing in the rain at a Gene Kelly film festival?" Calico dumped his chili dog and drove across the street to park behind the smashed van. Putting on their rain hats, both officers climbed out into the weather.

Calico approached the driver's side of the van while Wild John covered the passenger side, losing sight of each other because of the height of the vehicle. As he passed, Calico took a stab at opening the van's rear doors, but they were jammed shut. Water from the gushing hydrant poured down his neck as he reached the driver's door.

With his hand on the door handle, he was slightly off balance, no more expecting the door to fly open as it did than to take his next vacation on the planet of the horny and accommodating stewardesses. The muzzle of a Colt forty-five shoved its way out of the opening and spat a Gene Simmons' tongue as the first bullet struck home.

The second bullet should have put Calico in his grave, but the strands of Kevelar woven through his bulletproof vest dispersed the impact, as they had with the first bullet, causing major trauma to his chest but no penetration. Mental shock was immense, though, with all brain circuits kicking into survival mode. In front of Calico, the blurry shape of his assailant had turned his gun away and was pointing it through the cab of the van toward Wild John. Dredging his voice up from the depths of his balls, Calico finally managed to scream "Gun, John!" as loud as he could.

Pain jangled all through him as Calico peeled himself off the asphalt and unsteadily to his feet. He heard the muzzle blast from the forty-five again, but this time there was no impact, the assailant shooting at Wild John in the belief Calico was down for good. Grabbing a fistful of afro, Calico jerked the murderous bastard who had shot him out of the driver's seat and fell on top of him in the flood of the gutter. The forty-five clattered away and down a storm drain.

Anger overcame reason as Calico wrapped his hands around the neck of the black man underneath him, not caring that the bastard was six inches taller and sixty pounds of wire muscle heavier. He was going to choke the snot-piss out of him and then drown him in it. Hands grabbed at his shoulders to pull him away, but he fought against them. Other hands pried at his fingers, but he wouldn't release his grip until finally, by sheer weight of numbers, Wild John and two officers from a backup unit pulled him clear. The black killer's face had turned a distinct blue, his suddenly relinquished neck lolling back and vanishing the face's features beneath the rush of gutter flood.

Unfortunately, as far as Calico was concerned, somebody pulled King Carradine out of his watery coffin and kept him alive long enough for the paramedics to arrive and perform an emergency tracheotomy. Meanwhile, eager firemen applied the jaws of life to the rear doors of the crashed van, now known to be a two-day-old stolen with cold plates. Inside was a shipment of automatic weapons and rocket launchers stolen from a U.S. Army armory in Arizona a month prior. It was enough to make a terrorist cell or a tin-pot dictator drool. It was certainly enough to make the L.A. cops salivate when they realized what they'd stumbled on.

The incident almost made the rain worthwhile. Almost, because as soon as it became common knowledge who the local coppers had in custody, the brown wingtips and white socks brigade, otherwise known and despised as the F.B.I., stepped in. They claimed since the guns in Carradine's van had been stolen in Arizona and recovered in L.A. that made the charge Interstate Transporation of Firearms. And on top of that, the Feds already had a warrant out for Carradine for putting three of their agents in the hospital when he escaped from a trap sprung on him during the stake-out of a small-time gun runner playing footsie with Honduran rebels.

In court, the federal prosecutor slapped on a couple of attempted murder charges, for Carradine's assault on Calico and Wild John. But it was just window dressing, compensation to unruffle L.A.P.D.'s feathers after losing Carradine to the Feds. As soon as Carradine's A.C.L.U. lawyers started talking plea bargain, the attempted murder charges were the first things to go. The plea bargain, however, never came together and after eighteen months in the courtroom, Carradine got the shaft, his extensive past record helping to buy him twenty years in the federal penitentiary. He was told if he was a good boy, he'd be up for parole in seven.

Calico had been there the day Carradine was sentenced, as if wanting to make sure the man who had tried to kill him was put away. On the way out of the courtroom, Carradine, in handcuffs and accompanied by two federal marshals, stopped by Calico's chair. The two men locked eyes, Calico feeling somewhat intimidated as the standing felon towered over his own sitting position. Carradine bent from the waist to put the trachea tube in his throat on a level with Calico's face.

"Your white ass belongs to me, muthafucka." The whispered hiss of his ruptured voice sprayed out from the trachea tube in little drops of spittle which stung Calico's face.

Calico deliberately removed a handkerchief from his pocket, wiped his face slowly while listening to the rasp of breath which came from neck instead of mouth, and forced himself to look congenial. "And your ass, neck-breath," he told Carradine, "belongs to any group of cons who want to hold you down and stretch your asshole wide enough for you to fall through and disappear."

On the outside the seven years had passed quickly. Inside it had taken an eternity. Carradine had behaved himself, though. Behaved well enough, in fact, to get himself transferred from the Security Level 6, Maximum Security Penitentiary at Marion, Illinois, to the Security Level 3 facility at Terminal Island. If things went right for him he'd soon be making the rounds of the prison population, flashing the ace of diamonds from a worn deck of Bicycle playing cards to signify his last day in the pen.

As Calico entered the administration building at the north end of the penitentiary complex, he felt the fear of never being able to leave the institution crawl over him. There weren't many things Calico was consciously afraid of, but going to jail was definitely one of them. It always figured in his infrequent nightmares, which invariably followed a night of mixing liquors, and he knew he'd smoke his gun before it ever manifested itself in reality. Mentally shaking himself, he prepared for the confrontation ahead.

The parole agent at the prison was a heavyset

woman wearing cat's eye glasses, with tiny rhinestones in the frames, hooked to a chain looped around her neck. She regarded Calico through a haze of filterless cigarette smoke.

"I can understand your concern, Walker, but Carradine has been a perfect prisoner as far as the board is going to be concerned."

"Exactly what does that mean?"

Emma Grant set fire to another Camel from the butt of the previous one and then stabbed out the butt in her overflowing ashtray. Her short, bitten, colorless nails were an analogy of her surroundings.

"I mean his record's clean. There's a job waiting for him on the outside. We have a problem with over-crowding. And, on the surface, Carradine's the perfect example of a rehabilitated citizen."

"You must be joking."

"I'm not. Next Wednesday Carradine is out of here."

There was a pause which Calico spent thinking furiously, and Emma spent waiting with her chair pushed back and jean-encased legs crossed in a mannish fashion. Calico wondered for a fleeting second if she was a lesbian or had just adapted her style to the demands of her position.

"What about under the surface?" Calico finally asked.

Emma sighed. "Under the surface, Carradine is the kingpin of the black prison gangs here. Drugs, beatings, gambling, sex, cigarettes, and the rest of the contraband market are all conducted under his influence. He's got a piece of everything without being identified with any specific ideology."

"How the hell did he manage that with his physical condition?"

"If you didn't know the answer to that already you wouldn't be here."

Calico sighed audibly and paused for Emma to flare up another Camel. "It's because he's damn smart. He gets everybody else to do his dirty work. He has some kind of Mansonlike cult following, all the perverted sheep who need an evil shepherd to guide them. Did you hear what happened to the guy who backed out of delivering the guns we caught Carradine transporting because he was forced to deliver them himself? Carradine had him beheaded and his torso staked to the front door of his parents' home."

"I heard about the case on the news. There was never any evidence to point to Carradine. He was in custody at the time."

"Yeah, right. Prison walls have never been able to stop the jungle grapevine, though."

"Did they ever find the victim's head?"

"He was no victim. He was a jackal who got cut down by the pack. And, yeah, they found the head; although the press was never made aware of it. It came wrapped in a Christmas box, big bow and everything, delivered C.O.D. to my partner and me."

"Eewwww." Emma made a face.

"Yeah."

"So what do you want me to do? You can't fight the system."

"Life is hard and then you die. Is that what you're trying to tell me," Calico asked in exasperation.

"You got it in one."

"What if I can produce a witness at the parole hearing who will testify Carradine hired him to kill me during this last week before the hearing?"

Emma stared hard at Calico. "Not that I'm sure it matters, but are you being straight up about this?"

"It matters. And yeah, I'm straight up."

Emma leaned forward, put her elbows on her desk, and framed her face with her hands. She studied Calico intently. "You sure you didn't pull up outside with a lance and a broken-down horse?"

"I don't even know anybody named Sancho Panza."

"Want to tell me how you plan to pull off this miracle?"

"You've got the biggest balls of any white man I've ever come across. I'll give you that much." King Carradine's voice was still a whispered rasp, but surgery in the prison hospital had rebuilt his trachea so he no longer relied on a tube opening in his neck. "Do you realize I could have you killed anytime while we're out here?"

"You could try."

Carradine almost doubled over trying to hack for air and laugh at the same time. "Man, you do have balls. We're walking through the middle of a prison compound filled with assholes who'd tear you apart if they had any idea you were a cop, and you want to get in my face. Why'd you take the chance on talking out here? Where's the percentage in it?"

"We would have been playing games all day in an interview room. You would have assumed it was bugged and it probably would have been. Out here we can lay our cards on the table."

"Only got two cards, white boy. The ace of diamonds which I get to flash when I have one day left, and the ace of spades which I'm gonna personally stuff in your dead mouth."

"You're so full of shit, Carradine, you make a dog run smell hygienic."

"I told you my name ain't King Carradine no more. I am Eli Mohammed Kono."

"I forgot you found religion, King."

The two men walked slowly past a group of prisoners playing basketball. Neither said anything again until they were out of earshot. Carradine had changed his appearance while inside. His head was now shaved and gleamed in the midday sun, and wiry tuffs of hair sprouted from his upper lip and chin in a thick Vandyke-style beard. The round metal frames of prison glasses gave him a sixties revolutionary look. Calico was sure the impression was cultivated as the glasses appeared to be a clear prescription.

Carradine's musculature hadn't suffered in prison, despite the physical limitations initially leveled by his breathing tube. If anything, Carradine was more buffed out than when Calico had first encountered him.

"I've kept tabs on you, white boy, and the street is rumbling."

"Yeah. What's it say?"

"Says you is getting old. Thinking of packing it in, retiring."

"Is that right? I'm impressed. You jigaboos always did know how to run a grapevine. Guess it's all in your jungle heritage. You can take the pickaninny out of the jungle, but you can't take the jungle out of the pickaninny. I didn't know I was worth the effort, though." The two men had wandered into the weight-lifting area. Black faces exclusively surrounded the equipment and stared in anger and hatred at Calico. He knew the only reason they didn't go for his throat was because Carradine was keeping his cool. Out of the corner of his eye, Calico saw two prison guards with riot guns take up casual positions of advantage on either side of the weight-lifting area. Earlier, as they had been crossing the compound, he had seen the guard-tower staff double and take up a vigilance.

"You some kind of racist bastard, or are you just

trying to goad me?" Carradine waved his arms, like a farmer's wife shooing hens, the other cons using the weights backed out of the area leaving the two men alone. Carradine sat down on the bench press and easily lifted off the free weight bar loaded with two hundred and twenty pounds. As he pressed it he continued to talk. "I told you (pump), I got my two aces (pump) and I plan to play both of them (pump). So say what you want today (pump), but remember you'll pay later (pump, pump)." Calico was impressed. Both Carradine's voice and his breath were coming without visible effort. It was time, however, to bring things to a head. As Carradine pushed the bar up for another rep, Calico leaned forward and forced the bar downward, using his weight to slam the bar across Carradine's chest.

"Umphhh!" Air exploded from Carradine's lungs and he struggled to slide out from under the bar. Calico pinned him beneath it. Carradine had no choice. He had to keep his hands where they were on the bar, his muscles straining to push it upward, or Calico's added weight would crush his ribcage.

"What the hell are you doing?" Carradine's voice was strained.

Out of the corner of his eye, Calico could see the other black cons, who had been using the equipment, make a start toward him only to be brought up sharply by the riot guns of the compound guards. There was no noise or outcry. Prison is a place where private dramas can be carried out in public without fear of interference.

"I got two cards in my hand, too, King, or Mohammed, or whatever name you're playacting behind. The difference between your pair of aces and my cards is that mine are a pair of jokers bearing the faces of me and Wild John Elliot, two jokers who can beat even five aces." Carradine gave a sudden explosion of muscle effort to try and dislodge Calico. Calico grunted and forced the weight bar back down, this time dragging it back to rest across the scar tissue of Carradine's neck. The black con suddenly stopped his struggling.

"I've got news for you, hard man." Calico lowered his face directly over Carradine's so their eyes met, upside down, inches apart. "Me and Wild John ain't gonna wait around for you to come after us. Ain't gonna spend our retirement waiting for some scumbag to pop up from hell and drop the other shoe on us. The minute you leave this pen there's gonna be open season on your black ass. You ain't even gonna get the chance to cut some trim before we blow you outta your fucking socks. 'Course that might not bother you any since you've had seven years of being cock-stroked. You might not want no sweet pussy no mo'."

"I'm gonna fucking kill you, Walker. I'm gonna set you on fire and piss all over you to put it out before I gouge out your eyes and slit your throat." Carradine tried to push the bar up again, but Calico easily controlled him from his position of advantage.

"You ain't listening, shit for brains. I'm not gonna give you the chance to get close to me. You better start praying you don't get parole next Wednesday because if you do you'll be dead by Thursday." Carradine stared up into Calico's face, both men's eyes reflecting pools of hate. "They tell me you're a big shot inside these walls, so maybe you can suck enough cock around here to pull some strings on the outside to take a shot at me and Wild John before you hit the streets. Well, you better get your lips warmed up because that's the only chance you got."

"You're a walking dead man, Walker."

"You've been watching too many old movies while you've been away. You're the only dead man I see, and since I got no trouble with hunting down wounded game . . ." Calico suddenly released the bar causing the spring pressure from Carradine's arms to shoot the bar upward. The bar became unbalanced as the weary muscles in Carradine's arms failed to hold it, and the whole weight slammed downward before Carradine could roll completely clear. The bar caught one side of Carradine's throat, tearing the scar tissue there wide open and crushing seven years of surgical finesse.

Calico grabbed for the bar and rolled it to the ground. "Shit," he said loudly with feigned concern, and told one of the guards who had covered for him to radio for the doctor.

Looking back at Carradine's face he whispered, "Welcome back, neck-breath. Remember, if you get out of here while I'm still alive, you won't be."

"You overstepped. Way over." Emma Grant was angry.

"Accidents happen," Calico said from his seated position on the other side of the parole agent's desk.

"Bullshit! You had that planned from the start, knowing I'd protect you because of my involvement."

"Carradine is not a boy scout! He had to be forced to make a move on me now, before he gets out."

"Why didn't you just kill him out there? A little more serious 'accident.'"

"Despite what you might believe, I'm not a killer. I treat scum the only way they deserve to be treated. He belongs inside, where he can be controlled. What I told him was true, I'm not spending my retirement looking over my shoulder for him. You know as well as I do if he gets out he'll come looking for me. Tell me that isn't true, after all the time you've spent talking with him."

"He's given no indication."

Calico stood up, placed his hands on the front of Emma Grant's desk, and leaned forward. "That's not what I asked you to tell me. Based on your experiences behind these walls, behind this desk, behind the facade every con puts up when he comes in here, tell me you truly believe King Carradine would not have come after my partner and me."

Emma was silent. She sucked on her cigarette and exhaled through her nose. Smoke enveloped her face.

"I thought as much," Calico said softly and walked out of the office. The door clicked behind him with the finality of depressing truth.

TEN

FINAL MOVES

AFTER ATTENDING ONE in person for the first time, Tina decided there was nothing in the world like a funeral for a cop killed in the line of duty. A military burial didn't even come close. And the rites of a Hell's Angel's death, with the other members of the gang hauling the body out of its casket for one last family group photo, and the placing of the urine-soaked flying colors atop the cadaver's chest, is a travesty by comparison. A New Orleans-style interment with its jazzy, colorful procession, or a drunken Irish wake, guaranteed to end in a fight, have a certain flair but lack the decisive ingredient—*power*. Nothing, Tina thought, could match the power of a slain cop's funeral.

Blue suiters from across the state, and even across the nation, came to pay tribute to one of their own who had paid the ultimate price. The double-file procession of gleaming police motorcycles, ridden by road warriors wearing shiny jackboots and one-way sunglasses to hide the pain in their eyes, stretched for almost a mile. Following behind came row after row of freshly polished black and white units, their light bars silently flashing from red to blue—incongruous without the wail of a racing siren. At the rear of the procession glided the blackwalls and antenna farms of the plainclothes detectives' vehicles.

On the drizzly Thursday of Ed Martin's funeral the endless line of mourners snaked through the city like a python in search of prey. And God help any innocent who crossed its path. Waves of resentment and anger emanated above the crackle of the police radio band to which every cop's ears were unconsciously tuned even in grief. Resentment that some human aberration had taken the life of a cop attempting to do his job of protecting a public who always demands more than he can give. Anger at the public who shrugs its shoulders at a cop killing as if it is no more than a serf dying in the fields. Resentment and anger drawn from the frustrations of an imperfect society in which the human race cannot exist without preying on one another. In the grief of the procession there was a thrown gauntlet; the police mourning their dead in public, daring any outsider to challenge their right to do so, and holding the citizenry collectively responsible.

Three days after his blazing death in the early hours of Sunday morning, Ed Martin was lowered into his grave. The American flag was draped over his coffin and lay wetly plastered to the hard wood beneath it. Flowers surrounded the grave in huge numbers as if the mere presence of so many blossoms, ripped from the earth at their peak, could express the loss felt by the rank and file of gathered police officers who all wore a wide black band covering the identity numbers of their highly polished badges.

At the edge of the grave sat the grieving widow. She'd shared her husband's life for only three years, but that was still twice as long as either of the two ex-wives who stood discreetly to one side, veiled in black. Three children from the first two marriages look stoically down at the turf.

The ceremony progressed. "Ashes to ashes. Dust to dust" was lost in the rain long before reaching the back rows of the uniformed mourners. The guns were fired. Seven rifles. Three times. The police helicopters hovered in the missing-man formation.

A lone, tartan-clad warrior in kilt and busby brought the reed of a bagpipe to his lips. A second's delay as breath whistled down the blowpipe to the windbag. Steady pressure on the windbag, forcing the air up the tenor drones and down the chanter, and the ethereal wail of the pipes cried across the day.

"Amazing Grace."

Behind her mirrored sunglasses tears flowed from Tina's eyes as they did from many others.

Guy Stack and Thumper Thurman were staked out on Van Nuys Boulevard. Along with the other members of the Metro "A" squad, they were assigned to help reduce the day-watch residential burglary problem. What that amounted to was grabbing up all the juvenile truants which came within their reach, rousting the barrio hypes and gang members, and using shakey probable cause to stop anyone in a vehicle who looked like he had warrants because they needed to keep their arrest recap up.

"We've got to think of something soon. The damn run is only a couple of days away and we still don't have a car that's going to hold up to the speed and distance required." Guy Stack was dressed in jeans and a plaid shirt, his gun and handcuffs on a wide brown belt around his waist. He was slunk down in the passenger seat of the unmarked, dual-purpose car which most kids referred to as a "narc" car.

"What's wrong with taking this baby. It runs pretty good." Thumper watched the boulevard with sleepy eyes from their position in the driveway of a fast-food outlet.

"At the speeds we're going to have to travel to Vegas and back, this piece of shit wouldn't get us out of the division without shaking itself apart."

"You're exaggerating, man."

"Yeah, I know. But you can bet Calico will have something up his sleeve which will outclass a regulation police vehicle. No, we've got to come up with something special."

"If you say so. Tell me. Do you think this run thing is a good idea?"

"Don't tell me you're having second thoughts. Man, we've been challenged. That gook bitch and her partner made us look like a couple of assholes."

"We are assholes. Just ask any of the bad guys we put away."

"We might have the best arrest record in Metro, but those two made us look like a couple of doofusses. We got a reputation to protect. If we back out now, we'll never live it down. And not only that, there's the money at stake."

"Hey! Here we go!" Thurman pointed to an orange Dodge Charger which suddenly lit up its wheels in a parking lot and flashed recklessly out into traffic. "Idiots like him should be handed their heads on a platter."

"I'll hand it to him, all right, if you can get this thing in gear." Stack took the metallic-based red light off the floor, stuck it in the front window, and turned it on as he hit the dual-purpose vehicle's siren.

The driver of the Charger knew his car would be impounded if he was caught, but he had other ideas. Bad ones. The flashy car's exhaust roared the moment he spotted the flashing red light behind the windshield of Stack and Thurman's car.

"He's rabbiting!" Thurman yelled as he jumped on the gas as the Charger turned itself into a blur.

The Charger downshifted at the cross street of Burbank Boulevard and did a flat slide through the intersection before turning westbound.

"He's heading for the freeway," Stack exclaimed.

"You want to notify the Highway Patrol?" asked Thurman.

"No way, partner. This guy is ours!"

"If we can catch him," Thurman said, trying to use his size thirteens to push the accelerator through the floorboards.

Passing Sepulveda Boulevard, the Charger jumped onto the on-ramp to the southbound San Diego Freeway, sideswiping a traffic-light control box as it did so. The Charger was a faster car, but Thurman was a much better driver and kept the police vehicle within striking range of the fleeing vehicle. On the wide expanse of the freeway, though, the Charger began to pull steadily away, the police car topping out at well under a hundred miles an hour.

Stack turned around to look out his vehicle's rear window. Behind them, he caught a quick glimpse of the sleek lines of a Highway Patrol pursuit Mustang, specially designed by Ford for the C.H.P. to use in running down speeders. The Mustang, lights and siren wailing, blew past Stack and Thurman in pursuit of the Charger.

Hitting the dashboard with the palm of his hand, Stack swore, "Shit, the bastard's going to get our arrest!"

"He's welcome to him," said Thurman. He backed off the gas slightly, feeling the front end of the car beginning to mush out. "We were never going to catch him."

"I know," replied Stack, sitting back on the bench

seat in a sulk. "It's what I was talking about earlier. If we don't get a faster, better running machine than this, Calico and his partner are going to race the road out from under us."

Up ahead, the C.H.P. Mustang caught up with the Charger and forced it over to the shoulder with seemingly little effort. As Stack and Thurman pulled in behind the action, the two Highway Patrol officers already had the driver of the Charger proned out on the ground ready for handcuffing.

"Glad you boys could finally get here," chided one of the Chippys as his partner secured their prisoner. "We thought something had happened to you. Like when we blew your doors off, perhaps you stepped out of your car to find out why you weren't moving." His partner laughed.

The two Metro cops felt their ire rising. Stack stepped forward threateningly but was stopped by Thurman putting a big hand on his shoulder.

"It ain't worth it, partner," Thurman told Stack quietly. "Not this time. Just remember what goes around will come around. It will be our turn next time."

Ed Martin's funeral had left Calico in a thoughtful mood. He was glad he was retiring. It was time. He'd put in his thirty years and it was time to get out before the odds caught up with him. On the Friday the street racers came to town, Calico had driven down to police headquarters at Parker Center and paid a visit to the Personnel Department to sign his retirement papers. All the way down there he thought about his career, the run to Vegas scheduled for the Sunday morning watch shift, and about what kind of a threat Sal Fazio could be to his retirement if he caught him doing the run and could prove it. There must be a way to outfox Fazio, he thought, and then an idea popped into his head which appealed to him immediately.

When Calico reported for work at eleven P.M., Sergeant Zellof shouted to him in the locker room. "Move your buns, Walker. Captain Morrison wants to see you upstairs in his office."

"What's he doing here at this time of night?" Calico asked.

"I've got no idea. He's been hanging around, though, waiting for you."

Calico didn't like how that sounded, but he climbed into his uniform quickly, ran a polish cloth over his shoes and leather gear, patted masking tape over the blue wool of his uniform, and headed upstairs.

Outside the captain's office he knocked and entered the open door without waiting for a reply. Captain Morrison looked up from the paperwork on his desk. He was a large man, almost as big as Calico, with a full head of dark hair and a drooping mustache which underlined a drinker's nose. One portion of the pupil of his right eye had bled all the way over to the edge of the surrounding blue iris. When he looked directly at you, it gave the disconcerting impression he was looking over your shoulders.

"You wanted to see me, Captain?" Calico asked as he entered and stood in front of the city-issued veneer desk.

"Hey, how you doing, Calico?" Morrison stood up and extended his hand which Calico shook. "Sit down, sit down." Calico pulled up a chair and put it to use. "How's your partner holding up after the Torchsong shooting?"

"Fine. She's due to come back to work Saturday night for the Sunday morning watch shift."

"Just in time for your little out-of-policy escapade."

"What escapade is that, sir?" Calico asked with a frown.

Morrison sighed and sat down himself. He looked at the paperwork on his desk. "You ever disappointed you didn't try for promotion, Calico?"

"Can't say as I am, sir. I like working the street just fine. Pushing a black and white is more important than pushing a pencil in my book." Morrison looked up sharply. "No offense intended," Calico added quickly.

"How long do you have on the job now, Walker?"

"Thirty years, sir."

"And still pushing your luck?"

"It's the way I am. I don't know how to live or act any other way."

"You're a good cop. As smart mouth as you are, I wish I had a hundred more like you. Don't blow a thirty-year career doing something stupid on your last night."

"I don't intend to, sir."

"Sal Fazio is out to burn you any way he can. I don't know what it is between the two of you, but I'd watch my ass every second of every shift you've got left on this job."

"I will, sir. Is that all?"

"Don't do it, Calico. Fazio will have your pension, and you'll ruin your partner's career. Yours might be over, but hers is just beginning. She's also one of the good ones. We can't afford to lose her."

Calico sat silently.

"It had to be said," Morrison warned.

"You've said it, sir. I won't let you down."

"I'm sure you won't."

Calico stood up quickly and left the office. Morrison sat brooding in his chair for several minutes after, playing with a black marking pen. With a start, he realized he was getting ink all over his fingers and put the pen down in favor of the phone receiver. He dialed out a five-digit internal number.

"Van Nuys Vice Unit, Sergeant Buffet," came from the other end when the line was answered.

"Buffet, this is Captain Morrison. Are you handling the action on Calico's Vegas run?"

"Sir." The voice on the other end didn't want to commit itself.

"Never mind beating around the bush, Buffet. I'm not blind to what goes on in this division. Put me down for five hundred on Walker, and call up Captain Taylor over at Metro and tell him if he doesn't back his own team to the same tune, he's a bigger limp dick than I already think he is."

At the same time Calico was feeling uncomfortable in the captain's office, King Carradine was feeling a lot of pain in the prison hospital.

His windpipe had been ruptured again by the weight bar Calico had dropped across it. A trachea tube had again been inserted, and King lay on his back listening to his breath rasp in and out. Walker. Walker. Walker. One name continued to burn in his mind in pace to his breathing. Walker had to die, and die now.

A black prison orderly passed by Carradine's bed and stopped to change the bedpan. When he was done, Carradine's hand flashed out from under the covers and grabbed the orderly's arm in an icy, steel grip. The orderly's eyes bugged out of his head as Carradine drew him nearer. Carradine's lips moved, but no sound came out. The pressure increased on the orderly's arm forcing him to bend forward, closer to Carradine's mouth.

"Bring me Ketch," Carradine whispered.

"He getting out tomorrow, Mohammed Kono. He

don't want no one to bother him while he saying good-bye to his punch boy.''

Carradine increased the pressure of his grip until the orderly cried out. "Bring me Ketch!"

"I've been thinking," stated Thumper Thurman in a voice two octaves below normal due to the amount of alcohol in his system.

"Did you strain anything?" asked Stack who was in his usual slumped-down position on the passenger side of Thurman's restored sixty-five Cadillac.

"How would you like to take that C.H.P. Mustang pursuit vehicle on the run to Vegas?" Thurman kept his eyes on the road, trying to stop the white line from weaving from side to side.

"Are you just drunk, or have your brains slipped? What are we going to do? Ask 'em if we can borrow it for nine or ten hours?"

"No, I was thinking of stealing it."

"Stealing it?"

"Well, not us. I was thinking in terms of Harry Reeves."

"The car thief with the Ford fetish? You are crazy. Is he even out of jail?"

"Yep. Thanks to us. We gave him a break last time because he tipped us to that chop shop. He owes us."

After watch both Metro officers had downed a few brews too many at The Orphan's Home and were now headed back to their respective beds. Guy Stack was silent for a change, thinking about what Thumper had proposed.

"I don't know, man," he said finally. "Reeves is real weird. He's the only guy I know who can't get it up unless he's stealing a car. And not just any car. It has to be a Ford or he can't get off."

"What bees the difference? You like high heels and

garter belts. He be liking Ford seats and dashboards. Different strokes is all."

"Anybody ever tell you that when you get drunk you talk like a nigger?"

"Nobody be stupid enough to tell me that to my face."

"Oh."

"Well, how about it? You want that Mustang or not?"

"I'm thinking."

"While you're thinking I'm gonna stop and get us a couple more brews."

Thumper pulled the Caddy into the parking lot of a small liquor store and got out. "You coming in?" he asked Stack.

"No, I'll wait here."

Thumper slammed the driver's door of his car and pulled a thin windbreaker over the L.A.P.D. T-shirt he was wearing. Inside the liquor store he walked back to the refrigerator section and pulled out a six-pack of Heineken in cans.

Stack meanwhile had his eyes closed and didn't see the hop head enter the store about thirty seconds behind Thumper. Thumper saw him, though, when he got up to the cash register. He also saw the entrance to the Holland Tunnel which was disguised as the barrel opening of the gun in the hop head's hand. It was pointed straight at his face. Thumper was instantly sober.

"Freeze, mutha!"

"Yo, I'm frozen, man," Thumper spit out. "You'll get no argument from me. Take the honkie's money." The L.A.P.D. emblem, emblazoned across the front of Thurman's T-shirt, burned into the big man's chest like a branding iron. He was painfully aware that the windbreaker he'd put on was not zipped up the front and that most of the police department's emblem was visible. If the hop head saw it there was no telling what he would do. Thumper arched his shoulders forward in an attempt to bring the edges of the windbreaker closer together.

"Lay down on the floor, mutha, and do as I say and you won't get hurt."

Thumper moved down to his knees, keeping his arms in front of him to hide his T-shirt logo. His off-duty gun was in a holster on his ankle, but he didn't figure he could get to it without getting his head blown off. Where the hell was Stack?

Where the hell was Thurman was what Stack wanted to know. How long did it take to buy a six-pack? Guy opened his eyes and stared at the liquor-store entrance just as the hop head walked out, looked around without seeing Stack in the Caddy, and began to run. Stack's cop instincts reared.

He opened the passenger door and took off after the hop head. He didn't know what it was that made him do it. All he knew was it was the right thing to do.

The doper never knew what hit him as Stack tackled him from behind like death from the skies. The hop head's chin slammed into the pavement, driving his bottom teeth through his lower lips. The .38 Saturday Night Special with the bull barrel clattered away and spun to rest against a streetlight. Stack hit the robber once in the kidneys and once in the balls to be sure, folding him up like a baby trying to get back in the womb.

The Metro cop slapped on the cuffs he still had hanging from his belt, and pulled the brown bag of small denomination bills from the waistband of his prisoner.

"Okay, asshole," he said roughly. "You have the

right to swing first. However, should you choose to swing first, any move you make can and will be used against you as an excuse to beat the shit out of you.

"You have the right to have a doctor and a priest present. If you cannot afford a doctor or are not currently attending a church of your choice, one will be appointed for you.

"Do you understand these rights I've just explained to you, asshole?"

"I didn't do fucking nothin', man! Don't hit me again, man, please! I'm hurtin' real bad."

"I'm going to hurt you right into another zip code if you've fucked up my partner. Come on, get up." Stack hauled his prisoner to a standing position and half dragged, half pulled him back to the liquor store with him.

As he entered he was met by a jumble of sound. The store clerk was laying behind the counter counting in Farsi while, on the other side, the deep rumble of Thumper Thurman could be heard intoning, ". . . One hundred and fifty-seven. One hundred and fifty-eight. One hundred and fifty-nine . . ."

INTERLUDE

Citadel Casino—Las Vegas, Nevada
Tuesday—Sunday

Yes, I am a pirate
Two hundred years too late
The cannons don't thunder,
There's nothing to plunder
I'm an over forty victim of fate
Arriving too late
Arriving too late

—JIMMY BUFFET,
"A Pirate Looks at Forty"

ELEVEN

SETTING THE BLAG

M ORGAN WALES STARTED the caper from the position he liked best—scratch. His first move was to gather monetary capital. Even though he didn't have the price of a cup of coffee to his name, coming up with financing proved a doddle.

The Yellow Pages provided the address of the local methadone center, a state-sponsored institution where drug addicts were supplied with free doses of heroin substitute in order to help wean them off the real thing and hopefully to stop them from stealing to support their habits. Both goals of the program were a dismal failure, but the effort provided Morgan with a starting point.

The stakeout of the rehabilitation center quickly yielded results and Morgan was able to follow one of the hypes to a pawnbroker four blocks away. After an hour of watching the comings and goings through the grimy shop front, he was certain he'd located a business owner who possessed no qualms about receiving stolen property. Filing the information away, Morgan got on with the second part of his plan.

Cruising the neighborhood jewelry stores soon produced a number of easy marks, jewelry salesmen who hustle their wares from store to store. Morgan picked an obese man who locked his jewelry case in the trunk of his car each time he moved on to a new store.

Following the salesman, Morgan was pleased when the mark parked his car on a side street off the main drag and walked back to a medium-size jewelry mart to pedal his wares. As soon as the man was out of sight, Morgan walked up and punctured the front driver's side tire with his Swiss Army knife. It was time then to back off and wait.

When the salesman returned to his car, he stashed his jewelry case in the trunk, entered his vehicle, and started to pull away from the curb before realizing his tire was flat. Cursing, the salesman got out, kicked the tire savagely, took off his jacket, and opened the trunk to get out the jack and spare.

Morgan waited patiently until the vehicle was jacked up and the salesman bent over to remove the offending tire. Then strolling casually, Morgan approached the rear of the car, timing his arrival to coincide with the salesman's sweating efforts to line up the spare tire with the lugs. Reaching into the open trunk, he removed the heavy jewelry case without breaking stride, the salesman completely hidden from the action by the body of the car, and walked briskly away with his heart pounding pleasantly.

Three hours later he was back in his hotel room after striking a deal with the crooked pawnbroker. The stolen jewelry was already on its way to New York, Los Angeles, or even out of the country, and for his trouble Morgan put five thousand dollars in his pocket—ten percent of the jewelry's actual worth.

The police were left without a clue to solve the crime.

From the phone in his room on the Citadel's eighth floor, Morgan placed a collect, overseas phone call to a number in England.

"Claret's Wine Bar," answered a young voice on the other end of the connection.

"Will you accept a collect call from a Mr. Wales?" asked the operator.

There was a slight hesitation, during which the noise of music and glasses tinkling echoed down the phone line. Eventually the voice replied, "Yeah, all right."

Morgan waited until he heard the click of the operator hanging up. "Let me speak to Max," he said.

"Hang about. Is that really you, Morgan? We haven't heard from you in ages. Word was you'd retired."

"Word was wrong, mate. I've just been out of the country for a while. Now let me speak to Max."

"Sure thing."

The phone line went dead for a few seconds while the call was transferred back to Max's private office. Morgan could picture the fat man sitting there, surrounded by racks of wine, at his large rosewood desk in the middle of a room which looked like it had been carved out of rock, rough white walls and low domed ceiling giving the impression of a cave.

A voice suddenly came crisply across the transatlantic phone wires. "Morgan, this is a surprise."

"Pleasant, I hope."

"But of course. It's always a pleasure to deal with a professional who pays his debts on time." Max's voice was a deep, graveled rasp, like Velcro dragged across sandpaper. "You must be stone broke if you're calling me."

"It's how I work best."

Max laughed. "The infinite variety of the criminal mind never ceases to amaze me. What do you require?"

"I'm going to need a fly boy with access to a small plane big enough to carry three passengers and swag. One who's not afraid of mountain skimming and he must be willing to be a participant in the blag. A dope flyer is okay, but he has to be an independent, know the California/Nevada area, and not be strung out on his own toffee. I'll also need a sparks man with the same stipulation about participation, but that's it, I like to keep my teams small."

"What's the take?"

"It's a little rough to say, but somewhere in the region of a million to a million and a half. Possibly two."

"I like your style. How soon do you need this?"

Morgan thought briefly. Everything was moving smoothly, he didn't want to wait too long. "The blag is set to go next Sunday, very early in the morning, so I'll want the team assembled by Thursday night. Oh, and another thing. I need a rundown on a shark by the name of Merric. Comes from the Brixton area. Male, Caucasian, mid-to-late twenties, casino experience. His style and patter indicate he was probably apprenticed in one of Harry James' London clubs. I also need the rundown on a Vegas casino operator by the name of Ollie Sebastian."

"Augustus Sebastian's nephew?"

"I never said you weren't informed."

"I'll get on it. I can probably have the stuff on the Merric kid and Sebastian by tonight, but you'll have to call me again in the morning for the rest. This sounds like a big one. Are you thinking of using shooters?"

"Max, I'm surprised at you. Never used them, never will."

Max laughed again. "That's my boy. Your old man had guts, but you've got style and brains also."

"Flattery won't up your three percent," Morgan said and broke the connection.

That night, when Merric Bass finished his last twenty-minute dealing stint at the blackjack tables, he found Morgan waiting for him outside the employee's lounge.

"Hello, Brixton."

"Hello, Mitcham."

"You don't seem surprised to see me," Morgan said casually.

"I had a call this afternoon from a friend of a friend who said someone was asking questions for Max down the Piccadilly, so I expected a contact."

"I didn't know Max was so well known. He must be slipping. The Piccadilly is one of Harry James' clubs?"

"Yes."

"You must have pretty good contacts back home."

"I have to have. Harry still hasn't gotten over his losses. He still isn't sure it was me, but he could still get a bee in his bonnet and decide to settle accounts anyway."

"Max tells me you're a reliable lad once you've upped with a firm. Are you interested in some action on this side of the pond?"

"I don't see why not. Life's getting a bit stale taking punters' money and having to turn it all over to the house."

"Let's take a walk," said Morgan and the two men headed out the casino's employee exit.

As the large double door swung closed behind the two men, Merric asked, "How much are we going after?"

"The whole shooting match."

Merric laughed. "And you think Ollie Sebastian is going to let you walk away with it?"

"That's the beauty of the thing. Dear old Ollie is going to help us take it."

"Oh, yeah?"

"Yeah. That's where you come in. Can you get into

the casino's accounting office in the basement and snag a ream of computer printout?"

"Anything in particular?"

"Not really. Just anything dear old Ollie will recognize as coming from his own office."

"A walk in the park, me old son. A walk in the park."

"It's definite concerning Ollie then?"

"Yes, I'm afraid so."

"And Jonathan?"

"Clean down to the last penny."

Augustus Sebastian sighed and swiveled his huge leather chair around to look out the panoramic picture window at his back. He had the heavy, sad look of a bloodhound about him, large watery eyes and sagging jowls all connected by a bulbous nose. His body, inside the tailor-made Lacoste shirt and plaid golf pants, was heavy and soft. A full, flowing mane of silver-gray hair, however, gave him an aura of an old lion at rest, testament that not everything about the man was soft.

"You don't have any children of your own, do you, Dobbins?" Sebastian asked the other man in the room while continuing to study the Palm Springs landscape visible from the picture window.

"No, Mary and I have never been blessed." If Sebastian was a bloodhound, Dobbins was a badger, all wide-stunted body with a pointy face.

"Never been cursed is more like it. The only thing children are good for is taking what you've built and squandering it when you've left."

Dobbins remained silent. He'd heard the speech before.

"Lisa and I have never been 'blessed' as you put it either. Which means that, now I'm ready to retire, I've had to turn over the running of my casinos to my brother's sons. Neither of which would ever have amounted to anything on their own. Do you realize how hard it is to run a casino in Vegas or Tahoe without intervention from the organization boys?" Dobbins still kept his own counsel, knowing the question was rhetorical, his boss' way of letting off steam. "Sure we pay for the privilege of operating on their turf, but our operations have always remained clean in-house. And now little Ollie has taken so much out of the Citadel, he's sniffing around the mob boys for money to cover his greed. He dares to think he can outsmart me by letting me see the tip of the iceberg, making out he's just doing a little skimming. Does he think that once the mob gets its claws in, he'll ever see the back of them? Stupid with a capital 'S.'"

"What are you going to do?" Dobbins asked after Sebastian had wound down.

"Are you sure on the figures?"

Dobbins smiled sadly and picked up a sheaf of computer printouts. "We tapped into the computers a month ago. He's got some good help, but we finally found the weevil in the system which is transferring at least thirty percent of current projected profit increases into private accounts in Switzerland and the Bahamas. There is layer upon layer of misdirection in the system and it's hard to tell if we're even at the bottom of it now."

"I should know better than to question you, Dobbins. How long have we been together now?"

"Close to thirty-five years."

"Yeah. Well, there's nothing for it. I gave both nephews a chance. Jonathan is running the Tahoe setup below projection, but that's due to lack of flair and initiative rather than stealing. That is a problem which can be cured.

"Ollie, on the other hand, is making more money

than projected, but is stuffing it in his own cheeks. We can't have that, can we. It's time for Ollie to fall and fall hard. How would you like to come out of retirement and go back in the casino business, Dobbins."

"Whatever you say, boss. When do you want to move?"

"Let's say Sunday morning when everything is at its quietist."

Merric had been as good as his word, and so had Max. By Thursday morning, Morgan had a stack of printouts from the Citadel's accounting computers, and the two other element members of the blag team were due to arrive that evening. Chauncer, the electrician, would be arriving on a commercial flight from New York at eight o'clock. John Bolt, the pilot, would be arriving with his own transportation. Both had stated they could be left to their own devices to get to the Citadel's hotel.

Morgan had used separate couriers to make reservations at the Citadel for both men, varying the length of each man's projected visit and paying in advance for their stay, as well as his own, so there would be no questions asked later, during an investigation, to connect them.

"Did you have any problems getting these," Morgan had asked Merric when the latter had brought the computer printouts to Morgan's room.

"It was a right doddle, like falling off a log."

"Not that it really matters, but will they be missed?"

"No way. I scooped these out of the rubbish before they were sent through the shredder. As far as I can tell there was no log of what comes out of the computers and goes to the shredder."

"Great. What about Ollie's schedule?"

"He's set for a visit to his tailor this afternoon. While he's in the dressing room will be the only time he's away from his bodyguard. I've glimmed the place and figure it's our best shot. There's a delivery door at the back of the store which leads directly to the dressing rooms." Merric looked rightfully pleased with himself.

"You could get good at this," Morgan told the younger man with a smile. "Come on, we better get busy. We've got a lot of shopping to do before we become kidnappers, or nephew-nappers in this case."

When the time for the snatch came it was ridiculously easy. Ollie Sebastian walked around like a big man, with a bodyguard to watch over his every move, but neither the bodyguard nor Ollie ever expected anything to happen.

Morgan and Merric's shopping spree had been a success. At each of four different security stores around the city they had purchased model MTF76 tasers, police-type stun guns shaped like large flashlights. The tasers shot out twin barbs which, once embedded in the target's flesh or clothing, delivered a fifty thousand-volt jolt down the wires between the barbs and the battery in the holder and rendered the target unconscious. Four chain-name sporting goods stores had provided an equal array of hockey masks, used not only to protect the face of a hockey goalie, but also to turn him into an unrecognizable malevolent force designed to strike fear in the heart of an opponent. Fun stuff. A limousine had also been acquired, through the magic of Morgan's fingers, from a row of six parked behind a funeral home.

When Merric parked the limo behind Bannerman's Tailor Shop, entered through the unlocked service entrance, and stuck his hockey-masked face around the dressing room's curtain, Ollie Sebastian was literally caught with his pants down. His call for help was immediately silenced when Merric zapped him with the noiseless stun gun, sending the casino manager into temporary bye-bye land. Leaving the stun gun's barbs embedded in Ollie's naked ass, Merric took his finger off the trigger regulating the flow of voltage, picked up the unresponsive body in a fireman's carry, and dumped him unceremoniously in the backseat of the limo. He handed the taser housing to Morgan, who was also in the backseat, dressed in evening clothes and wearing a second hockey mask.

"It's amazing how you lose respect for a man once you've seen him naked," Merric quipped.

"Shut up, get in the front, and drive," Morgan responded, but not nastily. "And remember not to turn around. We can't have people looking in seeing you wearing a hockey mask while driving the limo, but we don't want Ollie boy here to see you face on."

"Aye, Aye, Captain. Do you want me to run up the Jolly Roger now, sir?"

"Get away with you." Morgan reached over and pulled the back door closed on Merric's laughing face. Within seconds they were underway.

Ollie Sebastian came around slowly. He groaned and reached for the barbs embedded in his buttocks.

"I wouldn't do that if I were you," Morgan told him. "You're going to need a doctor to remove those little devils, they're like fishhooks."

"Who the hell are you?" demanded Sebastian.

"Temper, temper," Morgan advised his captive, raising the taser housing from his lap and focusing Sebastian's attention on it. "You've already had one shocking experience this afternoon. I doubt you want another."

"Listen, asshole . . ."

Morgan pressed the trigger on the taser and shocked Sebastian into silence. After three seconds of watching the half-naked man convulse, he released the trigger, set the taser housing in his lap, and poured himself a glass of champagne.

"Pass us up a glass of the bubbly then," said Merric from the driver's seat. The partition between the front and rear of the car was still rolled down.

"Don't be silly. You're driving. Plenty of time for celebrating later."

Sebastian was coming round again.

"Shall we start over?" Morgan asked in a direct voice.

"What do you want?" asked Sebastian. "Whoever you are, I'm going to fry you for this . . ."

Morgan pulled the trigger on the taser again.

The next time Sebastian came round he was much more docile. Morgan handed him a glass of champagne.

"There, that's much more civilized, isn't it?"

Sebastian didn't reply.

"Now, Ollie, you've been a naughty boy, haven't you?"

"What are you talking about?"

"Your Uncle Augustus is going to be mighty unhappy when he finds out how much you've been stealing from him." Morgan threw several reams of Citadel's computer printouts in Sebastian's lap. He was gambling on the fact that Ollie Sebastian didn't know a computer printout from his elbow. He was also gambling on the conversation he'd overheard several nights before in the Lucky Thirteen club. It wasn't much of a gamble since most of his information was based on what Max had dug up about Sebastian's relationship with his uncle and with his brother who was running the Citadel's sister operation in Tahoe. Morgan had never known Max, or Max's information, to be wrong.

Sebastian looked down at the computer printouts in amazement. "Where did you get these?" he asked angrily, but immediately subsided when Morgan raised the taser housing.

"A little birdy dropped 'em on my porch, Ollie, and you're going to be glad he did." Morgan was getting hot under the hockey mask and decided to wrap things up quickly. "I'm going to do you a big favor, Ollie."

"You are?"

"Yes. First I'm going to relieve you of an awful lot of dirty money, and then I'm going to give you an excuse to wipe out all the data in your computer banks so your uncle will never be able to figure out just how far into the till you've dipped."

"Why?"

"Ah, I like a man who asks astute questions. First of all, I'm well aware that if I was to just take your money, sooner or later you or one of your associates would figure out who I am and come after me. I'm not particularly worried about the police in Las Vegas since they do exactly what the casino owners tell them to. So if you don't put any pressure on them to do a big investigation, they're not going to bust their humps. But I don't expect you to let all that filthy lucre slip through your fingers without getting a fair deal in exchange."

"And just what are you proposing?"

"When I hit your casino—never mind when," Morgan jumped in with when Sebastian opened his mouth. "I intend to screw up the entire electrical system of your casino and the alarm system of every other casino in the area. Now I don't need to do this, but as a favor to you I will. It's really amazing what a good power surge can do to a whole bank of computer chips. Vast sections of memory can be wiped out, left to float in space for eternity.

"Uncle Augustus won't be pleased when he turns up on your doorstep. You were a fool to think he'd never figure out the games you're playing. But he won't be able to prove a thing. Unless . . ."

"Unless, what?"

"Unless you decide to send the heavy mob after me and my troops anyway. Then instead of these wonderful accounting printouts being kept safe with me, they'll be sent off C.O.D. to Uncle Augustus along with an annotated description of each layer of your scam." Morgan sipped some more champagne. "So, there it is, Ollie boy. What do you say."

Sebastian was obviously thinking furiously. "How long do I have to get the computers set up?"

"Long enough. But don't think you can rip me, Ollie. I have people very close to you"—if you were going to run a good bluff you might as well take it all the way, Morgan thought—"and if you decide to fuck me it will be permanent bye-bye time." Pressure from Morgan's fingers was again applied to the taser's trigger and Sebastian convulsed with shock and passed out for a fourth time that afternoon.

"Okay, pull over quick," Morgan told Merric who immediately did as he was told.

"Do you think he bought it?" Merric asked after parking the car and turning around to take the worthless computer printouts from Morgan's outstretched hands.

"Time will tell, old son," Morgan replied as he ripped off his hockey mask, got out of the car, and walked away from the parked limo with Merric in tow. "It's a gamble. But that is what makes life so exciting."

PART THREE

THE RUN

Andiamo!

THE RIGHT REVEREND KENNEY BOB KAYES
LOVE CHAPEL OF THE PERPETUALLY REVOLVING
FOXY WOMEN
Las Vegas—Nevada

PART THREE

THE RUN

TWELVE

ANDIAMO!

MARSHA WALKER HAD worked herself into a tizzy and her voice could be heard well outside of the large townhouse she shared with her son Ren.

"Don't you see your father is jeopardizing his entire career to do something he thinks is macho? Even if he gets away with it this time, he'll do the same type of thing again and again until it eventually ruins him. And it will ruin you if you go into this crazy fishing business with him."

Ren was in his bedroom rapidly packing clothes and belongings into two suitcases and several big boxes. His mother was standing in the doorway trying, in her mind, to get him to see sense.

"Look, Mom. I'm sorry you and Dad couldn't work things out when you were married, and I'm certainly not saying it wasn't as much his fault as yours, but I'm tired of being caught in the middle between the two of you . . ."

"He has poisoned you against me, hasn't he? What has he told you about me?" Marsha was becoming insistent and grabbed her son by the arm. Ren whirled on her in sudden anger but struggled suddenly to stay cool.

He removed his mother's hand from his arm and

then put both of his hands on her shoulders. "That's the funny thing, Mom. He has never said anything about you but good things." Ren pushed his mother to a sitting position on the bed and then sat down beside her. "You've done a good job of bringing me up, and I love you very much. I always will, no matter what. But I have to do this. All these years he's been a part-time father and I've been a part-time son. Now it's time for both of us to try it full-time. If it doesn't work out it won't be the end of the world, but at least we will have tried."

Marsha sighed. "But why this fishing thing? It sounds so risky."

"It is risky"—Ren laughed—"but if it wasn't neither Dad or I would be interested in trying it. We're very much alike that way. Neither one of us is ever attracted to the easy route. Besides, other than police work and getting his butt bruised on the back of obnoxious animals, the sea and fishing are the only other things Dad knows or gives a damn about. He can't go on being a policeman forever, and this gives him something to go to. He'd curl up and die if he didn't have something to challenge him every day."

"You're your father's son all right. You know him too well."

"I'm also my mother's son. I know you too."

"Oh, God, Ren. I'm going to miss you," Marsha said in a quieter voice. Impulsively she hugged her son tightly. A single tear rolled down her cheek.

"Hey, come on now," Ren said, hugging his mother back. "Is that what this is all about? It's not like I'm going off to sea forever. I'll just be down at King Harbor, thirty minutes away. I've tasted Dad's cooking, and I won't go near my own, so do you think I'm going to be a stranger around here? I love you, Mom, but it's time for me to do this."

"Yes, I know it is, but every mother hates to cut the apron strings." The two of them laughed together suddenly. "Hey, you better get going if you want to get this stuff down to the boat and get back to the station to see your father off on his big run," Marsha said, taking a look at her watch.

"I'm not going to the station. I'm hitching a ride with a couple of the tow-truck guys from the police impound yard. They're going to meet the units at a rest stop near the halfway point of the run in case they need anything." Ren paused and then added, "Do you want to come along?"

Marsha thought about it for a moment, "Yes, but I won't. If I did your father would never let me live it down."

"It's too bad you guys have such a war going on." Ren shook his head sadly. "If you declared a truce you'd probably find out you still loved each other."

"There's no doubt we still love each other," his mother told him. "We just can't stand to be in the same room."

The phone rang early Saturday afternoon. Calico hadn't been out of bed long, but he was at least awake and working on his first cup of coffee. Working morning watch always put your schedule at odds with the normal world of nine to fivers.

"Hello," he said, answering on the fourth ring.

"Hello, asshole."

"Is that you, Fazio? What a pleasant surprise."

"I just wanted to let you know, I'm going to be on your ass all night tonight. You fuck up just once and I'm going to be on you like stink on shit."

"Sounds like you; stink on shit."

"You do this run tonight and your ass, and your pension, will belong to me."

"Funny thing, Sal. I thought they belonged to the city just like yours." Calico hung up. When the phone began to ring again, he took it off the hook and stuffed the receiver between the cushions of his couch.

He drank another cup of coffee while thinking about his situation. Sal Fazio was a definite spanner in the works. Steps had been worked out to anticipate and deal with him, but there was still a question whether they were enough.

Another monkey wrench in the situation was his feelings toward Tina. Or more exactly trying to figure out what his feelings were. Since they had made love neither one had called the other and their paths had crossed only briefly at Ed Martin's funeral. It was as if each of them was waiting for the other to make the first move, set down the ground rules for whatever it was which had developed between them. Was this a continuing affair, or did they just carry on like nothing had happened? Tonight was the first night they would be paired in a patrol car since the Torchsong shooting. It was also the night of the run which could jeopardize both of their careers.

Calico briefly considered calling the whole thing off. What the hell did he care? He went to work tonight, put in his eight hours, and tomorrow morning at seven forty-five he'd walk away from it all. What was the big deal?

The walls of his small apartment began to close in on him and he began to feel a cold sweat slither across his skin. Damnit, he thought, it was a big deal. If he walked away without doing this he'd regret it every day for the rest of his life. It would eat at him like a cancer, leaving a hole in the pit of his stomach every time he thought about his police career. He'd spent thirty years on the streets avoiding being shot out of the sky. If he went down tonight, lost everything on one last fling, at least he'd go down in a blaze of glory of his own choosing. That didn't mean, however, he had to take his rookie partner with him.

Picking up the phone, he depressed the plungers to cut off the wailing which was chastising him for leaving the receiver off the hook, and tapped out the number of the police station. Once connected, he got one of the desk officers he knew slightly to give him Tina's home number. He hung up and tapped it out quickly.

"Hi. This is Tina. I'm not in right now, but if you leave your name and number at the tone I'll get back to you. If this is you calling, partner, I feel wonderful and I want to talk to you, but if you're thinking of trying to talk me out of tonight, forget it. I'll see you in roll call and then it's 'andiamo!' That's Italian for 'eat my dust!'" There was a brief pause followed by a high-pitched "beeeeep." Calico hung up without leaving a message.

Half of him felt terrific because she felt wonderful and wanted to talk to him. His other half, though, was pissed off because she had anticipated him trying to call her off the run. He punched out another number on the phone.

"Hello, Wild John?" he asked when the receiver on the other end of the line was picked up. When he received an affirmative, he continued, "I need another favor . . ."

There was more than one way to skin a beautiful Japanese cat who was given to strange Italian sayings, he thought to himself cheerfully.

Harry Reeves was a very strange man. His looks were normal enough—thin but curly gray hair over a mottled sixty-six-year-old scalp which topped five-foot nothing of stooped, reedy frame dressed in baggy khaki pants, worn tennis shoes, and a frayed blue workshirt, but his mind was strange. Not all of it. Just the part which dealt with his sexual proclivities.

It was that part of his mind, driving him mad with sexual desire, which had made him a career criminal, a marked man unable to help himself, and, as the doctors at San Quentin had diagnosed, unwilling to help himself.

He had gone to jail over his weakness for the first time at the age of sixteen, graduating to state prison when he was nineteen. Since then he'd spent twenty-five of his last forty-seven years as a resident of the gray-bar hotel.

He didn't really care. He knew how to survive inside. If truth be told life was easier for him behind bars except for the fact he could never achieve sexual satisfaction inside prison. The peach-fuzzed first offenders did nothing for his libido like they did for many of the other cons. Bun boys did less for him than the scantily clad women he looked at in magazines or noticed in the flesh when he was on the outside, and they did nothing for him at all. The only way he could have achieved sexual satisfaction in prison was if the warden had allowed him conjugal visits with a stolen Ford motor car. It didn't have to be a fancy one. It didn't have to be new. But it had to be stolen and it had to be a Ford.

On Saturday night when Thumper Thurman banged on the front door of the rooming house he was staying at, Harry Reeves had been out of prison for his longest stretch in years. He'd been out for eight months.

"How you doing, Harry?" Guy Stack asked as he stepped out from the opposite side of the door. It was getting on for ten P.M., but the night still retained some of the heat from the Indian summer day which had preceded it.

"What are you guys doing here? I ain't stolen a car

since I been out." Harry didn't hate cops like many cons did, but he was still a little suspicious when a pair of L.A.'s finest turned up on his doorstep without known provocation.

"Sure, Harry, that's why we got reports of someone matching your description hanging out around the Ford sales lot on Ventura Boulevard."

"It wasn't me, I'm telling you . . ."

"Come on, Harry. Don't lie to us. This is me and the Thumper." Stack put his arm around Harry's shoulders and guided him away from the front door and down the steps of the porch. "We know all about your dirty little secret. I bet if we turned your room over we'd find all kinds of pornographic car magazines hidden under your mattress."

"Hey, that's not funny," Harry retorted, beginning to look distinctly upset. "I don't do that stuff no more."

"Sure you do, but it's okay." Stack opened the backdoor of the unmarked police cruiser and pushed Harry into the backseat ahead of him. Thumper climbed in the front and pulled the car out onto the street.

Harry didn't put up any resistance, acting more like a disconsolate puppy on the way to visit the vet. He wasn't a violent man. Nor was he unintelligent or untalented. His skill at tinkling the ivory piano keys and his willingness to act as a peer counselor had made him an integral and valuable part of the prison population.

"Where you taking me?" Harry asked. He was feeling distinctly nervous. Cops didn't just come and take you out for an evening drive. There was something up.

"Can you still file a Ford key from memory?" Thumper asked from the front seat.

An inkling of thought stirred in the back of Harry's

head, and down in his groin a little twitch of anticipation, a faint jolt of electricity, ran through him. "It's something you don't forget," he said craftily. "You tell me the year and model, give me a blank key, and in two minutes I'll file a master for you. Hey, you guys ain't settin' me up or nothin'. . . ?"

"You know us better than that, Harry. We can get better arrests than you just by driving down the street with the backdoors of the police car open. People are lining up to get arrested by us," Stack said with a smile. "You should relax. After all, wasn't it us who got those twenty-eight felony charges of driving without owners' consent dropped to one misdemeanor count?" The truth of the matter was Harry had stolen the same car twenty-eight times before he had gotten caught. Each time he stole the car he kept it only long enough to fulfill his need for sexual satisfaction and then returned it to the location he had stolen it from, always with a topped-up tank of gas. He'd admitted to all the thefts when Thumper and Stack had caught him red-handed the twenty-eighth time. When the case was presented to the Deputy District Attorney it had been referred directly to the City Attorney's office due to lack of evidence to show Harry had planned to permanently deprive the owner of the vehicle. The City Attorney had seen fit to combine all the charges in one count. Thumper and Stack had nothing to do with how the case was filed, but Harry didn't know that, and at the time Harry had thought they were his best friends in the whole world.

"Yeah you guys were okay, but I still did a year and a half back in the pen."

"It wasn't our fault your parole officer violated you because you were still up to your old tricks. We tried to talk him out of it, but you know how those guys are. They're tough." They are also swamped with work, thought Thumper in the front seat, and Harry's parole officer wouldn't have done a thing if he and Stack hadn't stayed on top of him. But again, Harry wasn't to know that.

"You say you haven't boosted a car since you've been out this time?" Stack asked.

"That's right, I've been staying clean, Mr. Stack."

"You must have a lot of repressed sexual tension built up by this time, or have you started playing the ladies?"

"No, I still don't like girls, Mr. Stack. Sex is dirty with girls."

"Is that what your momma taught you?"

"You know it is, Mr. Stack. I told you all this before." Harry's mother had been a staunch southern Baptist. Raising her family in Mississippi, where Harry was born, she'd allowed Harry's father to sweat over her exactly six times during the course of their marriage before he up and left the family to the poverty lines. Harry knew it was exactly six times because he had five older siblings, and the last time Harry's father screwed Harry's mother was the night he left home for good, the night Harry was conceived. From that day on, Harry's mother never let the word sex, or any mention of anything having to do with sex, be talked about in the house again. It was a heathen sin to think about sex. It was even worse to participate in it.

He was thirteen when he had his first sexual experience. Since his mother had refused to speak about the subject, the only reference he had to the terrifyingly exciting new feelings he was experiencing was his surroundings at the time of his first orgasm. He had been offered a ride home in the new Ford owned by his school math teacher. Harry had accepted, and when the teacher asked Harry if he wanted to sit in his lap and steer, Harry knew it was the wrong thing to do but couldn't help himself. While he steered the car excitedly down the back roads of his Mississippi town, the teacher had unzipped Harry's pants and masturbated him to orgasm.

From then on Harry would always return to Ford cars for his sexual gratification, avoiding the sexual guilt his mother had fostered by getting his satisfaction from an inanimate object. Eventually, in an effort to recapture the illicit feelings of his first orgasm, Harry found stealing a car gave him the same type of thrill.

"It's been a long time then since you got your rocks off, Harry boy, and sex is like a misdemeanor—the more you miss de meaner you get."

Thurman laughed nastily from the front seat. "Yeah, abstinence makes the heart grow fonder, or is that absence makes the dick grow harder. Something like that."

"You guys are scaring me. What are you talking about?" This was really getting weird, thought Harry.

"You got nothing to worry about, pal. We thought we'd give you a chance to have a little fun." Stack took a blank Ford key out of his pocket and pressed it into Harry's right palm which immediately began to sweat. "You got your files with you?" Stack asked.

Harry's testicles began to feel like they were attached to a live wire which ran straight up his body to the key in his hand. "N . . . N . . . No. I don't have 'em. I . . . I threw 'em away." Harry stammered as he tried to hand the key back to Stack.

"Come on. Don't bullshit me, Harry. Those files and lock picks are your whole world, your whole reason for living. You'd never throw them away. You put them in your pocket in the morning like you do your wallet." Stack reached over and manhandled Harry around until he could pull a thin leather purse from a rear pocket. He zipped it open and spilled the contents out into his hand. "Hey, must be magic, man. Looky what I found." Stack rolled the selection of files and lock picks around in his hand.

Harry smiled nervously and gave a small strangled laugh. "Please, Mr. Stack. Don't tell my parole agent you found those on me. I don't want to go back to the joint yet. I'm trying real hard."

"I know you are, Harry, so I'm going to give you a chance to do what you do best and not have to get in trouble for it."

"We're almost there, partner," Thumper said from the front seat.

Stack looked up to see where they were at. "Don't sweat it, Harry is going to do his thing for us in nothing flat and we're going to have us a car."

"You want me to steal a car for you?" Harry looked both worried and excited at the same time.

"That's right. But not just any car. We want you to steal a cop car."

Harry looked crestfallen. "But you guys all drive Chevys or Plymouths."

"We don't want you to steal an L.A.P.D. car, we want you to steal a Highway Patrol car."

"You're kiddin'?"

"No we ain't," said Thumper, pulling into a parking lot across the street from a doughnut shop. "And there it is. All eight cylinder, four hundred and fifty-one cubic inches, of custom-ordered, freeway flying, bastardizing, asshole-puckering Ford." He pointed across the street to where the sleek lines of a C.H.P. pursuit Mustang crouched, waiting like a sleeping cat for the two officers who patrolled in it to finish up their coffee and fat pills inside the doughnut shop.

"Shit," said Harry with awe.

"Yeah," said Stack with obvious glee.

Harry's hands started to itch and began to move almost like they had a mind of their own. The left one crept out and snagged a file from the cluster still in Guy Stack's hand. The right hand maneuvered the blank key around so its blade was captured between middle and index fingers. Never tearing his gaze away from the car across the street, Harry brought the file into contact with the soft metal of the blank and began to work magic.

"You guys know that Ford is an eighty-five, don't you? You can tell by the taillights. The ones on the new models are larger and more square. They also have the third eye in the middle of the back window."

"Does it make a difference?" Stack asked with sudden concern.

"Shit no! It's a Ford, ain't it? I can steal any Ford on wheels in under sixty seconds." Harry's hands were flashing along the length of the key, gouging here, cutting there, filing and smoothing. He seemed to be judging his work by nothing more than the pressure of the file on the dry, cracked skin of his right hand's fingers.

"Are you sure you can do this?" Thumper asked.

"No sweat. What do you want me to do with the car once I've got it?"

"You know the abandoned garage over on Kester between Hatteras and Oxnard?"

"Yeah. It's an old Shell station. Been closed up for about two years now."

"That's the one," Stack told him. "The rear bay door is unlocked. You do your thing and then get your ass out of here and over to that garage. Slide that beauty inside, close it down, and then get the hell out of there. And remember, you even think of telling anyone about this caper and your ass is grass. Me and Thumper will deny everything and then we'll bury you in a prison hole so deep there'll be more sunlight inside your asshole. You got that?"

"You don't have to worry, Mr. Stack. I'll do it just like you told me. All I got to do is steal it and I'll be happy . . . if you know what I mean."

"Yeah, I know what you mean, Harry. Just don't be leaving no mess on the seats or steering wheel."

Thumper turned around in the front seat. "Okay. Enough of this bullshit. We ain't got much time. Harry you get out of the car over here. Me and Stack are going to go into the doughnut shop and keep them two chippys busy. When you take the car you're going to have to move your ass to get to the garage before the info gets on the air. We'll stall for you by faking radio trouble with our car. It will buy you a little time, but somebody will eventually get the bright idea of calling it in on a pay phone. You don't have far to go, so just make sure you get there without hitting anything."

"Okay, okay." Harry's face was shining with sweat. He reached down and adjusted the obvious erection tenting the groin of his pants.

"Get out of here," Stack said loudly, repulsed by the action, and pushed Harry out of the car.

Stack got out of the car as well and then reseated himself in the front next to Thumper.

"We got to be crazy puttin' it on the line with some sex pervert right out of a dirty book. If he screws up, we gonna be fucked." Thumper wiped a huge hand over his shovel-shaped face.

"You worry too much, partner," Stack said as he slid down in the seat and put his feet up on the dashboard. "Let's do it."

They drove across the street, parked, and then entered the doughnut shop. One of the C.H.P. officers looked up and recognized the two L.A.P.D. officers.

"Well, if it isn't Molly and Moe the Slow twins. You guys need help catching road racers again?"

Stack and Thurman looked at each other. It couldn't have worked out better.

Reaching out with the catcher's mitt which was his right hand, Thurman planted it on the chippy's shoulder. "Hey, you know what they say, man: Some days you eat the bear, and some days the bear eats you."

And tonight, thought Stack delightedly, us bears are going to have a feast.

The Van Nuys roll-call room was alive with tension and apprehension as the uniformed rank and file slid into their seats. For the first time in years everybody was in their seats five minutes prior to the eleven P.M. Saturday start of the Sunday morning watch shift.

Earlier, Calico had waited for Tina to pull into the parking lot prior to getting into uniform.

"Hi," he'd said as she slid out of her Honda.

"Hi, yourself," she'd responded with a brilliant smile as if his being there waiting for her was exactly the right thing to have done.

Calico still hadn't sorted through all the emotional changes he'd experienced since making love to his partner. He had never slept around while married to Marsha, and since the divorce his several low-key affairs were never anything of great duration.

He'd resisted falling prey to the succession of easy women the morning watch regulars referred to as "twelves," or a six and a six-pack. Twelves were most often cop groupies, willing to spread for anything with a badge. They were also referred to as coyote ugly— women who, if you woke up next to them in the morning with your arm around them, you'd rather chew your arm off than wake them up in order to leave. The only thing worse than waking up next to a woman who was coyote ugly was waking up to find a woman's chewed-off arm under you own head.

The easy response to Calico's situation would have been to ignore it completely. But he couldn't, or wouldn't, do that. Tina had never been very far from his thoughts since the night they had made love. A fact which both bothered and excited him. It also made him very wary of being hurt in case she would think him an old fool and pass off their lovemaking as nothing more than a notch on the bedpost. He knew that was an unreasonable emotion; he'd worked with Tina long enough to know what her standards were, and he knew free love without commitment wasn't one of them. But he was still scared, both of being rejected and of being expected to make a commitment.

In the end, Tina had made it easy for him. Standing in the parking lot, looking at each other like a couple of love-sick puppies, she had taken a quick look around, to see they were alone, and then moved up on her toes to kiss him quickly on the lips. He'd reached for her, but she had darted out of range with a light laugh.

"You look like a boy trying to work up the nerve to kiss the girl after his first date."

"I feel like a fool."

"For heaven's sake why?" She had moved back into range and took his hand.

Calico shrugged. Her hair was pulled back into a long ponytail and her face was scrubbed free of makeup. Calico decided she was so pretty it hurt his eyes, and then felt even more foolish for the pounding of his heart in his chest. He was in his fifties for crying out loud.

"My mother once told me that if you have strong feelings about a person, then chances are they probably feel the same about you and are just as scared to let you know it," Tina related with a smile.

"Your mother sounds like a very smart woman."

"Yes, she was."

There was a moment of silence before Calico took a

deep breath. He was on the verge of telling Tina how he felt but just couldn't do it yet.

Tina laughed. "You coward," she said to him lightly. "Let's get out of the parking lot or we'll be late for roll call." She'd kissed him again and then darted away to the station entrance.

In the roll-call room, Lieutenant Heller cleared his throat to get everybody's attention. "Time to get started. It looks like things might get lively tonight, so I want you all on the street pronto." Heller was well aware of what the night held in store and, as crotchety as he could be sometimes, he was only sorry he wasn't going along on the ride.

Sal Fazio stepped in through the front door of the roll-call room. "Calico, I've got . . ." he started to say but was cut off by a voice from the back of the room.

"Oh, there you are, Sal. I've been looking for you." Everyone in the room turned around to look at Captain Morrison who had entered the backdoor of the room unobserved. He walked to the front and put his arm around the stymied sergeant. "Come on up to my office, will you. I've got an important audit that needs your special attention." Morrison guided Sal Fazio gently, but firmly, away.

All the morning watchers looked at one another. You could have heard a pin drop. Then a huge cheer went up and everybody went into motion at once.

Shotguns and cars had all been checked out prior to roll call to save time. Van Nuys to Vegas was a long run. The round trip was slightly over eight hundred miles, and the two police units would have a little under nine hours and forty-five minutes to cover the distance, eight hours of regular shift, forty-five minutes of Code-7 lunchtime, and the extra hour tacked on when the clocks were turned back.

The police parking lot was swelled with bodies as

Wild John pulled in with the souped-up sixty-five Plymouth. It sparkled and gleamed under a new wax and polish job. Wild John jumped out with a huge grin plastered across his features.

"Whoooo-weeee!" he whooped, bounding up to Calico and guiding him quickly back to the car. Tina followed in their wake.

"I put four spare tires on the backseat for you"— Wild John pointed into the rear of the car—"and there are a couple of extra additions under the seat which you can check out on the way."

"What kind of additions?" asked Calico suspiciously.

"Oh, just a few 'tools' to help you straighten out any curves those two jerks you're racing with might throw at you."

As if on cue, Stack and Thurman pulled into the far end of the parking lot in a roar of exhaust. Stack, who was in the driving seat, stuck his head out the window and yelled down at Calico, "Are you and Blanche ready to go, or are you ready to back out with your tails between your legs?"

"What the hell are they driving?" asked Gina Goodwin, a female officer who had been an Academy classmate of Tina's.

"I'm not sure," replied Wild John, squinting across the distance that separated the two units in the parking lot. "It looks like a C.H.P. chase car, but it's got L.A.P.D. markings on the doors."

"Magnetic stick-ons," said Calico. "All the plain Metro units carry magnetic door signs with the L.A.P.D. emblem so they can be used in areas where high visibility is needed. They must have slapped them on over the C.H.P. markings."

"Where did they get a C.H.P. unit from?" Tina asked.

Stack again stuck his head out the window of the menacing-looking unit he was driving. "Hey! What are we waiting for? Let's do it!" He punctuated his statement by punching his accelerator and laying a line of skid out of the parking lot and away into the street.

"Come on, partner!" Tina yelled at Calico. "They're getting the jump on us!" She turned away from the driver's side of the sixty-five Plymouth and made to head around the front of the car for the passenger side.

Calico nodded his head at Wild John who stepped sideways and bumped Tina into the front quarter panel of the unit with his hip. The total unexpectedness of the movement caught her off balance and the top part of her torso sprawled over the unit's hood. Wild John moved in with practiced ease and slipped a wrist cuff come-along over her hand and twisted it tight. Tina gasped with the sudden pain and had no choice but to follow when Wild John pulled her away from the vehicle.

Calico had already jumped into the driver's seat and fired up the unit with a throaty growl. Power surged through every cubic centimeter of the engine and car.

"I'm sorry, Tina. You've got too much to lose if we don't make it back without being caught or wrecked."

"Calico. . . !" Tina screamed as the Plymouth took off in a cloud of burning rubber. "Shit. . . !"

Spinning in toward her restrained hand, Tina lunged her mouth down on Wild John's arm and bit hard. Her captor yelped in surprise and let go of the wrist cuff. He made a grab for it when he realized what had happened, but Tina was too quick for him as she smashed an elbow into his chest, driving him backward to trip over the foot she had locked behind his right ankle.

Breaking free, Tina knew she only had a few seconds, but there was no way Calico was going to leave without her.

THIRTEEN

LOSERS REAPERS

T HE SHOTGUN CLOSEST to her was in the lax grasp of Gina Goodwin. With a quick flick of her right wrist, Tina shed the binding wrist cuff and grabbed the shotgun. Gina shouted, "Hey!" in surprise, but made no effort to chase after Tina who was sprinting across the parking lot at a right angle to the direction Calico had taken in the unit.

Tina's heart was pumping heavily in her chest as she tried to picture Calico's progress. The station's police vehicle parking lot was on the northwest corner of Tyrone Avenue and Delano Street. Calico would make an immediate right turn out of the east exit to southbound Tyrone Avenue. At the stop sign fifteen yards farther, he would execute a California rolling stop and another right turn to westbound Delano Street. If she could time it right, Tina figured it might be possible to head Calico off at the pass; get in front of him as he raced down toward Van Nuys Boulevard and a left turn toward the freeway. It would be her only chance to stop being left behind.

Like smoke, Tina flowed over the low retaining wall which separated the parking lot from the street. A screech of tires rounding the stop sign at Tyrone and Delano invaded her ears and she looked up to see Calico accelerating toward her.

Moving at top speed, she raced into the middle of the street and turned to face the oncoming police unit. Her ears picked up the sound of rising rpms and knew Calico had spotted her and was trying to bluff her out of the way. She brought the butt of the shotgun hard against her right side, pumped a round into the chamber, pushed the safety off, and blasted a flock of pellets down the barrel into the roadway to the right of the oncoming police car.

Calico responded by accelerating harder.

The other morning watchers began to yell at Tina to move, but she stood her ground. An emotional calm floated over her as she pumped another round into the chamber, brought the shotgun up to a shoulder position, and pointed it directly at the front grill of the black and white Plymouth heading right at her.

Calico slammed on the brakes.

The Plymouth's tires dug in, laying rubber all the way. Calico released the brakes slightly to keep control of the skid and turned the steering wheel sharply to the left. The unit turned broadside but continued on line toward Tina. It finally rocked to a stop two feet short of her shotgun-aiming figure.

Calico threw open the driver's door and jumped out, yelling at Tina over the roof of the car. "Of all the stupid stunts! What the hell are you trying to prove? Get the hell out of the way!"

"If you get back in that car without me, I'll put so much lead into the engine the only thing it'll be good for is a paperweight. I'm your partner, and if you're going to Vegas, then I'm going to Vegas."

"You're nuts!"

"And you're not, I suppose? Now back off and throw me the extra set of keys."

"There isn't an extra set."

Tina fired another round into the ground near the

front tires of the unit. The soft asphalt of the street absorbed the power of the pellets and stopped them from ricocheting. Chewed up chunks of asphalt, however, did splatter against Calico's ankles.

"Shit!" Calico screamed.

Another round was pumped into the shotgun's chamber.

"Yo! All right, all right!" Calico grabbed the second set of keys from where they were nestled in the front of his Sam Browne and tossed them to Tina who caught them one-handed.

"Now back away from the door."

"Come on, damnit. Stack and Thurman are getting away."

"Back off!"

Throwing up his arms in exasperation, Calico stepped back from the car.

Tina turned toward the onlooking police crew and gave them a quick curtsy. She then ran quickly over to the passenger door of the Plymouth, unlocked it and climbed in. She looked out the open driver's door. "What are you waiting for?" she asked Calico. "Stack and Thurman are getting away."

"I'm beginning to understand why Stack hates women," Calico said loudly as he clambered back into the car and fired the engine. Tina leaned over and kissed him on the cheek which sent the onlookers into a frenzy of war whoops.

"You're a pain in the ass, rookie," he said, pushing her away from him and wiping his cheek.

"Yeah, I know," she said, settling back with a bump as Calico accelerated away.

Delano Street spat the pair out onto Van Nuys Boulevard. They headed southbound toward the freeway.

"Is that them, about three blocks ahead?" Calico asked Tina, referring to Stack and Thurman.

"What's the matter, are you going night blind or something? Of course it's them. Let's get this hunk of metal in gear."

"Hey, listen, if you're going to get smart I can tie you to the bumper and let you come along for the drag."

Tina started to retort but Calico cut her off.

"Great, they're turning on Burbank! Heading for the San Diego Freeway . . ."

"Sure they are, they're taking the back route out through Little Rock and Pearblossom. It's the fastest route to connect with Highway Fifteen to Vegas," Tina stated with a puzzled look as Calico sped straight across Burbank Boulevard and continued straight down Van Nuys toward the Ventura 101 Freeway.

Calico grinned. "Oh, no, it's not. It might be the shortest route, but it isn't the fastest. Going the back route is like a rollercoaster ride. It's about five miles shorter than the front route, but the road has more dips than a nerd convention." Calico stopped talking for a moment as he entered the oncoming, but clear, traffic lanes to pass two civilian vehicles with a case of black and white fever, refusing to either pass one another or go over the thirty-five mile an hour speed limit. Once he was in the correct lane again, Calico picked up his monologue. "We're going to be traveling most of the way at over a hundred miles an hour. If Stack and Thurman try to maintain that speed over the back route, they're going to tear hell out of their car. They'll be lucky to make it to where the two routes converge at Victorville . . . hold on!" He turned the steering wheel sharply, ran a red light, and hit the freeway on-ramp doing forty miles an hour. At the top of the ramp he was doing eighty. As he entered the freeway the unit topped the one hundred miles per hour rate.

Tina reached over and turned on the cherry top light and the two separate amber flashers. She didn't bother with the siren, knowing full well they would be outrunning its warning sound. "Where did you find this old heap?" she asked, looking around the interior.

"Watch your mouth, woman. This car is a piece of history. The fastest police pursuit unit ever built for the L.A.P.D. It's an antique, and if we treat it with respect it will get us to Vegas and back in time for coffee and doughnuts at end of watch."

The small plastic statue of Jesus swayed violently back and forth as it hung from the unit's rearview mirror on its short chain. Tina took her Buddha out of her top uniform pocket and went to hang it on the mirror as well. Calico stopped her, took the Buddha in his hand, and then removed the plastic Jesus from the mirror. He tossed both statues over onto the backseat.

"We can't rely on those guys tonight. They try to jump out of the vehicle at anything over fifty-five miles an hour. Tonight it's just you, me, and this bullet train we're riding."

"This is bullshit," Sal Fazio said to himself, sitting in the captain's office auditing the patrol recap figures back to the first of the year.

Not only was he bothered that what he was doing was just busy work, designed to keep him off the streets and away from trying to catch Calico, but the figures he was auditing reflected Calico as having the highest felony and misdemeanor arrest rate in the division on a monthly basis. Plus over fifty percent of Calico's arrests were observation arrests, a direct result of self-initiated police work on Calico's part as opposed to arrests resulting from radio calls.

There was no getting around it. Calico was a hell of a policeman, admired and liked by his peers, and respected by his superiors, including Captain Morrison, and those facts lay like a festering lump in Fazio's stomach. He'd lived with the lie of blaming Calico for the breakup of his marriage for so long now he actually believed it. He hated Calico and must do something to screw him over before his nemesis retired. He needed to expose the Vegas run in such a way even Calico's friends in high places would take action in order to cover their collective rear ends.

Feeling sourly definite about his objective, Fazio threw down his calculator. He quickly flipped through the reports in front of him and scrawled his signature at the bottom of the last page, verifying he had checked all the figures and found them correct. It was a lie, but there wasn't going to be an audit to check the audit. The department was paranoid, but not that paranoid.

Downstairs in the parking lot, he started up his police car and pulled out onto the city streets. Plugging his rover into the convert-a-com unit, he used the car mike to request Calico and Tina's unit status.

"Nine-A-twenty-one is on a disturbance call at one five zero zero three Victory, the Pussycat Bar," replied the RTO.

Fazio frowned. He was certain Calico's unit would have been unassigned—the girls at communications fully aware of the Las Vegas run and, he assumed, in on the conspiracy which seemed to condone it.

Putting his foot onto the gas pedal, he sped up Van Nuys Boulevard, turned right onto Victory and was three blocks from the Pussycat when he heard Calico's voice over the radio, "Nine-A-twenty-one, we have a Code-four at our location," advising the situation at the bar was under control. Fazio was confused, Calico should have been well on his way to Vegas by now.

The Pussycat's parking lot held a dozen or so vehi-

cles seemingly parked with random abandon. Fazio
slid his unit in next to the black and white already
there, and entered the topless bar. He spotted Ray
Perkins and his partner, Walt Huntly, talking to several half-dressed girls and the bar bouncer. On the
floor next to them was a burly, handcuffed patron
wearing a red lumberjack shirt, worn Levis, and heavy
work boots.

"What happened?" Fazio inquired.

"Oh, hi, Sarge," Perkins said, turning around to
face his supervisor. "Mr. Herriot"—he indicated the
handcuffed man using the overly polite tone of voice
and address which is the L.A.P.D.'s sarcastic trademark rudeness—"figured looking at the girls on stage
wasn't good enough and decided to have some more
personal contact." Perkins looked over at one of the
bare-chested girls standing next to him, "Darla is making a citizen's arrest for battery."

"Yeah, that creep should be locked up in a cage.
Where does he get off puttin' his hands on me?"
Darla's voice was like that of a screeching parrot. In
the dark bar light she looked good enough to screw
despite her tattoos, Fazio thought, but you would have
to gag her. It was unusual for one of the girls in a
place like this to press charges, though, and Fazio
pulled Perkins aside and said as much in a quiet voice.

"Yeah, I know," said Ray. "But you see, Mr. Herriot wasn't just satisfied with touching Darla, he decided he wanted a share of her tips as well and started
pulling dollar bills out of her snatch. We should actually book him for robbery, but Darla is just mad now,
she'll never show up in court, so we might as well just
make it a battery so the detectives don't have to waste
time messing with it."

Fazio nodded his head. A battery was a simple misdemeanor, the patrol officers' report being sent di-

rectly to court. If Herriot was arrested for robbery, a felony, the detectives would get involved by first presenting the case to the District Attorney who, because there was no weapon involved, would refer the case to the City Attorney for a misdemeanor filing. At the C.A.'s office, the detectives would re-present the case which would then be filed as a battery because that was the easiest charge to prove. The detectives would waste hours of manpower and end up back at square one with the same filing charge they would get if Herriot had been booked for battery in the first place.

"You going to take him in?" Fazio asked Perkins suspiciously. "Where's Calico and Tamiko? I thought this was their call."

Perkins slapped an innocent look on his face. "We got here first. They took off just before you got here. I'm surprised you didn't pass them in the parking lot. Calico put out the Code-four."

"Yeah, I heard." Fazio knew something was fishy, but he couldn't figure out what. "If you've got this squared away, I'm going to take off."

"Sure thing, Sarge. No sweat. See you later." Perkins couldn't help the small smirk stretching across his mouth.

Outside in his patrol car, Fazio picked up the radio mike.

"Nine-L-twenty, ask nine-A-twenty-one to switch to tac five." Tac five was the radio band used by field units to communicate with each other while not clogging up the frequency used to assign calls for service.

"Nine-A-twenty-one switch to tac five for nine-L-twenty."

"Roger, switching," Calico's voice replied.

Fazio was getting mad now. There was no way Calico and Tamiko should be in radio range.

"Nine-L-twenty to nine-A-twenty-one. Give me a location for a meet."

There was nothing but static over the radio and
Fazio had to make his request again before Calico's
voice came through in reply.

"Nine-L-twenty, roger. We're on a station call
checking out the mountain racers. How about meeting
us at Beverly Glen and the start of dirt Mulholland."

Fazio acknowledged the location and headed in the
direction of the division's southernmost border.

Mulholland Drive, because of its twisting, dangerous progress along the crest of the low mountains
which separated Van Nuys division from Hollywood
division, was a favorite location for kids in souped-up
cars playing king of the mountain. Mulholland was
well paved for the entire length of its slash across the
Valley except for one section of approximately five
miles which was still not much more than a wide dirt
trail. Dirt Mulholland, as the unpaved stretch was
known, started at the intersection with Beverly Glen,
which ran up from the Valley and then draped over
Mulholland before descending to the Hollywood area
on the south side, and continued its windy path westbound to White Oak Avenue in West Valley division.
There were no turnoffs along the entire stretch. You
entered on one end and continued until you spat out
the other.

At the start of dirt Mulholland, Bill Kerouac and
Gina Goodwin waited in the squad car assigned to
Tina and Calico.

"I hope this works," said Gina.

"Me too," replied her partner. "I almost had a
heart attack when we couldn't find the tape giving this
location for a meet."

On the bench seat between the two officers rested a
pocket-size cassette player and a mound of tapes.
Each of the tapes was labeled with one or two sentences of conversation Calico had taped on them in
the hopes of throwing Fazio a curve. When a situa-

tion, like Fazio requesting to meet with Calico and Tina's unit, presented itself, Kerouac would place the tape with the appropriate reply in the cassette deck and play the response through the police radio microphone. Calico tried to cover every conceivable situation with the tapes, including a fail safe where he reported his radio was malfunctioning.

Calico figured it was inevitable Fazio would try to set up a meeting with him at some time during the shift. Obviously when he and Tina didn't show up, it would give the sergeant the ammunition he needed to blow them out of the water. With that in mind, setting up a meeting became an important part of the plan to take Fazio out of the play.

About fifteen yards east of the start of dirt Mulholland a cherry-red Mustang with a teenage driver sat revving its engine while Kerouac and Goodwin were parked on Beverly Glen watching for the first sight of Fazio. The youth in the Mustang was excited about what was coming and couldn't wait to tell his buddies about it when it was all over. You never could figure the fuzz, he thought to himself. Some of them were a real pain in the ass, but Kerouac and Calico were okay, they had both given him breaks in the past, so he was happy to help out.

Gina shifted nervously behind the cruiser's steering wheel. She had restyled her hair into a bun on top of her head so her backlighted silhouette closely resembled Tina's. "How did I let myself get conned into this? If Fazio catches up with us, we'll be in as much trouble as Tina and Calico for acquiescing."

Kerouac suddenly sat up straight behind in his seat. "There's no time to back out now. Here comes Fazio. Let's hit it!"

"Get ready with those tapes," Gina told her partner as she quickly turned the black and white's engine over.

The headlights of the police car flashed twice in a signal to the cherry-red Mustang. Gina looked out the rear window and saw the outline of Fazio's unit approaching them as Kerouac fumbled with the first of the needed tapes.

A screeching of tires accompanied by a flaming light show, as the teenager lit up his tires, preceded the Mustang's progress as it cut across Beverly Glen and entered the start of dirt Mulholland.

"Here we go!" yelled Gina as she slammed the police cruiser into gear and took off in pursuit. Behind him, she saw Fazio's unit fall into position to follow the chase.

Finally, Kerouac got the tape he wanted into the machine, switched on the radio mike, and listened to Calico's voice flow over the police frequency to broadcast the chase.

The three-car procession raced along the dirt road, the Mustang and the first police car raising a cloud of dust so thick it forced Fazio to drop off the pace a bit in order to see. Potholes and large rocks in the roadway threatened to tear out undercarriages at the first opportunity, and steep dropoffs to the right side threatened to demolish completely any vehicle which lost control.

As her speedometer edged toward sixty, Gina swore at the kid in the Mustang. "Shit! He's crazy. Didn't you tell him this wasn't for real and to take it a little easy?"

"Just keep him in sight, partner," Kerouac said to her as he almost bounced off the roof of the car when they flew over a particularly deep rut. "It isn't too much farther before we hit the trap point and hopefully lose Fazio."

"I just hope we don't get stuck."

Kerouac was having trouble bracing himself safely while using one hand to stop the tape player from jumping off the seat and operating the radio mike with the other. Calico's prerecorded, untroubled voice, however, was still broadcasting smoothly.

Behind the Mustang and the first police cruiser, Fazio fought to stay close to the chase. He'd been surprised at Beverly Glen when he saw the outline of Tina and Calico in his headlights. He was very confused, but didn't have a chance to get things straight before the Mustang blasted past, dragging Tina and Calico away in pursuit. He tried to contact Tina and Calico on the radio, but was constantly overridden by Calico's broadcasting.

Ahead of him the dust of the pursuit was still thick, but Fazio drove through it as fast as he could, determined to be in on the kill at the end of the chase. He had to confirm Calico and Tina were in the cruiser. His eyes told him one truth, but his instincts told him different. In his gut he knew Calico was halfway to Vegas by now. Yet if that was true, how in the hell was he able to broadcast the pursuit?

CRUNCH . . . SPLAT . . . SCREECH . . . SPLUT . . . THUD . . . . Fazio was suddenly thrown forward against the restraint of the seat belt which held him firmly as his car shuddered to a stop. Dust filled the air in a veil that was far too thick for his headlights to penetrate. The engine of the cruiser was stalled out and Fazio quickly ground it to life again. It didn't feel like he had hit anything. Rather it was like a giant magnet stopped his forward progress. He put the car into drive and gunned the engine. His only reward was the sound of his rear wheels spinning while Calico's voice continued to emanate from the radio speaker as the pursuit of the speeding Mustang continued.

Two things happened when Fazio climbed out of his car to investigate his situation. His flashlight failed him, and his feet sunk up to his ankles in muddy clay.

"Mother Fucker!" he screamed and tried to walk out of the huge mud puddle he was stuck in. It took Calico, Kerouac, and Ray Perkins three trips with a fully loaded county water truck to achieve the right size and consistency of mud puddle they knew would trap someone driving through at speed. On the north side of the roadway was a dry strip wide enough to drive across which both the Mustang and the first patrol car used. Fazio, however, not knowing the mud puddle existed, drove straight into it as planned. It would take a tow truck to get him out.

"No way are you going to leave me stuck here, you asshole Calico," Fazio said out loud to the pitch-darkness of the rural area. There wasn't a house or a phone for miles, and it would take him forever to walk back to the station or even to an area where he could call for help. He sloshed back across the mud puddle and grabbed the radio microphone through the driver's window.

"Nine-L-twenty, I need a OPG tow at my location three miles into dirt Mulholland."

"Unit attempting to broadcast. The frequency is restricted for a pursuit in Van Nuys area." The RTO's voice echoed through the silence of Mulholland.

Fazio fumed as he listened to Calico's voice continue on the air. Eventually Calico, in compliance with established procedures, declared he was terminating the pursuit due to the dangers of the speeds being reached. He requested other units to be on the lookout for the Mustang since a roadblock at the far end of dirt Mulholland had not been established in time.

Fazio screamed and picked up the mike, repeating his request for a tow truck at his location.

The RTO's bored voice returned, "Unit attempting to broadcast, your transmission is breaking up. Please repeat."

"Argggh," Fazio was becoming inarticulate. He

knew the RTO could hear him. He'd been set up. He kicked the door of the cruiser in frustration before repeating his request again, and again received a reply from the RTO that she was unable to understand him due to static. The sergeant screamed loud and long and threw the mike back into the car where it bounced off the bench-seat cushion and jumped up to crack the windshield. Fazio covered his face with his hands. Swearing and mumbling under his breath, he slogged through the mud to the back of the cruiser and opened the trunk.

"I won't let you beat me, you bastard! I'll get out of here and beat you at your own game." He fumbled around in the dark, feeling objects in the trunk to find something suitable to jam under the tires for traction. Eventually he found four hard, oblong block shapes. In the blackness of the night it was impossible to identify them and in his eagerness Fazio didn't even stop to think what they might be. All he knew was they were his ticket out of the mud hole.

Dropping to his knees, he scooped mud out from under the buried rear tires. He didn't care how dirty he got. It would be worth it if he could dig out in time to foul up Calico.

Thirty minutes later he had the blocks wedged firmly under the tires. He clamored back into the cruiser and started up the engine. Excitement pounded in his chest and he knew he had to control himself, take things slow and easy or he'd only dig himself in deeper. He applied pressure to the gas pedal and heard the rear tires begin to spin. He backed off and tried again. Still the wheels spun again, but the car rocked forward slightly.

Releasing the accelerator, Fazio let the car settle back. His heart was pounding somewhere in his throat, making it hard to breathe. He was so close to getting out. He stared straight ahead through the cracked windshield and tried to concentrate on nothing but putting the right amount of pressure on the gas pedal which would drive him out of the hole.

The driver's side window had been wound down so Fazio could also hear clearly what was going on. Any clue to his progress could be critical. His ears were tuned, his sight focused ahead in concentration, his sense of feel focused completely on the gas pedal.

Consciously, he believed he had closed down his senses of smell and taste in order to concentrate more fully on the others, but the gremlins in his nose and along his taste buds suddenly sensed smoke and fire and sent an emergency message to his brain . . . *FLARES! The fucking oblong blocks are boxes full of flares!*

His foot flew off of the gas pedal as his eyes flicked up to the rearview mirror. But it was too late. The smell of burning rubber became overwhelming and flames burst up from the rear of the cruiser. Fazio bailed out and rolled away from the flaming death trap. He scampered through the mud on his hands and knees, diving over the drop-off on the southside of the road and rolling away through the brush and brambles as the gas tank blew.

Down on Ventura Boulevard at the local doughnut stand, Kerouac, Gina, and the youth who had been driving the Mustang looked up at the sudden glow on the skyline.

Kerouac grimaced. "I don't know what he's up to, but it looks like Fazio is burning mad."

With Stack at the wheel, Thumper Thurman and his partner blasted across the Los Angeles–San Bernadino County border in a shower of sparks, their rear bumper grabbing the concrete when the shocks bottomed out.

"Yahoo!" yelled Stack. "Ride 'em cowboy!"

"Slow down, you mutha." Thumper's eyes were as wide as ping-pong balls, his feet stamping imaginary brakes on the passenger side floorboards, his ham hock-sized hands bracing his arms against the ceiling.

"Pilot to copilot." Stack made his voice crackle like static before continuing. "Prepare for turbulence ahead. Please extinguish all smoking materials and return the stewardess to her normal upright position."

"It's no wonder you crazy folks is white. Saves the coroner having to cover you with a sheet."

"Beats being brown because you're full of shit like you."

"If you ever drop that speedometer below . . . Shiiiit!" The Metro cop's stolen pursuit car bottomed out through another dip and then launched into space over a sharp hump. ". . . a hundred, I'm gonna turn what's left of your brains into scrambled eggs."

The sign for Palmdale whipped by as the speeding Highway Patrol cruiser aimed for the intersection of Highway Fifteen, at Victorville, where Stack and Thurman's route would intersect with Calico and Tina's. Stack continued to maintain speed on the two-lane back route to Vegas whenever possible. He turned the flashing red light in the cruiser's window on and off whenever necessary to buy safe passage past the sparse traffic heading in the same direction, but the humps and bumps in the road forced him to go slower than he wished in order not to tear the cruiser to shreds.

Thumper lent support with a continuous flow of directions, blasphemy, and insults. "Look out for the jack rabbit!" . . . "You asshole, you're going to kill us!" . . . "If I ever catch up with the guy who issued you a driving license, I'm gonna tear his head off and shit in the hole!"

Stack cut him off, "Pilot to copilot. Bandits dead ahead."

"What are you talking about?" Thumper squinted into the darkness pierced by the cruiser's headlights and picked out a string of red lights.

"Reapers, man. It's the fucking Reapers on a run."

The string of red lights quickly materialized into a mass of denim, leather, hair, and tattoos fused to the gleaming metal of two-wheeled iron horses. There were fifteen chopped Harleys draped with various dregs of humanity all flying the colors of the Reapers outlaw motorcycle gang.

Over the previous ten years the Reapers had become a particular thorn in the side of the L.A. Police Department. While the Hell's Angels had tempered their street activities somewhat, in favor of the more profitable crimes of drug running and munitions dealing, the Reapers had filled their ranks with the lunatic fringe of the Angels' followers who longed for the old days of raping, pillaging, and terrorizing. Most of them had teethed on cycle myths blown out of proportion with constant retelling. Most of them were crazy. All of them had made their bones by committing rape and murder in front of other Reaper witnesses in order to earn their colors.

"Yahoo! Let's have us some fun . . ." Stack goosed the accelerator and hit the red light and siren. The motorcycle riders at the back of the pack gave a startled look over their shoulders.

The front bumper of the Highway Patrol car almost brushed the rear wheel of the first Harley in range. At the last second the rider made a sharp left into the empty oncoming traffic lane and laid his bike down with a shower of sparks that lit the night like Fourth of

July. There were screamed warnings among the bikers as Stack and Thurman blew past them, scattering the Reapers in all directions. One rider on a custom three-wheeler, his momma riding high behind him, clipped the wheel of another Reaper and spun away wildly.

Stack and Thurman raced down the road ahead of the pack. Stack's laughter was almost insane, and Thurman's face glowed with a mean sweat. "Again, man," he said softly to his partner.

"You can't be serious," Stack said.

"Bet your ass on it, boy," Thurman replied, reaching his long left leg over to stomp on the brake pedal. His arms jerked the wheel out of Stack's hands and spun the car through three and a half rotations until they were faced back the way they had come.

"Hit it! I hate these muthafucking scum."

Stack laughed wildly and jumped on the gas.

The Reapers saw the cruiser coming and scattered to either side, not believing what was happening. Stack and Thurman sped through without incident. Once past, Stack stomped on the brakes and spun the cruiser around for a third pass.

This time the Reapers were ready. Several of them slashed out with heavy link chains which smashed across the roof of the cruiser. One Reaper, however, was too slow to pull his chain back and Thumper leaned out the window to grab it. A single jerk of the black officer's powerful shoulders and the Reaper became part of the highway tarmac. Stack goosed the hopped-up pursuit cruiser and blasted away into the night.

"You are the craziest . . ." Stack said to his partner. "You could have killed the bastard."

"No better 'n what he deserved, man. You know that." Thurman stared straight ahead through the windshield. "Look," he said, and pointed at an oncoming road sign. "Highway Fifteen a mile and a half ahead."

"We haven't seen any indication of Calico and the cunt behind us," said Stack. "They must have gone the front way. We've lost a little time on these bumps and messing with those jerks. I hope they ain't ahead of us."

"It don't matter, man. We'll catch them if they are. No way we gonna lose this race. Too much riding on it. I need the cash we staked to pay my bills."

"If you're that broke why did you agree to put the money up and do the run?" Stack took his eyes off the road for a second to glance at the dark silhouette of his partner.

"We've been partners for a long time, man. Do you really need an answer to that question?"

Stack thought for a moment, looking back at the road and steering into the oncoming lane in order to avoid a major pothole. "No, I guess I don't. You're a lot like me. There was no way to back out of the challenge without losing face. You'd think we were a pair of fucking Orientals."

"It's more than that and you know it." Thurman's voice had dropped to even a lower octave than normal. "We lay it on the line every time we go out on the street to play cop. The assholes hate us because it's our job to keep them on a leash or beat 'em back into their cages. The liberals hate us because having us around is an admission that their views on life are invalid. Average Joe Citizen thinks we're a pain in the ass because the only time he has contact with us is when he's been the victim of a crime and holds us responsible for not doing our job, or when we hit him in his wallet by writing him a ticket when we should have been out stopping the criminals who victimized him.

Nobody wants us around, but you should hear 'em yell when we aren't.

"Doing a good job as a cop is like pissing in a dark suit—it feels good, but nobody notices. It's a no-win situation which drives us to look for stunts like this run to Vegas so we can make like a bunch of butch Girl Scouts—posturing and mouthing off for our peers, looking to show how crazy and tough we are. Policemen are no different than any of the warrior classes throughout history. The crazier you are, the tougher you are, the more you show you don't give a damn, the more respect you get. And that's what it's all about. Respect. We all want it. And the only way to get it is by being larger than life. Doing things everyone else is afraid to do. And if the public doesn't like it, then fuck 'em if they can't take a joke."

Stack was amazed at his partner's insight. "That's the longest speech I've ever heard you make."

"Yeah. Well, we all didn't just drop out of the trees yesterday."

The highway underneath the two officers suddenly smoothed out and the intersection with Highway Fifteen, which would take them straight into the heart of Vegas, cut off to the right. Stack steered into the interchange and put his foot down.

Traffic on the four-lane highway was heavier than it had been on the back route and Thumper turned the red light in the cruiser's window on and left it on.

Stack's eyes flipped to the rearview mirror.

"Hey, hey. We've got company."

Thumper turned around in his seat and looked out the rear window.

"Is it them?"

"Has to be. Who else?"

Coming up fast, Calico and Tina knew they had the power under them to pass their competition and leave them in the dust.

"Let's do it," Tina said to her partner. They had both been holding their breath in anticipation, hoping Calico hadn't miscalculated by taking the longer route.

Calico grinned, seeing Stack and Thumper swing through the interchange. "Hold on," he told his partner, and gave more juice to the engine. The cruiser responded with a low-pitched growl of suppressed power. The speedometer was buried somewhere over a hundred and twenty miles an hour.

"What's that ahead?" Tina asked, pointing toward two parallel lines of revolving red lights.

Calico didn't respond right away. Instead he pulled a hidden microphone out from under the cruiser's dashboard.

"Hey there, good buddies, you got your ears on? This is Big Blaster coming at ya."

"CB unit?" Tina asked, amused at the corny accent Calico's voice had assumed.

"That's a big ten-four, good buddy," Calico replied to his partner.

"Next thing you'll be picking hay out of your hair."

The CB unit under the dash cackled in response to Calico. "Good to hear you, Big Blaster. This is the Pick 'Em Up Guys. It looks like the Slime Bucket beat you down the back route." The voice over the CB was Ren's.

As the two racing police units approached, the parallel lines of flashing red lights lit up the rows of tow trucks beneath them. Ren was in one of the front trucks waiting for his father to pass by.

Calico spoke back into the CB, "The Slime Bucket isn't going to be in the lead for long. What's the situation with the smokies?"

"We had a word with them over the air, Big Blaster, and you're clear through the Nevada border. After that it's anybody's ball game."

"Ten-four, Pick 'Em Up Guys. And thanks for turning out."

"No sweat, Big Blaster." Ren's voice was excited. "Looking forward to seeing you on the waves. But watch your tail. Word is the Slime Bucket is going to play dirty."

"I'd be disappointed if they didn't," Calico replied and hung up the CB mike. Both he and Tina waved and sounded their siren as they passed between the two rows of pickup trucks, each one representing an official police tow yard from each of the seventeen L.A.P.D. areas.

Tina picked up the regular car mike. They were well out of range to be heard back in the division, but she was banking Stack and Thurman had the Highway Patrol radio tuned into the city police frequency and she would be able to communicate with them from car to car.

"Play time is over, ladies. Time to make way for your betters."

There was a short pause and then Stack's voice came back to her.

"Is that you, Blanche? Shouldn't you be at home cooking or changing diapers? You might get your hair mussed out here playing with the big boys."

"I think 'boys' is the key word there. I'm glad you recognize your genetic limitations," Tina sent back.

Calico had pulled alongside Stack and Thurman, and Stack looked over and gave a one-finger salute to Tina, who laughed. Pissed off, Stack cut the front of his cruiser over, forcing the other car to break or collide.

Swearing, Tina grabbed hold of the dashboard with both hands. Calico pulled out to pass again, but Stack kept cutting over in front of him, almost unending Thumper who was climbing over to the backseat of the Highway Patrol cruiser.

"What's Thurman doing?" Tina asked with concern.

"Who knows," Calico replied, concentrating on his driving. He knew he had the power under the hood to get away from Stack. The problem was getting by him.

The two units raced on for another mile, Calico and Tina half a car length back in Stack's blind spot.

"Look out. Thurman is up to something," Tina said as she watched Thurman roll down the closest side window to them in his car.

"Holy SHIT!" Calico jumped on the brakes but it was too late. Thurman had chucked several large iron bars with tire-ripping spikes onto the highway.

Calico missed the first one clean and avoided the second as it bounced and clipped his bumper. But the third one was unavoidable as it slipped under the right front wheel and slashed the tire to shreds. The steering wheel had a life of its own as a fourth spiked bar tore the offside rear tire out, and a fifth bar caught the left front tire.

Avoiding the brakes altogether, Calico fought to steer the cruiser which slid from one side of the highway to the other and back again with his efforts. Eventually the cruiser slowed enough to make braking feasible, and Calico brought the limping unit to a stop on the right highway shoulder. He slumped forward over the wheel in shock.

"See you later, alligators." Stack's voice came mockingly over the radio.

"You okay?" Tina asked.

"Yeah. You?"

"Fine. But I need to switch to brown panties to hide the stains."

Calico laughed. "I know what you mean. What a pair of bastards."

"What do we do now?" Tina asked.

"Well, we aren't done for yet. Thankfully Wild John

supplied us with spares. How fast can you change a tire?"

"Let's make like the pits at Indy."

"Funny, you don't look like Bobby Unser."

"Yeah. And you don't look like an old lady, but you drive like one."

Before Calico could retort, Tina was out of the cruiser and dragging the spare tires out of the backseat. Calico followed her out of the car and stretched his back. A familiar, but faint noise grabbed at his ears. Something about the noise made him uneasy, and as he sifted his memory to identify it, the hair on the back of his neck lifted.

It was the thunder of distant but angry Harleys.

FOURTEEN

PAYBACK

―――――

"ARE YOU GOING to help with this, or do you figure changing tires is woman's work." Tina slid
the jack under the front bumper of the police cruiser.
She had hauled one of the spare tires out of the backseat and set it down next to the front passenger side.
A wisp of hair straggled across her brow, sprung loose
from the bun on top of her head, and a smear of dirt
marred her forehead above her right eye.

With his back turned to her, Calico spoke to his
partner. "Tina, get the shotgun out of the car and find
some cover."

"What are you talking about?"

Calico spun around and moved fast. The noise of
the approaching motorcycles had him spooked. He felt
vulnerable, stranded as they were on the side of the
road. Traffic was so sparse the only thing to pass them
since they had pulled over were two eighteen-wheelers
and a VW bug trying to build up enough speed to take
off.

"I've got a bad feeling," Calico told Tina with
enough urgency in his voice to grab her attention. He
clambered into the cruiser's front seat and unlocked
the shotgun from its rack. "Here, take this and get off
to the side of the road," he said, handing the weapon
out the passenger door to Tina.

Tina still didn't know what was going on, but she knew enough to realize her partner was serious and she better do as he told her.

The flat desert landscape on either side of the highway offered little in the way of concealment, but there was a low ditch on the far side. She ran quickly across the roadway and rolled into the ditch behind a bushel of low scrub and twisting manzanita. A large rock at the bottom of the gully bruised her knee and she shoved it out of the way with her foot as she jacked a round into the shotgun and slid the safety off.

Back at the cruiser, Calico removed the second shotgun from the trunk, unsnapped the leather loop over his holstered .38. He moved around to a position of advantage at the front of the car where he could keep the engine block between himself and any flying lead coming his way. He didn't know why the sound of the oncoming Harleys made the blood race so fast in his veins that his skin was itching, but after thirty years on the street wearing a target, he trusted his gut instincts.

Facing down a pack of biker scum in the middle of the night on the straight stretch of desert highway between the nothing towns of Victorville and Barstow was not exactly Calico's idea of a good time. On the other hand, he had always admired Evel Knievel's prospective—"When I die, I want it to be glorious."

The ragged line of the bikers' headlights coalesced into a nightmare vision of death's-head helmets, studded boots, strapped-down Bowie knives, iron-twisted muscles, Reapers' colors, and mutated values. The choppers slowed at the sight of the stranded police car and the four passenger vehicles behind them sped past, their inhabitants looking straight ahead, glad they were no longer the focus of the outlaw's attention.

The bikers were silent except for the revving of their motors as they assessed the situation. It was easily clear this wasn't the same cop car which had harassed them earlier, but it was still a pigmobile and they had the taste of blood in their mouths.

Pushing his Harley closer to the back of the cruiser, the lead biker's attention was riveted when Calico ran a round up into the chamber of his shotgun. The singular "click-klatch" sound rose without effort above the noise of the motorcycle engines.

"Well, howdy, Officer. Do you need some help?" The leader of the pack was lean and tall. A bushy mustache hung down on the side of his twisted top lip to connect with an ugly untrimmed goatee. His hair was long and looked like a rat's nest from blowing in the wind. His eyes were hooded and sunken in shadows. Greasy jeans were topped by a black T-shirt and a Levi jacket with the sleeves cut out. On the back of the jacket were the Reapers' colors, a skull inside a black cowl framed on two sides by the staff and curving blade of a scythe. Along the handle of the scythe were strips of different colors, each one earned for a different act of violence or perversion.

"Hey, pig. I asked you a question."

"Go fuck yourself," Calico replied.

The biker laughed and turned back to his cohorts and gave a hand signal Calico couldn't see. On cue the other bikers gave throttle to their engines and moved around to circle the cruiser. Chains came into sight as did several handguns and a sawed-off double-barrel shotgun.

A line of sweat popped out across Calico's brow, but he surprised himself by feeling remarkably calm inside.

"I don't like your attitude, pig." The head biker turned to talk to Calico again from the rear of the car.

"Take it or leave it, pal. Your choice."

"How about we just take you apart?"

"You can try." Calico's voice was firm. From behind him came a whizzing noise. He ducked instinctively and rolled away to his left as a three-foot length of chain twirled through the space he had been inhabiting and crunched onto the hood of the cruiser. Calico came up on one knee, the shotgun taunt against his right side, his back to the flat tire still attached in the passenger-side wheel well. He had a full range of targets, but it was too soon to move and he held his fire.

"What's your name, asshole?" he asked the lead biker. As he did so he stood up slowly and contemptuously turned his back on the bikers who had thrown the chain at him.

"What's it to you?"

"Not much. But when I write out the death report, I'd like to know what to fill in for the name of the scum who's so scared of the police he has to hide behind an army of other scumbags. By yourself you couldn't intimidate Cheese Whiz."

The biker spokesman shoved down his kickstand and angrily hopped off his Harley. "The name is York. And I ain't scared of you or any other pig. I ain't scared of anything."

"Then how come you need all these other assholes to help you take on one real man."

"Hey, fuck you. We didn't start this." York walked around to confront Calico who turned his back to the cruiser, using York as a shield between him and the other bikers. "Some of your buddies spread a couple of Reapers over the roadway earlier tonight and it's your luck to be the payback. Nothing personal, man, just a payback."

"Are you willing to be cut in half as part of the payback?" Calico asked. "And how many of your re-form-school mates are going to be willing to die just to take down one cop?"

"Don't kid yourself, old man. You're dead where you stand anytime I give the word."

"I might be an old man, but I'm a tough old man. I'm not going without taking somebody with me."

York and Calico stood facing each other down.

Calico broke the silence. "What are you waiting for filth bag? Let's rock and roll."

In the darkness, with all the outlaws' eyes on Calico and York, Tina had come out of the gully and was halfway back across the highway when she felt she'd waited as long as she could. Bringing her shotgun up to her shoulder, she squeezed the trigger and blasted two rounds off in quick succession.

A few shotgun pellets on the farthest edges of the firing pattern scattered stingingly among the closest group of bikers, but the main thrust of the shots thudded into York's Harley and turned night into day as the gas tank blew apart.

Calico was the first to recover from the shock of the explosion and butt-stroked York across the jaw with the stock of the shotgun in his hands. The collision of York's face and the shotgun stock dropped York to the ground like a sack of rocks and caused the shotgun to discharge into the air, adding to the confusion.

A blast from a sawed-off shotgun wielded by one of the other bikers chased Calico's fleeing frame as he scrambled for cover under the cruiser. A second shot blew the weapon up in its owner's hands in a symphony of screams.

Tina had her hands full as she waded into the confused flank of outlaw bikers on the highway side of the cruiser. She didn't even notice the cavalry arrive until one of the bikers was pulled out of her grasp by a tire iron-waving tow-truck driver.

The tow trucks from the official police garages had arrived in a flurry of emergency lights and squealing tires and plowed into the bikers before discharging their drivers and passengers into the fray started by Calico and Tina. Knees and elbows flew in furious clashes punctuated by tire irons and screaming.

Calico rolled out from under the cruiser and kidney-punched a biker who was putting the boots to a downed tow-truck driver. He grabbed a handful of greasy hair and pulled violently backward before bringing an elbow down on the biker's sternum.

"Thanks, Calico," said the tow-truck driver, wrapping an arm around his sore ribs as the policeman helped him to his feet.

"For what? You guys saved our asses."

"You okay, Pop?"

Calico looked around and saw a disheveled Ren walking toward him. He smiled at his son and was glad to see all of the bikers were down and being herded into a group by the other tow-truck operators.

"I'm fine," he said to his son. "Where's my partner?"

"Right here," Tina replied from beside him.

He was glad to see she was in one piece. "You left that a bit tight, didn't you?" he asked with a smile. "They almost had us."

"Had you, you mean. Anyway, 'almost' only counts in horseshoes and hand grenades."

"Or atom bombs like the one you set off in York's Harley."

"Yeah."

Calico turned back to Ren and shook his hand. "I'm certainly not complaining, but where did you guys come from?"

Ren smirked. "We saw those assholes cruise by after you went through. I had a bad feeling about what

Stack and his partner were going to do, so we decided to follow your trail for a while."

"Damn glad you did."

"Ditto," said Tina.

"What happened to the cruiser?"

"Thurman dumped some spiked bars under our tires. We got three flats. Can you guys help us get them changed before we lose too much ground?"

"You got it," Ren said and turned away to organize the chore.

Five minutes later Calico and Tina were back in the cruiser with the engine thrumming away at idle. Ren was leaning through the driver's window talking to Calico.

"What do you want us to do with the Reapers?"

"Slash their tires and leave them to it. There are two things you can depend on with outlaw bikers: they'll take any opportunity to go on you, but if they lose they'll go away and lick their wounds without complaining."

"Okay. We'll see you when you get back."

"You got it. And thanks, you're a smart kid."

"Runs in the family."

The two men looked at each other and nodded.

"Enough of the family reunion," Tina said in mock exasperation. "Let's get out of here."

"Yes, Blanche," Calico replied and hit the gas.

Thirty minutes later Tina rubbed her eyes like a three-year-old awakened from a deep sleep.

"I see it, but I don't believe it. It's a mirage," she said, slightly awed.

"Ain't it a sight," Calico said, laughing. "I've always thought my name should be up in lights, but in this case I'll settle for phosphorescent rocks."

On a steep mountainside off to the left the name CALICO glowed eerily in the dark night.

"Where did it come from?" asked Tina. "It's an omen."

"No, it's a ghost town. Back in the late 1800s it was the sight of the richest silver strike in California history. They took about eighty-six million dollars of silver out of the mines and another nine million in borax, but it had played itself out by around 1907 and rolled over to play dead until it was revived as a tourist attraction in the fifties."

Tina kept looking out of the window at Calico's name in giant-size letters made of rocks on the hillside. It made her feel as if even the mountains were rooting for them. "I still say it's an omen."

Calico looked out at the letters. "Let's hope you're right because we've got a tough row to hoe to catch up."

Jack Ketch sat on the edge of the bed in the dingy downtown hotel. A fifth of Jack Daniels stood on the battered dresser, a half-empty glass of the same libation on the chipped nightstand.

Ketch's small body frame was wrapped with cable-corded muscles, the result of hour after hour of workouts inside prison walls. In actuality he'd put in very little time fighting for the privileges of using the free weights to pump iron. Instead he concentrated on isometric-type exercises as well as other basics such as push-ups, pull-ups, and sit-ups. He could easily rip off two hundred push-ups without breaking a sweat, and a thousand sit-ups barely caused a tremor in the case-hardened bands of alligator muscles rippling all directions across his midsection.

Ketch believed in the basics of his exercise routine. In fact he believed in basics in all things. Prison reduced life to basics. When you were outside you always wanted "things," cars, money, clothes, trim, whatever. Inside prison "things" didn't exist. All you wanted was to survive. And to survive, especially when you were small, you had to be tough. So Ketch became tough, through exercise, through the martial arts which were taught every day, in plain sight, on the prison compound by cons to cons, including favorite moves such as how to take a cop's gun away while he is searching you, or how to take a cop's baton away and feed it back to him. Ketch also became tough by becoming "smoke," a freelance prison hit man. He was neutral, available for hire to any segment of the prison population who wanted a shiv twisted into a kidney. He was a tiny whisp of smoke both feared and revered for his skills.

Looking at himself naked in the hotel-room mirror, Ketch could see little that was as big as his reputation except for the huge afro exploding wildly from his black skull, and the length of meat swinging between his legs. The latter was recovering from the workout given it by the blond whore titivating herself in the smelly bathroom.

"Whew-wee, baby. You'd been holding that load a long time," the whore called out in a mock sexy voice in hopes of garnering a tip she wouldn't have to report to her pimp.

"Don't kid yourself. I did more than pull my pud in prison, and your ass isn't half as tight as the bun boys inside."

"Then why'd you come looking for some honey-bunny first thing you got out?"

"Just put your clothes on and get the fuck out of here. I don't need the Q and A."

The whore came out of the bathroom and crawled onto the bed. Her sagging tits hung pendulously down, her nipples grazing the coarse bed sheet and coming erect, as she nuzzled her face down into Ketch's crotch. "Ah, come on, baby. Don't be like that. Let's see if we can do it again for Pookie."

Ketch threw his right hand into her hair and yanked her head backward. "What are you playing at, bitch. I ain't never met no whore who'd come back for seconds after the job was done." A Filipino butterfly knife sung in his left hand before he brought the blade tight against the girl's prominent left cheekbone. "Talk to me or I'll cut you a new vagina right here in your face."

"It was Purple, man. Purple!"

"Who's Purple?"

"My pimp."

"What's he want from me?"

"Nothin'. He told me to make sure you were satisfied. Told me word had come down from the King that you were to be treated special and then given a message."

"What message?"

"Don't cut me. Please, I'll tell you, but don't cut me."

"You'll tell me whether I cut you or not. Getting cut don't depend on you telling me, or me liking the message. Getting cut depends entirely on how I feel. You got that?"

"Yes . . ."

"Now tell me."

"The King, Eli Mohammed Kono, he told Purple to tell you to do the favor he asked for or when you came back inside you wouldn't have no dick to fuck with anymore."

Anger flowed through Ketch's muscles and a thin trickle of blood appeared under the knife point. The whore whimpered and began to move her lips in silent prayer, her eyes shut tight.

The two bodies stayed frozen in that position until

Ketch pulled the knife away and stuck it in the night-stand. With his other hand he pushed the whore's face back into his crotch, forcing his huge member between her lips.

"Okay, baby. Message delivered. Now suck that beauty off for all you're worth and maybe I'll let you live."

Later, after the girl had left, Ketch sat on the bed with his back resting against the headboard. A tinny-sounding radio tuned to a Spanish music station could be heard from the room next door.

From a bag the girl had left behind, he took out an oilskin-wrapped 9mm Beretta with two extra maga-zines and two boxes of ammunition. Holding the gun in his left hand he wrapped fingers around the cross-checked grips. He popped the magazine out of the butt and ran back the slide to eject the round in the chamber so he could practice dry-firing at objects in the room. When he was satisfied he had blasted every inanimate object which could possibly pose a threat, he stripped the gun down and began to clean it. He reloaded, putting a round in the chamber and leaving the de-cocking device off before sliding the gun under the left side of the thin mattress where he could get to it quickly.

The serial number had been filed off the gun, but it didn't occur to Ketch to worry about it. The mere pos-session of the gun by an ex-con was enough of a charge to get him sent back to the joint, but he wasn't concerned about that either. Sooner or later he'd be going back anyway.

He'd just finished a seven-year sentence for armed robbery of a federal armored van. Prior to that he'd served a total of five more years on a variety of charges in a variety of institutions. He was well ac-quainted with prison life, even enjoyed it because inside he commanded far more respect than he did in the straight world. Life was a breeze inside compared to out.

Ketch served his full sentence this time, literally spitting on the chairman of the parole board when they tried to force him out to make more space in the prison. There was no way he was going to play their games when he was outside, having to report in every time he wanted to take a shit.

He'd done his time and now he was out and free—free of the recognized establishment anyway. He still had a debt to fulfill to the people inside. They had provided all the information he needed and supplied him with a weapon from their outside contacts. They also made it clear what would happen if he didn't follow through. He didn't mind. It was a snap job anyway. The only problem was the rush factor which had been placed on the job. But it would get him back into the swing of surviving on the outside.

The only thing he didn't really like was being expected to use the gun. It wasn't basic enough. He would take it along as insurance, but it wasn't going to be his initial approach. Moving with fluid grace he opened the scarred drawer of the hotel nightstand. From it he withdrew another bag of items he'd purchased earlier in the day with the gun-cleaning equipment. He emptied the bag onto the bed. Two foot-long lengths of half-inch metal pipe threaded at one end, two metal end caps which he'd doctored at a machine shop so a rotating eye bolt protruded out from the middle of each one, and an eight-inch length of steel chain fell out.

He screwed the end caps over the threaded ends of the metal pipes and snapped one end of the chain onto each eye bolt to connect the two pipes. Now he had a basic weapon, nunchaku, developed centuries earlier by oppressed peasants in the Orient who were not allowed to possess ordinary weapons and needed to rely upon basic implements for defense.

Standing up from the bed, still naked, Ketch held one half of the weapon in his left hand and began to swing the other half in front of him in a slow circle at the other end of the chain. He built up the speed of the circle slowly, at the same pace he was building his concentration, and then suddenly he cried out with an explosion of breath which shook the walls of the room and began to whip the weapon in a blur of movement over his shoulders and around his waist. His hands moved from one length of chain-connected pipe to the other with sure, flowing, blind speed. The lamp on the nightstand became an enemy in Ketch's mind, and with a sudden flick, like the tongue of a snake, one end of the nunchaku swung out and shattered the ceramic base, plunging the room into darkness.

Yes, Ketch thought to himself, the basics were best. And they would be all he needed to do the favor the King had requested—kill a cop.

"I'm going to pull over into that rest stop ahead," Stack told his partner as he slowed down the steaming Highway Patrol car. "She's overheating like a son of a bitch."

The two police officers had passed over the border line into Nevada about ten minutes prior and everything had been running smoothly. They'd waved at the Nevada State Police trooper who was parked at the border checkpoint watching them in astonishment as they cruised by at well over a hundred and twenty miles an hour. The first or last of the Nevada casinos, depending on the direction you were traveling, flashed by them in a blur of lights, looking like street whores who were too broken down to work the main lines anymore, settling for making a living on the fringes of the game.

The trouble with the car started shortly after that when Stack noticed the temperature indicator creeping up toward the red zone. He didn't say anything to Thumper for a while, but when the pointer edged into the danger area and steam began to rise from the hood of the car, it became inevitable. Fortunately there was a closed tourist information center just up ahead and Stack steered toward it.

"What do you think the matter is?" Thurman asked, the rise in his voice expressing concern.

"Let's just pray it isn't the water pump or we're going to be stuck but good. Could be the fan belt and that can be a problem too."

The information center was a small wooden building with a closed sign in the front window. The area around it was parched grass with a couple of picnic tables and two portable toilets. The tiny parking lot contained an abandoned sedan of indecipherable make, and a motorhome parked next to a pickup and camper rig, both apparently settled in for the night. The motorhome had two mopeds strapped to the rear bumper.

Stack pulled the cruiser into the parking lot and stopped at the far end. Both he and Thumper got out and walked around to the front of the car. Steam billowed out from under the hood, making both men cough and wave their arms around wildly. Stack finally stuck his head in over the engine.

"It's the fan belt," he said, reaching in with one hand and removing the remains of the fiber belt from the hot engine. Gingerly he pulled up the pressure release tab on the radiator cap and jumped back when steam billowed out anew.

"What do we do now?" Stack asked his partner who had slid into a silent funk.

"I'm thinking."

"That's a first. Don't hurt yourself."

Thurman's manner turned threatening. "You want to get out of this mess, or piss me off with old jokes?"

"Sorry. You got any ideas?"

"Let's have a look at the junker parked over there." Thurman indicated the abandoned car at the other end of the parking lot. The two officers walked over to it and opened the hood. The car was an old fifty-six pink and white Chrysler Windsor with a push-button unit mounted to the left of the steering wheel to work the transmission. It had all the grace of a tank painted with a sad clown's face. The impression of sadness was intensified by the flat tire on the driver's side.

"Doesn't look like this will be much help," said Stack. The car's fan belt crumbled under the pressure of his fingers.

Thumper shook his head disgustedly. "The way some people take care of their vehicles. There ought to be a law."

They looked at the other belts in the car, but none were in better shape and wouldn't have fit anyway. The trunk of the car was tied down by a piece of nylon cord, which Stack cut with a small pocket knife.

"When was the last time you saw one of these?" he snorted after lifting the lid to expose the trunk's contents.

Thurman stepped around to look inside. "Must be the original spare," he said as he poked the flat, treadless tire. "They haven't produced inner tube tires for passenger vehicles in thirty years. It's no wonder it wasn't full of air when the owner needed it most."

"What now?" asked Stack. "Do you think the camper or motorhome over there would have a spare belt which would fit?"

"I doubt it, but we'll have to check."

The result of their efforts was strange looks from

two different families and a big goose egg as far as a new fan belt was concerned.

Stack kicked the side of the offending Highway Patrol car. "We're sunk. There is a deep tide of shit about to race in over our heads."

"Give me your pocket knife."

"Suicide is not going to help matters."

Thumper wrapped one of his mitts around his partner's shoulder and squeezed so hard the collarbone started to grind. "Cut the crap and give me the knife."

Stack handed it to him hastily and then rubbed his shoulder. Thurman stalked off across the parking lot. Following him with his eyes, Stack watched as Thumper went back to the old Chrysler and opened the trunk again. He heard a low grumbling of swear words as Thumper appeared to be wrestling a python in the trunk area, but it was too dark to see what was actually happening, and Stack's feelings were hurt enough that he was not going to go over and help unless he was asked.

Eventually Thumper walked back toward him. "This should do the trick," he said and held up a one-inch-wide circle of rubber cut out from a cross section of the inner tube from the Chrysler's spare tire. It looked like a fat, flat rubber band.

"You're crazy," Stack told his partner, but turned to watch with interest as Thumper went to work in the engine area of the cruiser with a large screwdriver and an adjustable wrench he had also brought back as booty.

"Crazy like a fox," Thumper replied in his characteristic low monotone. With surprisingly deft fingers, the black officer folded the thick rubber band in half around its circumference and stretched it between the space the traitorous fan belt had once occupied. He sweated and swore, taking the skin off almost to the bone on several knuckles, but at last he grunted success.

"Did it!" he said in short-lived victory as he pulled his head out from under the hood and caught his partner's gaze to the highway where Calico and Tina were zipping past.

"Shit! Water, we need water," he said and ran to the driver's side of the car, pushing Stack out of the way. He started up the engine, got out of the car to check if his handiwork was holding. The jury-rigged fan belt was spinning happily. Thumper slammed the hood and told Stack to pull up next to the water hose on one side of the information center while he cut another circle of inner tube just in case. With luck they could be on the road again in a couple of minutes.

"Did you see that?" Tina asked her partner as they sped past the information center/rest stop.

"Where?"

"Back there. I'm certain that was Stack and Thurman parked in the rest stop. What the heck are they doing? Playing tortoise and the hare?"

"I don't know, but this is too good an opportunity to pass up. It's time for what goes around to come around."

"The payback," Tina said maliciously, "is a bitch."

Calico laughed. "Have a look and see what Wild John threw in the backseat for us."

She leaned over the seat and Calico found himself looking at her backside as she rummaged around. "I think I've found just the thing," said Tina's muffled voice.

Me too, Calico thought to himself.

Thumper and Stack were straining their eyes so hard to the front, to catch a glimpse of their adversaries, they failed to notice the squad car pull out behind them and slip up on their rear, running without lights.

Tina unsnapped her seat belt and wound down her window. "Just a little closer. A little closer. Oh, God, please don't let them see us. A little bit more . . ."

With athletic grace she thrust her torso through the passenger window and brought the stock of the tear-gas gun to her shoulder. The wind stream buffeted her about as if she was in a duel with the air conditioner that ate New York. She gave up trying to open her eyes and instead trusted to instinct for her shot, knowing Calico was keeping them only inches away from Stack and Thurman's rear bumper.

The recoil of the shot drove her back against the pillar post of the car while the noise was torn away by the wind.

"Bull's-eye!" yelled Calico as he watched the tear-gas projectile shatter the rear window of Stack and Thurman's cruiser and begin to spray its blinding ingredients inside.

With two hands, Calico did three things simultaneously. His left hand turned the steering wheel to move around the rapidly slowing car in front of him, and his right hit the lights and siren switches as it reached over to haul Tina back through the window by her gunbelt.

"You did it. You did it. Beautiful shot," he enthused.

Tina yelled and screamed in delight along with her partner. Both watched as Stack and Thurman's car weaved all over the highway, the interior a solid fog bank, until it finally stopped and both officers bailed out with their hands over their eyes.

"That was great." Calico extended his right hand palm down and Tina reached over and slapped her own palm across it.

"What a team," she said.

Calico laughed again. "Next stop Lost Wages, Nevada."

FIFTEEN

E.T.A. LAS VEGAS, NEVADA

L AS VEGAS SPREAD out in front of them like a multicolored bug light in the middle of the desert. The
land around the city was flat and lifeless in the pale
moonlight which had finally broken through the thick
cloud cover. Calico and Tina were still a few miles
outside of the city, but it seemed to beckon their
cruiser like a siren, a seductive nymph, part woman,
part bird, luring ships to the rocks of destruction.

"You know we'll never get away with this. They'll
be waiting for us when we get back."

"I knew that from the start," Tina said gently.
"Even with all the precautions we took and all the
people we have pulling for us, I figured we'd get cop-
ped in the long run. Is that what you've been brooding
about for the last half hour?"

"Well, if you knew, why did you come?"

"Easy. Being Oriental and female, I meet the department's minority recruiting quotas in two areas.
They can't afford to fire me. Also I'm off probation.
Barely off, I know, but still off, and that makes it even
more difficult for them to fire me. The most they'll be
able to do is give me a handful of days off without
pay. I can handle that standing on my head.

"Additionally, you're my partner. The challenge to

Stack and Thurman was as much mine as yours. This run will be talked about for as long as L.A.P.D. exists. I had to come. The chance to be part of a legend doesn't happen often."

Calico had the accelerator of the black and white stuck to the floor, the speedometer needle off the dial, but steering was easy on the straight swoops of the highway. "Is that why you hired on the job in the first place?"

"Part of the reason. Other parts had to do with my family and upbringing. It was the kind of job my mother would have understood. It was also the kind of job which, in the long run, would prove to my father I am the equal of his sons."

"No desire to help mankind?"

"It's never been a prime consideration. Selfish, huh?"

Calico shrugged his shoulders.

"Sure, I like the feeling when we take an asshole off the street," Tina continued. "And there is a certain satisfaction, not only in helping an individual in a crisis, but in being the person where the buck stops. But you've taught me, and a year on the streets has shown me, there is no helping mankind.

"Being a cop offers challenge and diversity. I like being part of the biggest and toughest gang in the city, and this is one of the few jobs where being good at what you do has far more impact than your skin color or your sex. It's kind of tough to expect anything more."

"Life is hard and then you die?"

Tina laughed. "Yeah, something like that."

"Do they give classes in cynicism at the Academy now?"

"I wouldn't have any trouble passing it if they did."

The cruiser was silent except for the strong throbbing of the engine, and the city of Las Vegas was almost upon them when Tina asked, "What about you? Will you miss all this when you've left it behind?"

Calico thought before replying. "I don't think you can leave it behind. I've been a policeman for so long it's completely ingrained into my way of thinking. I'll never think like a straight. I wouldn't want to if I could.

"I guess I'll miss the beat of the street. There's nothing like it; going into a house where you know a burglar is hiding, taking an asshole to jail who has just spit in your face and told you he ain't going anywhere, keeping all the weasel scrotums in line while they're on your assigned turf. As a street cop you aren't supposed to solve crime, that's the detective's job. A street cop is supposed to put his butt on the line and stop crime before it happens, while it's happening, or immediately afterward. If it gets past that point you've failed and all you can do is pick up the debris and pass it on.

"But things are falling apart on the street. The lid is already off the trash can and I'm glad I'll be out fishing when somebody manages to spill the whole thing over on its side."

"Now who's being cynical?" Tina asked.

"Come on, it's inevitable. It's history. Everything goes in cycles. The Greek empire fell, the Roman and British empires followed suit. What makes you think the American empire will be any different? Every day another wrong suddenly becomes acceptable behavior. Felonies become misdemeanors, misdemeanors become infractions, and infractions disappear into the great morass. Vice laws are always the first to go. Once a society's morals are corrupted they're hanging over the abyss by fingertips only."

"Whew, you're depressing."

"Life is . . ."

"I know. 'Life is hard and then you die.'" Tina repeated Calico's epitaph, but in a darker manner without irony. "But don't worry," she said quickly in a much lighter tone, "I'll dance at your wake."

Calico laughed, breaking the mood. "If you promise to dance on my grave, I'll make arrangements to be buried at sea."

Tina groaned.

Calico looked at his watch and fiddled with the stem. "What time do you have?" he asked.

Tina twisted her wrist and glanced at it. "Coming up on three A.M."

"You should have turned your watch back an hour ago; it's only two A.M."

Tina reset her watch. "You're right. I forgot we get an extra hour tonight with the time change."

"Can't afford to forget it," Calico said. "With everything that has happened so far, we're going to need it. It's going to be tight getting back on time already."

"We'll make it," Tina said with confidence.

"I wish you hadn't said that out loud."

McCarran International Airport appeared in the flat lands off to their right and the famous Las Vegas Strip stretched out in front of them, parallel to the highway, exploding with colored lights, neon, and promise. "Hold on," Calico told his partner, concentration and authority back in his voice as he exited the highway. "Here we go."

It was almost time for the "off" and the men were getting fidgety, but Morgan Wales knew they would pull together when it counted. Feeling the edge of your nerves before a big blag was often sweeter than the consummation of the job itself, like the anticipation before making love to a beautiful woman for the first time. Electricity in the nerves helped to stimulate perceptions, made you more efficient. Only a moron didn't feel the butterflies, and morons could only be relied upon to do one thing consistently—make mistakes.

The previous few days had been a hornets' nest of activity for Morgan and his crew. Merric had been keeping a close but surreptitious eye on Ollie Sebastian, reporting back to Morgan that Sebastian was far busier than usual with Ellis, the casino's computer and financial wizard, but security hadn't been noticeably changed or increased.

"What's your gut feeling?" Morgan asked Merric at one point. "Do you think Ollie knows we bluffed him about having the inside track on the financial scam he's running on his uncle?"

"Yes and no."

"You're a big help. Remind me to ask for your opinion more often."

"What I mean," Merric said, his eyes rolling in exasperation, "is if he wasn't running a scam on his uncle, he wouldn't be running around like a centipede shopping for socks as he checks all his figures. He might not believe we know all about the scam, but the fact we know it exists is enough to have him running scared. You've also given him the perfect cover-up by offering to screw up the computers. Ollie is greedy, but he isn't stupid. He knows his uncle will discover the rip-off sooner or later. However, if the casino's computer's accounting memories are wiped out, it's going to be very tough to prove anything and will give him the opportunity to take the money he's stolen and run, or if he's got the nerve, to set up another type of scam.

"I don't think he gives a damn about the money we're going to steal. After all, it belongs to the same uncle he's been stealing from. All he's worried about is cleaning his own house so he doesn't get splattered when the crap hits the fan. Our blag is giving him a made-to-order cover-up and he intends to take full advantage of it."

Morgan nodded his head twice, thinking about Merric's assessment. "What do you think his attitude toward us will be after the blag?"

"Gut reaction?" Merric asked rhetorically. "Live and let live. He'll make a show of coming after us. He has to. But it will be all bluster and fanfare. He's going to get away with far more money than will ever be sitting in the vault when we hit."

"Hmmmm. I wonder where he's got his bundle stashed?"

"Come on, Morgan!" Merric was alarmed. "You can't be serious. We can go after Ollie Sebastian's stash another time. Let's not complicate the blag."

Morgan shook his head, as if to clear it of wistful thinking, and then smiled. "Yes, you're right. Things are complicated enough. Still . . ."

"Morgan," Merric said in playful threat.

The captain of the small crew of cutthroats had found Merric to be an extremely useful first mate. He was an intelligent and constructive sounding board and often helped to temper some of Morgan's more flamboyant tendencies as he had done in this instance.

Merric was also an expert scrounger. He'd switched to working days at the casino and began to chat up one of the girls who worked in the basement computer room. From her, he established the manufacturer and the type of computer and alarm systems which the Citadel utilized. Fortunately both had originated from the same source.

Using part of the seed money, he caught the next red-eye round-trip flight to the manufacturer's home base in Chicago. There, he presented himself as the representative of a business consortium looking to start a new casino in the Lake Tahoe area. He explained he was interested in a computer alarm system similar to the one his good friend Ollie Sebastian used in Las Vegas. He was given the red-carpet treatment and returned to Las Vegas frayed and frazzled, but in possession of a full set of technical papers to help explain the system to his fictional consortium partners. The diagrams meant nothing to Merric, but he knew they would provide everything needed for Chauncer, the sparks man.

Chauncer, too, had been a pleasant surprise to Morgan. Soft-spoken with gentle mannerisms, the slightly built man was good company. He had a solid reputation according to Morgan's sources for being a stand-up guy when part of a blag team. Twice in Chauncer's career jobs had turned sour—it was inevitable in the thieving business—but both times he had kept his mouth shut and refused to cut a deal with the authorities. The first time had resulted in a three stretch inside California's Chino prison. The second time he'd walked away. Not because he'd turned informer— none of the other blag team members had taken a fall—but because without incriminating himself there wasn't enough evidence for the police to convince the D.A. to file charges. Chauncer knew the value of keeping his mouth shut. He knew that eighty percent of captured villains who believed the lies about cutting deals ended up worse off.

When Merric presented him with the diagrams from Chicago, deep lines brewed up across Chauncer's usually smooth forehead. He took a pair of wire-rim glasses from the breast pocket of his shirt and worked them over his ears behind the thinning friar's ring of hair which hung there. After a short period, Morgan had tried to get an assessment out of him, but Chauncer just grunted, looked up in irritation, and went back to his own room to study the information.

A couple of hours later, while Morgan was going through his daily ritual of isometric exercises, Chauncer knocked quietly and stuck his head around the door to announce he was going out on the street to look over some of the other casinos and to look at the city's power transformers. He appeared to be preoccupied, but Morgan knew it was the sign of an expert's mind taking in all possibilities. He also knew when Chauncer returned he would bring with him a feasible plan to serve the blag team's needs.

There was one aspect of the blag, however, with which Morgan was not overly pleased. John Bolt, the pilot, was a rangy cowboy type with a head of straw-thatched golden hair and a pair of vacant blue-green eyes inherited from some long-forgotten Swedish ancestor. He had a surly and superior attitude which would one day be knocked out of him, but until then would continue to rankle everyone he came into contact with.

Morgan immediately phoned Max, his contact who had sent Bolt, and asked for a replacement. It could have been arranged, but Max assured Morgan that Bolt was the best low-profile pilot available, known for keeping cool in bad situations, and could fly anything anywhere.

Sometimes it was important to make allowances for individual attitudes if it would lead to the success of the blag, so Morgan put off judgment of Bolt on Max's word, which had always been good. But he wasn't happy about it, believing harmony in a team was as important as technical expertise.

Things almost came to a head again a short time later when Morgan laid out the basis for the plan to Bolt.

"What kind of guns are we going to be taking?" Bolt had asked.

"None. I've explained to you about the tasers. We'll back those up with tear-gas spray and a twelve-ounce beanbag gun which will knock any resistance on its ass."

"The beanbag gun is only good for one shot before reloading. I don't like it," Bolt insisted. "You need some real firepower in case things turn sour. Anybody who is really determined to stop us isn't going to worry about a little electric shock or a case of teary eye."

"Fifty thousand volts is not a little electric shock. If you want me to, I'll demonstrate it on you." Morgan was feeling testy. "And we'll be using CS tear-gas spray which has proved effective even on the majority of PCP suspects. We have some extra of that around too if you'd like a sample."

Bolt grunted. "I still don't like it."

"Tough," Morgan told him. "You do it my way or you walk away now. No hard feelings."

"You need me."

"No, you need me. I can have another fly boy here tomorrow by making one phone call. I already made that call once, but I was told you're very good at what you do. I can make allowances for attitude but not for shooters. Are you in or out? Tell me now while the overseas phone rates are still low."

Bolt smiled briefly, more a surly grin than anything else, and stuck a mint-flavored toothpick between his teeth.

"I'm in. I just wanted to see if you could be pushed."

"Satisfied?"

"For now."

"No. Forever. If you push again we'll call the game on account of rain."

"Going to take your ball and go home?"

"You betcha. And it's an expensive ball. Your cut is a quarter to a half of a big M. If you want to make a stand on principle it's okay with me."

"For that kind of bread, I'll make a taser my best friend."

Morgan was still a bit unsettled, but it quickly became clear that, technically, Bolt was exactly what the crew needed. He grasped the main thrust of Morgan's plans on first telling and added several suggestions to the escape segment which was his responsibility.

"We've been over this ground before," Bolt told Morgan and the others shortly before the zero hour when the crew was all gathered in Morgan's suite, "so you're all aware that one of the reasons Las Vegas casinos are considered hard robbery targets is because of the escape factor. Plopped down here in the middle of nowhere, Las Vegas has very few exits, and even if you get through them there are long stretches of empty roads or highways before you come to anywhere useful. The police here may be manipulated by special interests, but they are still efficient and can have this whole town bottled up in next to no time. Any blag men still inside when that happens are then faced with a tightening-net effect which leaves no place to run."

Morgan spoke up when Bolt paused to light a Camel cigarette. "I considered holing up somewhere in town for however long it took for the heat to blow over, but that scenario has built in problems of its own."

"People get too edgy," Merric said from his seat on one of the room's two couches. "Lots more time for something to go wrong."

"Right," agreed Morgan. "So I want us to get clear of here as soon as possible. Tell us again about the plane you're flying," he asked Bolt.

"It's a Norman NAC One Freelance. A British plane derived from the BN-Three Nymph. Room for the four of us plus the booty. It has integral long-range fuel tanks and is designed for short takeoff and landing situations. It's a dope smuggler's dream, not large enough to run grass, mind you, but now cocaine is the drug of choice it's the perfect border hopper."

"Are you sure about getting us out of here?" interjected Chauncer. He seemed slightly nervous and Morgan thought he might have a fear of flying.

"The plane was hangared over at McCarran International. I filed a flight plan to L.A. and took off about four this afternoon. I flew according to the plan until I got off the radar screens and then turned around and came back low behind the hills to the east. There is a dope runner's flat in a patch of desert to the east of here; I landed there without much problem. It's isolated and very few people know about the strip. The plane is safe there."

"What will happen when you don't land in L.A.?" Merric asked.

"I've got that covered. Another pilot, who deals in Mexican imports with me, has an identical plane to mine. He's being paid a flat fee, without knowledge of our caper here, to take off from his private strip and land in L.A. to cover me. His papers are the same as mine and won't be questioned."

Morgan smiled in approval. "And getting back from where you landed to the hotel?"

"I did what you told me," Bolt replied. "I flew to Reno very early yesterday, on a commercial flight, and stole a Jeep. I put cold plates on it which I picked up from a junkyard. Next, I drove it back here and hid it in some scrub near the runner's flat. Merric met me there and drove us back. Today when I landed the plane, I used the Jeep to get back to town and we'll use it again tonight to return to the plane."

Morgan looked over at his first mate who expressed his approval of Bolt's actions. "It's a good setup," Merric said. "The plane is set for immediate takeoff. The Jeep is parked in the Citadel's garage near the exit we plan to come out. After the hit we'll pile into the Jeep and avoid the streets by driving out across the desert directly to the plane. If Chauncer causes all the commotion he's promised us, the police will be far too busy to be worrying about four guys in a Jeep."

"Don't worry about the distractions," Chauncer spoke up again. "There are two main generators which supply the Strip with power. Each of the casinos have their own secondary generators, but they don't kick in for at least five minutes after the main generators shut down. Each Casino also has a main alarm system tying in directly to the police station, which has its own power source.

"The weak link in the system is the fact that each casino alarm runs through the same switching point to the police station. Overload the switching point and all the alarms will go off at the same time. When we enter the Citadel, we will be coming in through a rear basement door which Merric will open for us. Unfortunately, if we call the private elevator to The Lucky Thirteen down to the basement it might tip our hand too early since nobody is supposed to be in the basement area. So, we'll have to go up to the first-floor gaming level to page it. This is the make or break spot because we will be exposed to the overhead cameras briefly. Just remember to keep your faces down to the floor and we shouldn't have any problems. Bolt will be in charge of convincing the elevator guard to come with us."

"No problem," said Bolt, hefting one of the tasers in his hand. This model was different from the type Morgan had originally used on Ollie Sebastian, better for close-up work, relying on two stationary prongs to make contact with the target's skin instead of the barbed hooks which shot out of the other model. Each crew member would carry both types to use depending on the situation.

"Before we move up to The Lucky Thirteen," Chauncer continued, "I will manually activate the Citadel's secondary generator and plug it directly into the alarm system and their computer setup. The oversurge of power will blow the switching station and set off all the alarms along the Strip as well as sending the Citadel's computer to micro-chip heaven. I'll put all of that on a short fuse to give us time to get up to the private club so we can make maximum use of the confusion. There will also be a lot of lights flashing and sirens sounding as secondary alarms are automatically set off by the silent alarms being activated. With alarms ringing at all the casinos the cops won't know which way to run first.

"After the alarms are tripped we will have about ten minutes before the timed charges at the two main power generators blow and turn off this town."

"Will we be able to get all the cash we need out of The Lucky Thirteen in that time period?" queried Bolt.

Morgan answered, "We're just concerned with the paper money. The coin is of no practical use to us and will be far too heavy and cumbersome to transport. A million and a half to two million in bills stacked and bound as it is in the vault should not prove too much of a problem. Four large duffelbags will do the trick with Merric and Chauncer carrying two each, while you and I, John, cover the retreat. We'll firebomb the stairwell to stop pursuit, and Chauncer will rewire the elevator to take us on an express route directly to the basement. Any problem with that, Chauncer?"

"None. It's as easy as pie using one wire and two alligator clips. And I'll take out the phone system before we go up."

The four men looked at each other. Morgan looked at his watch.

"Okay, that will do it. Any other questions? No? Good. Has everybody set their watches back to accommodate the time change?" The crew all acknowledged in the affirmative. "All right," Morgan continued. "We've got time to shoot one across the bows, and then it's time to board the gunwales of this casino."

The four men stood up and raised short glasses which Merric had just filled.

"To the blag," said Morgan.

"To the blag!" came the echo.

Two black stretch limousines tooled quietly down the wide strip of Las Vegas Boulevard at a discreet twenty-five miles per hour. Inside the first limo, Augustus Sebastian and Dobbins, his right-hand man, were squashed between several large simian types in expensive suits tailored to accommodate bulges under arms or in waistbands. A similar team of heavies followed in the second limo.

"You were very quiet during the flight here, Dobbins. And since we left the airport you've been positively silent. You don't approve of our actions?" Sebastian spoke out of a respect for his friend which had been etched in the past to sustain through the future.

"Augustus"—Dobbins so rarely used Sebastian's first name that the old man's usually unexpressive face registered surprise—"we are the old guard. The young turks are running the business now and they are like sharks—constantly on the move in search of fresh prey. I am concerned that they will tear Jonathan apart in a feeding frenzy of greed. Jonathan has run the Tahoe casino for you competently but without inspiration. If you cast out Ollie and bring Jonathan in, I think Jonathan will lose everything for us."

"And you think it is better to let Ollie steal from me like I was a blind man selling pencils on a street corner?"

"No. But you are far from handicapped poverty. What Ollie has stolen from you has not hurt you . . ."

"You are wrong," Sebastian interrupted his friend. "It has not hurt the operation as a whole, but it has hurt me as a person. He took my trust and twisted it into something ugly. If he'd have asked for the money I would have given it to him. But he just took it. I could even have tolerated that, it would have shown strength, but he tried to deceive me and that I cannot accept."

"You would rather take a chance on losing everything instead of letting this ride?"

"You know me well, old friend. Besides, I am bored. You are bored." Sebastian looked at Dobbins who shrugged his shoulders. "We might be old, but we are not weak. We will have to take Jonathan in hand and fight off the sharks."

The driver of the limo pulled to the curb in front of the Citadel. "We're here, Mr. Sebastian."

"Thank you, Garrett," Sebastian told the driver and then turned to the men who were with him in the limo. "You all know the drill. You move in quietly and take over the key security positions. Do it discreetly so as not to upset the patrons. Garrett will come with Dobbins and I to locate Ollie. If one of you find him before we do, I want him held but not bruised. That will come later. Do you understand?"

The three other men in the back of the car nodded

and got out to join the men from the other car who were standing on the curb listening to Sebastian through the rolled-down rear window.

The men turned to go, but Sebastian stopped them again. "And remember, I want the computer room secured first, even before the first-floor vault and the vault in The Lucky Thirteen, right?"

"Yes, sir," replied one of the heavies who appeared to be nominally in charge of the others.

"Good, let's do it." Augustus Sebastian looked down at his watch and exited the limo.

Behind his boss, Dobbins checked his own watch, realized he had forgotten to adjust it, and rolled the hands back from three A.M. to two A.M. before following the entourage into the casino.

The Citadel glittered like a giant phallic symbol standing hard and erect over its domain on the Strip. From its domed roof three single-beam spotlights spurted their golden streams into the night sky. Calico thought the effect was pornographic, but he didn't have time to dwell on it as he turned the cruiser around two black limos, which had pulled up in front of the casino, and slid into a "no parking" space on the building's side.

"Do you have the camera?" Tina asked as they both scrambled hurriedly out of the car.

"You betcha," Calico replied, holding up the black case of a Polaroid Land Camera.

"That isn't one of those pieces of crap the department uses which never works, is it?"

"Nope. This is my own."

"How about film?"

"Damn it, woman. Save the third degree for the bad guys."

"Sorry . . ."

The two uniformed officers turned the corner and ran up the three low steps which led to the casino's lobby. A doorman pulled open one of the heavy glass entries for them, and they moved through quickly, almost bumping into the backs of several large men in dark suits who appeared to suddenly disperse about their own business.

"Don't you think it's odd?" Tina asked.

"What's odd?" Calico replied, looking after the big men as they moved away.

"The doorman . . ."

"What?" Calico turned his attention back to Tina.

"The doorman," she said, slightly exasperated. "He didn't even blink at our uniforms and nobody else around here seems to be taking notice of the fact we're carrying guns."

"We're policemen," Calico replied as they walked rapidly across the lobby floor to the huge and imposing Wheel of Fortune table set off to one side. "We're invisible, like mail carriers or bellboys. We're part of the everyday scenery. People look at us without seeing us. It doesn't matter that we have badges which say City of Los Angeles instead of Las Vegas. All anyone sees and ignores is the uniform."

Around them the clinking of coins in the slot machines went on nonstop in the background, occasionally overrun by the sound of a small jackpot tinkling into metal cups. The casino floor was less populated than normal due to the hour and day, but there were still enough players around to keep half the card tables and machines busy. One of the three roulette tables on the main floor was operating for a sparse crowd.

Calico saw one of the large men who had preceded him and Tina into the lobby tap one of the obvious floor-security men on the shoulder and engage him in a brisk conversation before leading him away. Calico frowned.

At the Wheel of Fortune an older woman with bleach-blond hair and too much eye makeup smiled at the two officers through bee-stung lips which revealed a surprisingly beautiful set of white teeth. Her body, slid into a white-sequined sheath, didn't show the mileage which was revealed in the lines around her eyes, but Calico was willing to bet the condition was due more to the plastic surgeon's knife than to any aerobics instructor.

"Hi, my name is Laura," she said in a pleasant voice which Calico hadn't expected. "Do you want to try your luck?" She spun the big wheel behind her with one hand and then stopped it again before indicating, with a feminine wave of her other arm, the playing positions at the small table in front of her.

"No thanks," said Calico. "But you could help us out." He laid a ten-dollar bill on the gaming table.

Laura frowned at him. "If you've got something kinky in mind with those uniforms and nightsticks, it's going to take a lot more long green than that before I feel like playing along."

Calico's face turned red which made Tina laugh. She took the camera from Calico's hand and held it out toward Laura. "Anyone who can make him turn that color can't be all bad," she said, indicating her partner with a movement of her head. "We just need a quick picture taken."

The Wheel of Fortune spun around again with a push from Laura's hand as she laughed with Tina and took the camera. "Sure thing, honey. You guys must be having a wild weekend up here. I love the uniforms. Where did you get them?"

"We . . ." Calico sputtered before Tina stepped on his foot.

"Trade secret," Tina said with a wink and boosted herself up to sit on the gaming table and pulled Calico over to stand next to her. Laura moved around in front of the two officers after disappearing the ten spot down her cleavage. She brought the camera up to her face and peered through the viewfinder. "Smile big," she said.

Tina giggled. "Come on, honey," she said to Calico. "This shot should really give you something to talk about with the boys at the Elks Lodge when you get home."

Calico grunted, his attention suddenly drawn to the opening of a private elevator across the casino floor on the opposite wall. He saw four men, all looking down at the floor, their jackets bulging in odd shapes, step aboard. The casino employee who had been guarding the elevator had a strange and sickly look on his face. One of the men pressed the up button. As the flash of the camera went off in his face, and the doors of the elevator moved shut, there was a split second in which his mind took its own photo of two of the men inside pulling hockey death masks down over their faces.

He stood stunned for a second and then was distracted by a loud noise from his side.

"You bastards," Stack yelled, attempting to break loose from Thurman's grasp. "Were you trying to kill us with that tear gas?"

"Tear gas?" Laura said, still holding Calico's camera. "And two more johns in uniforms. You really are kinky, honey," she said to Tina. "You should go far in this town."

"Shut up," Stack said to her and reached for the camera and the developing photo in her hand.

Laura kicked him in the right shin. "Back off, sucker. You haven't paid the fee to crease my merchandise."

Stack howled and grabbed his leg. Tina jumped off the gaming table and kicked him in the other shin, dropping him to the floor. She twirled and took the camera from Laura. "Thanks, honey. Got to run." She grabbed Calico by the sleeve. "Let's go."

"Yeah," Calico said as Thurman hauled his partner off the floor, placed him in front of the Wheel of Fortune, and snapped his picture with his own Polaroid.

Tina pulled Calico away, but he grabbed one of Laura's arms and dragged her along. As he did so a wailing alarm sounded through the casino making everyone look away from the tables. Lights began to flash around the ceiling. "Is there another floor in the casino which has gambling on it?" he asked Laura.

"What's happening?" she asked.

"Answer me!"

"You're hurting me."

Calico pulled away from Tina and took hold of Laura with both hands.

"If you don't answer me, I'll break you in half. Is there another floor with gambling on it?"

"Yes . . . yes. The Lucky Thirteen club."

"Can you get there on the regular elevators?"

"No. You have to use the private elevator over there." Laura pointed toward the shaft where Calico had seen the men with the hockey masks enter.

"Shit."

"What is it?" Tina asked. "Come on. Stack and Thurman are already out of here." She dragged her partner away and out of the lobby through the heavy glass doors.

Calico's mind was spinning with possibilities, but it wasn't until he got outside and heard sirens sounding from other casinos up and down the Strip, a cacophony of jungle animals warning others of danger in their midst, that he decided on a course of action.

"It's a robbery hit," he said to Tina. "We can't leave."

"What are you talking about?"

"Just before the alarms started going off, I saw four guys get into the private elevator which leads up to that Lucky Thirteen club Laura was talking about."

"So?"

"They were wearing hockey masks and the bulges under their jackets weren't lumps of money."

Tina was silent for a moment. Calico didn't figure he had to explain anything else to her. She was smart enough to put two and two together and come up with an answer.

"We aren't cops in this town," she said. "If we get caught here, we are well and truly fried."

"Bullshit," said her partner. "We're cops wherever we are. City or state border lines don't make any difference. There is a robbery going on up there"—he pointed an arm and an extended finger up the side of the casino building—"and people could be getting killed. The local cops are going to be running around like beheaded chickens with all these alarms going off. We're the only ones who know where the action is. I can't walk away."

Tina looked at him and saw the pleading in his eyes. Thirty years of doing what a cop does poured out of them. "What if there are hits going on at the other casinos at the same time?"

"It doesn't change anything. We know about this one and we have to do something."

A squealing of tires drew their attention as Stack and Thurman roared away from the confusion.

Calico looked after them. "They don't matter. It's what's inside you that matters. What you instinctively know is wrong or right. Are you in or out?"

"What do you think?" Tina asked and turned back to run into the casino.

SIXTEEN

COLLISION COURSE

U PSTAIRS IN THE Lucky Thirteen things were going
well for Morgan and his boarding party. The elevator guard had been trussed up and moved out of the
way before the elevator doors had opened into the private club. As the four robbers had stepped out onto
the floor of The Lucky Thirteen, hockey masks securely in place, their apparition had coincided per-
fectly with the confusion of the alarms sounding.
Morgan and Bolt had immediately zapped the two
main-floor guards with tasers, sending both targets immediately to dream land. Merric followed up to take
the guards permanently out of the play by securing
their wrists, elbows, knees, and ankles with white surgical tape, while Morgan and Bolt ejected the pods
which contained the spent taser barbs and reloaded.
One of the patrons decided to play hero and made a
move on Chauncer only to be coolly hosed down with
tear-gas spray by the sparks man.

Several women started to scream as Morgan moved
quickly to the center of the room. He used his tear-gas
spray liberally to cause confusion and temporary pain
to several of the pit bosses as he zeroed in on Ollie
Sebastian's position. The bodyguard standing next to
Ollie dug under his shoulder for the hogleg buried

there, but before he could withdraw it his eyes lit up like Christmas bulbs, courtesy of two long-range taser barbs. Memories of the taser's shocking pain were still fresh in Ollie's mind and he had no wish to experience them again firsthand, so when Morgan turned the skull design on his hockey mask in Ollie's direction, the portly casino manager threw his hands skyward without any hesitation. Morgan smiled behind his mask, but all Sebastian saw was the death's-head grimace on the outside.

"Tell everyone to sit down." Morgan's voice was muffled from behind the mask. "Do it," he insisted as he brought the close-range stun gun up under Ollie's neck but did not activate it. Merric had moved in and done his taping job on the bodyguard. Throwing the half-empty roll of tape away, he jogged quickly over to join Chauncer who had already jumped the cashier's counter and was stuffing money from the open vault into one of his duffelbags.

"Everybody please calm down," Ollie said in a nervous voice.

"Climb up on the gaming table and tell 'em louder," Morgan told him. "I want everybody on the floor with their hands on their heads or you get a dose of what your bodyguard got and I find myself another spokesman."

Fear passed across Ollie's face but he did what he was told, climbing up onto the table in front of him and regaining some of the baritone timbre of command in his voice as he repeated his request.

"Better," said Morgan, "but it needs to be louder. Make them understand. Tell them nobody gets hurt if they do as you say."

Ollie looked down at Morgan. "The computers. . . ?" he asked in a quiet voice.

"You're going to need a whole new system."

Ollie felt better and again turned to face the confusion on the floor of the private club. "Please calm down," he asked, this time eliciting some response as the crowd began to react to the command in his voice. "There is no need to panic. If you sit on the floor with your hands on your heads I have been assured no harm will come to you. They are only after the money in the vault."

The voices of the crowd became a low rumble. One or two of the patrons began to sit down as Ollie had instructed, their acquiescence sparking the same response in the other gamblers who also moved onto their haunches or fannies before lacing their hands across the dome of their skulls. Several of the women were crying and, for the life of him, Morgan couldn't figure out why. He'd made no threat directly to them and the coup so far had been bloodless.

"Get down," he told Ollie who stepped off the table to stand next to Morgan.

Morgan looked over to the vault area where Merric gave him a thumbs-up sign indicating everything was going well.

"I'm a bit surprised," Morgan said to Ollie.

"About what?"

"I was sure you would try to pull something with the cash in the vault. Short us on the take or even have the damn vault locked up."

Ollie smiled. "I believe in giving money for value. You did me a valuable service with the computers. If the vault had been closed or short, my uncle would have twigged something was wrong. It didn't make sense to stiff you."

Movement by the stairway door caught Morgan's attention in the corner of his eye. He instinctively dove forward, driving his shoulders into Ollie Sebastian's gut and followed the corpulent casino boss to the floor as the crack of a .45 auto reverberated across the room.

"John!" Morgan screamed at Bolt, but it was unnecessary as the tall, laconic pilot had already swiveled to meet the threat, bringing what looked like an unholy union of a shotgun and a bazooka to his shoulder, and fired a twelve-ounce beanbag directly into the chest of the casino guard who was making his play for fame from the stairwell.

The impact of the beanbag lifted the guard off his feet and slammed him into the opposite wall of the stairwell four feet away. The heavy door he had hidden behind swung closed quietly on its pneumatic arm. There was screaming and a general wailing from the patrons again as Bolt reloaded and Morgan jumped to his feet.

"Sparks," Morgan yelled over at Chauncer. "Get those firebombs down the stairway now. We don't want any more surprises."

Chauncer moved quickly, dumping his two duffel-bags of cash into the private elevator which had been wedged open, and taking two ominous-looking, grenade-type objects from the pouch attached to his side. Merric was still stuffing money into his second bag while Bolt had turned his attention back to cover the patrons sitting on the floor.

Once at the stairwell, Chauncer put both of the firebombs in his left hand and reached for the handle of the door with his right. Observing the stunned casino guard still propped up against the opposite wall, he wedged his foot against the door to stop it from closing. As his eyes and attention moved from the guard to the implements of destruction in his hands, Tina burst through the opening and slashed the heel of her palm downward across the bridge of Chauncer's nose.

Blood spurted out two feet and splashed across

Tina's uniform blouse as she followed up her initial attack by driving the tip of her Monadnock baton into Chauncer's sternum. The sparks man dropped the fire-bombs, with their pins still intact, and threw his hands up to his face.

Calico followed Tina through the doorway, his blue steel .38 held out in a two-handed grip, his eyes taking in the situation around him in a split-second glimpse. He got the word "Freeze . . ." out of his mouth, but Bolt was already bringing the beanbag gun into play, the sound of the cartoon-shaped gun's explosive force overriding everything. Calico's shooting stance had not been the two-foot spread, body front, gun-centered tradition both favored and taught by the L.A.P.D. Rather it had been the Weaver side stance which he had seen demonstrated several years earlier and had adopted for the sole reason that it made more sense to make as small a target of yourself as possible. As a result the twelve-ounce beanbag caught him in the arms, sending his gun flying and numbing the feeling in his upper extremities, but it did not do the crushing damage to his chest that it had done to the casino guard. Nevertheless, off balance and stunned, he fell unceremoniously on his rear.

The door to the stairwell, which had been pneumatically closing with the removal of Chauncer's foot, suddenly flew open again as several of the large security men who had come with Augustus Sebastian burst through. Tina had wrapped Chauncer up with a spinning round kick and a baseball swing follow-through of her Monadnock before rolling away from the blag man to assess the situation. Her gun was drawn, but the patrons standing behind both Bolt and Morgan forced her to hold her fire. Augustus Sebastian's bully boys had no such compunction, however, as they let lead fly at everything in sight.

"Hold your fire, you shitheads," screamed Calico as he dug his two-inch backup gun out of its ankle holster.

"Move," yelled Morgan at Merric and Bolt as he zapped Ollie Sebastian with the close-range taser and leaped for the elevator.

Merric followed his boss, but Bolt was busy clawing out a machine pistol from the folds of his long jacket where it had been hiding on a sling down and across his back. He fired a short burst which took out one of Augustus Sebastian's security men and forced the others to dive for cover. Tina still didn't have a clear shot, as Bolt grabbed a woman off the floor to use as a shield, but Calico brought his two-inch to bear in a shaky grip.

"Don't do it, man. Don't add murder to robbery," Calico called out to the now crazy-eyed pilot.

Bolt turned the woman in Calico's direction. "Fuck you," he said and fired off another burst of bullets from the machine pistol, the first of which tore into Calico's forearm before the others raced to the casino ceiling as the woman in Bolt's arms fainted and spoiled his aim.

When the woman's dead weight slid away from Bolt's torso Tina fired two shots. Her aim was low, one bullet chipping out the floor at Bolt's feet, almost hitting the woman there, and the other doing little more than tag the meaty part of the blag man's buttocks. Bolt didn't even know he'd been hit.

Rolling away from her shooting position, Tina scrambled for cover as Bolt turned the machine pistol toward her. She heard Bolt scream, followed by a long burst from the machine pistol, and screwed her eyes tight, holding her breath, anticipating the ventilating pain of bullets ripping into her body. For a long second afterward, she couldn't believe she hadn't been hit, and then realized a strange silence had descended over the casino floor. She risked a quick opening of her eyes.

"I said no shooters, you asshole, and I meant no shooters," said Morgan Wales, standing upright over Bolt's body, connected to it by the twin barbs of a long-range taser. He hit the trigger on the housing unit in his hands again and Bolt began to flop around on the floor like a dying fish.

People were slowly coming to life again, moving around cautiously. Tina moved quickly across to Morgan with her gun held on the robbery mastermind who made no effort to stop her when she took the taser from him.

"Hello, my pretty," Morgan said to her, his clipped English still muffled by his hockey mask. "Any chance of getting a drink before you put the cuffs on?"

Tina spun Morgan around without saying a word, put one of her feet into the crease of his knees and forced him to the floor. She holstered her gun, drew her cuffs out of the pouch on her Sam Browne, and slipped them over the Englishman's slim wrists. She didn't, however, ratchet them down as tight as she might have done. She bent over close to Morgan's ear. "I don't know who you are or what your game is, mate," she said in a false but pleasant imitation of Morgan's accent, "but thanks for saving my ass. Look me up when you get out and I'll stand you to the coldest beer in town."

Morgan laughed quietly through his mask.

It took close to two hours before sanity returned to the Citadel and to the Strip. Chauncer's explosives had gone off at the city power generators before anyone could get to them, but within fifteen minutes secondary power sources had kicked in and Department of Water and Power crews had been sent out to repair the damage.

Before heading for Humana Hospital on Mayflower Parkway, Augustus Sebastian had taken command of proceedings at the Citadel with the firm hand of long experience. The security men he had brought with him took over key positions as he had originally arranged, and his nephew, Ollie, had been whisked away in Dobbins' care to be dealt with later.

The casino owner was put out when he realized the computer had been wiped clean by Morgan's crew, but he certainly didn't need to operate toward his nephew like he was conducting a court of law. He already knew what Ollie was about and didn't need any further evidence. Ollie would pay dearly for underestimating his uncle, figuring Augustus was still completely unaware of the scams he was running while managing the casino. But that could all be sorted out later, Augustus thought to himself, there were more pressing matters at hand.

Three of the four hockey-masked robbers were in the custody of the Las Vegas Police Department, but the fourth had disappeared down the private elevator with the two duffelbags of cash which had been tossed in there by the one called Chauncer. The L.V.P.D. had shut down the city within minutes of the alarms going off, but there was still no sign of the fourth robber. If he was still inside the city limits the police would catch up with him sooner or later, but something told Augustus the bird had flown. It didn't bother Augustus too much, though. He admired a good caper, and this one had been excellent even though it had come unraveled in the end. After all, he himself came from a long line of family members who had earned their money the old-fashioned way—they stole it.

The hospital walls were a filmy green color, reminding the casino owner of bile as he walked with a slow gait from the waiting room toward the emergency treatment room where an older doctor was busy caring for Calico's arm.

"Sir, you can't go in there," said a young bucktoothed nurse, laying a soft hand on Augustus' arm as he passed her station.

"It's all right, nurse," interjected the doctor without looking up from the suturing job he was performing. "Mr. Sebastian is expected."

"Sorry, Doctor," said the nurse, a miffed expression crossing her face as her authority was overridden.

"Hello, Foster," Sebastian said to the doctor.

"It's been a long time, Augie. I've missed you."

"I don't suppose your wallet has though. You never were able to break even at our weekly poker sessions."

The doctor laughed. "Money comes and goes. Friends, however, are another story."

"You must be the Calico Jack Walker I've been hearing so much about." Augustus spoke directly to Calico for the first time, noticing the sweat beads across the policeman's forehead.

Calico only grunted in reply, preferring to concentrate on a corner of the room as the doctor finished the stitches.

"If I didn't know you better, Foster, I'd say you didn't use enough local to kill the pain."

"I didn't use any," the doctor replied. "He refused it. Cops and cowboys—you can't figure them."

"Why?" Augustus asked Calico in amazement.

Calico winced. "Pain is nature's way of saying you fucked up, but you're still alive. If you live with the pain of your fuck ups, perhaps you won't make the same mistake again somewhere down the road."

"Cops and cowboys," said the doctor again as he finished his patch job.

"How bad is it?" Augustus asked.

"He was lucky," Foster replied. "The shot tunneled a graze down his forearm and then blew through the right biceps. Tore up some of the muscle, but no permanent damage done. Need a sling for a while though."

"No sling," said Calico.

"Listen, cowboy," said Foster with a sigh. "I'll go along with no anesthetic, but you're not leaving this hospital until you've got a sling round that wing. Your choice—no ticky, no washy. No slingy, not walky out of here."

"Can he travel?" asked Augustus.

"With a sling."

Calico grunted.

"I've just spent the last ten minutes talking with your partner," Augustus said. "She's a very impressive young lady."

"She'll do," said Calico.

"She also explained to me what staying around to stop the robbery of my casino could cost you."

"You play, you pay," said Calico. "It all evens up in the end."

"What happened to your 'life is hard and then you die' line?" asked Tina as she too stepped into the emergency room.

Calico looked at her with a smile. "Must have leaked out through the hole," he said, moving his crippled appendage gingerly.

A thoughtful look flitted across Augustus Sebastian's brow as he came to a decision. "I think I still have enough sway in this town to square you with the police department here, and I'd hate to see you lose this race you're involved in on account of my casino . . ."

"That's right nice of you, Mr. Sebastian," Calico stated. "But there is no way we're ever going to catch Stack and Thurman now. We don't even stand a chance of getting back by the end of our shift."

"Are you a betting man, Mr. Walker?"

"I'll give you odds on it."

"In that case, I think I have the solution to your problems. That is if you're willing to play a longshot?"

Calico looked from Augustus to Tina whose eyes widened slightly in encouragement.

"No guts, no glory," he said finally. "What do you have in mind?"

SEVENTEEN

THE SEBASTIAN SOLUTION

T HE DIFFUSED LIGHT of the false dawn crept slowly over the Shadow Mountains before suddenly spilling down into Victor Valley like a lioness stalking and then attacking her prey. Highway Eighteen, the shorter but more punishing route to the finish line of the run, bisected the arid, little populated area as it raced toward the Los Angeles County line and, beyond there, the Antelope Valley Freeway.

"Any sign of them?"

"For the tenth time in five minutes, no," Thurman told his partner as he craned his neck around to check through the shattered rear window for any signs of Calico and Tina in pursuit. "Would you calm down. We're home free. Ain't no way they can catch us now."

"Bite your tongue . . ."

"Wait," Thurman's voice filled with alarm. "What the hell is that?"

"Oh, shit," said Stack, taking his eyes off the road for a second to hang his head down without even looking around to see what his partner was talking about. It had to be bad. Eventually he raised his eyes to look in the Highway Patrol cruiser's rearview mirror, seeing nothing behind him but empty road. There was noth-

273

ing in front of the speeding cruiser either except for a sign announcing the L.A. County line.

"I don't believe it," said Thurman in awe.

"What? What?" asked Stack, confusion making him angry. And then the first sounds of heavy, beating blades entered his body through his ears and seemed to reverberate his vital organs inside him. "What is it?" he asked again, anger now giving way to the first inklings of irrational panic.

"I'm seeing it, but I don't believe it. You better put the pedal to the metal, partner. Calico and Blanche have just bought back into this race."

Behind and above Stack and Thurman's cruiser, a huge Sikorsky S-64 Skycrane helicopter was a black silhouette against the orange glow of the dawn light shafting across the mountain crests. The Skycrane's six egg-beater blades cut through the morning air in great, thumping swaths. It was a beautiful sight of power and beauty, one which had been a constant comfort to the U.S. troops in Viet Nam as part of assault-support companies before coming home to be put to commercial use hauling huge loads of raw materials. Hanging under the cut-out belly of the Skycrane was Calico and Tina's black and white police unit, suspended from the mother ship on a taut umbilical cord of steel-belted straps.

"There they are," said Tina from her position in the driver's seat of the cruiser as she pointed a finger down at the highway below them.

Calico was sitting next to her, nursing his sling-supported arm. With his good hand he reached over and picked up the hand-held walkie-talkie which they had been using to communicate with Augustus Sebastian and the pilot who were in the two-seat bubble of the helicopter above them. Never particularly fond of flying, he wasn't real happy with Sebastian's solution to the problem of catching up with Stack and Thurman.

But he had been impressed with the masterful way Sebastian organized the Skycrane, leased by one of his other business interests in Las Vegas and hangared at McCarran International; the pilot, forced out of bed with his girlfriend; and the loading of the police cruiser, as if it were all an everyday occurrence. By the time Sebastian finished making the necessary phone calls from the hospital's staff room, and escorted Calico and Tina to the airport, the blades of the Skycrane were already warming up and everything was ready to go. Calico almost balked when he realized he and Tina would be riding in the cruiser suspended below the helicopter, but she dragged him inside and told him to quit whining. "Do you expect to live forever?" she'd asked him. It was a question he'd never really considered.

"Yo, Big Bird," he said into the walkie-talkie. "That's our quarry in front of us. Set us down anywhere along here and we'll take over, just do it gently. We don't want to burst our tires."

"Whatever you say, Walker," Sebastian's voice returned over the radio. "I have to say it's been interesting. You certainly know how to add spice to an old man's life. Give me a call and tell me how things turn out. And next time you make a Vegas run, plan to stay at the Citadel's expense."

"Thanks for the ride," said Calico as the gigantic helicopter, which had sped them back toward L.A. as the crow flies, descended from the sky to set the cruiser down on the desert hardpack near the side of the highway about a hundred yards in front of Stack and Thurman. The pilot released the ratchet lock on the straps which attached it to the police unit, and Tina put the cruiser in gear and sped out from underneath the hovering Skycrane like a tasty morsel escaping from the clutches of a dragonfly.

The tires of the squad car spun clouds of dust skyward to compete with the dust storm created by the prop wash from the Skycrane. The rear tires broke loose for a second to fishtail the cruiser's rear end as Tina accelerated toward the highway tarmac where Stack and Thurman had just sped past.

"Can you handle the power of this baby?" Calico asked Tina as she bounced the unit onto the roadway.

"I'll certainly be able to do a better job than you can with that busted wing. And if you're going to backseat drive from here to home base you're going to have to show me your license to do so."

Calico grunted and then winced as Tina drove through a dip, causing him to jostle his injured arm against the car door.

"You better hold onto that arm 'cause things aren't going to get any better till we hit the Antelope Valley Freeway."

"Don't fuss, woman, just drive. I can take it."

"Suit yourself," Tina said and accelerated into a particularly vicious dip.

Calico let out a yelp and grabbed his arm. "Son of a bitch! Are you trying to kill me?"

Tina laughed. "So you do feel pain. I was beginning to wonder."

"Yeah, I feel pain. If you're satisfied now, how about you do something about catching up with and passing those two bastards in front of us?"

"Yes, bwana."

The dissipating darkness of the night still hugged the roadway, refusing to give ground without a fight to the ever-lightening sky. The cars of early risers began to appear with more frequency along the highway. Stack and Thurman, still in the lead of the procession, had their lights and siren working full-time keeping the roadway clear, scattering passenger cars and trucks onto the soft shoulders ahead of them like startled sheep.

Tina tried to use Stack and Thurman's progress to judge her speed and anticipate most of the dips in the highway as they fell away from under the cruiser's wheels like rippling ocean waves. The police frequency radio in the console had begun to crackle faintly again as they came within range, but neither Tina or Calico picked up on their unit designation among the few calls which were being assigned.

Calico eventually broke the silence which had descended between him and his partner over the last few miles.

"About the other night . . ." he started.

"When we made love?" Tina asked, not turning her head to look at him.

"Yes." He was constantly surprised at how aware Tina was on the peripheral, almost always knowing what he was referring to even if he started a conversation in the middle of left field like he had now.

"You picked a strange time to bring it up."

"I couldn't wait any longer for the right time to come along. It has been building up inside me until it just popped out."

"If you would have held on another two heartbeats it would have popped out of me."

Calico looked at her and smiled, but Tina had her eyes concentrating strictly on the road, both hands firmly on the steering wheel at ten and two o'clock. The soft morning light backlit her hair and shot shadows off of her sharp cheekbones. Calico thought she was so beautiful it made his teeth hurt.

"These types of emotions aren't supposed to happen to me anymore."

"What do you mean?" Tina asked. Her own emotions were expressed only through the fact the cruiser was beginning to pick up speed and close the gap with Stack and Thurman. "Do you think you are too old to fall in love?"

"It's what I've thought for a long time. Marriages which work these days are an exception to the rule, and I'm not just talking about police marriages. The ones which work are in a constant state of negotiation, concessions being given on both sides, a monument to compromise. I'm not good at marriage."

"Do you have to have marriage to have love?"

"It's the logical conclusion even if the marriage is without the legalities of church or state."

With the increase of speed the dips in the roadway added jarring punctuation to the partners' conversation. Ahead of them Stack and Thurman appeared to be running full out, while beneath Tina's foot there was still a quarter of the gas pedal left before she touched the floorboards.

"Your problem, partner," she said as she pulled out into the oncoming eastbound traffic lanes and put her foot to the floor, "is you think your soul is older than your heart." As she pulled the cruiser alongside Stack and Thurman, an eighteen-wheel tractor-trailer rig filled the girth of the eastbound lanes lumbering directly at them.

"Tina . . ." Calico started when he began to realize his partner was not backing off the gas.

"Face it, damn it," Tina said, her mind refusing for once to acknowledge the change in direction of Calico's comment.

"No, that's not what . . . Tina!" Calico braced himself as the semitrailer's air horn blasted a panicked warning over the caterwalling sirens of the two police cars.

Calico closed his eyes tightly and forced all the air out of his lungs.

"I said face it," Tina screamed. "I don't know when it happened or how it happened, but I love you and damn it you love me."

"Yes, I love you!" Calico screamed as the semitrailer roared past them, forced to scrape the shoulder of the road on one side while Stack and Thurman were forced to the shoulder on the opposite side with Tina splitting the difference. In a fractional second of time which lasted for eternity, the three vehicles all seemed to share the same road space and then Tina and Calico's cruiser spurted loose, like a bar of soap held too tightly in the bathtub, and slid back into the proper westbound lane ahead of Stack and Thurman.

"Well, I'm glad we have that settled," said Tina calmly.

Calico opened one eye. "Thousands die," he said, quoting the make-believe headline he thought should have ensued from Tina's driving habits.

Ahead of them, Tina could see the entrance for the Antelope Valley Freeway. "Fifteen minutes to the finish line, partner. Let's put paid to these cowboys."

To their rear, Stack's voice reached them with the aid of his P.A. system. "It ain't going to be that easy, Blanche."

The parking lot at Van Nuys station was crowded with cops from both the morning shift and the oncoming day shift. Anticipation was in the air as everyone kept checking their watches and looking out at the various street approaches to the station in hopes of catching the first glimpse of the racing cars. Several of the units were being assigned nonemergency calls. The calls were acknowledged, but still nobody left the parking lot. The response-time average was going to be shot to hell.

"There," shouted Wild John as he hopped off the low retaining wall which bordered the lot and pointed a callused finger toward a roar of noise, a cloud of dust, and a vague black and white shape which seemed to be flying toward the station in a blur of speed.

"Who is it?" asked a voice from the crowd, but it was too soon for an answer.

Looking out of the picture window of his office on the third floor of the police building, Captain Morrison crossed his fingers and offered up a little prayer.

A second blur of black and white roared onto the home stretch behind the first, but it was clear there was no way it could run down the bullet in front of it.

"Come on, come on," Wild John whispered to himself before shouting, "It's Calico!" when he was three-quarters sure of the identity of the lead car.

A squeal of tires as the cruiser turned into the parking lot, scattering cops in front of it, confirmed the identity as Tina braked to a halt on the slick surface of the lot. By the time Stack and Thurman had pulled in behind the leaders, the assembled cops had hauled Tina out of the car and were carrying her around on their shoulders accompanied by wild cheers. Calico too was surrounded by friends and coworkers. Wild John was pumping Calico's good hand and saying over and over again, "Hot shit, I don't believe you did it. Hot shit."

Metro coppers who had come down to support Stack and Thurman were gathered around the purloined Highway Patrol cruiser giving support to the two men who, even though they had lost the race, were still a part of the legend which had just been forged. Plans were already being hatched to return the Highway Patrol cruiser in a fashion which would best embarrass the C.H.P. while covering Stack and Thurman's rear ends.

As the congratulations built to a crescendo the door to the police building unexpectedly burst open, crashing against the wall behind it, and Sal Fazio stepped out into the parking lot like a knife into the back of the celebration. His uniform was smeared with mud, his pants bagged around his knees where normally rested a razor-sharp crease. One tail of his shirt was out and soot still marred one cheek. His hair was on end, slightly singed, and the smell of smoke emanated around him in an invisible aura.

"You. You bastard," he said in a quietly dangerous voice to Calico who had turned to face him. "You're responsible for this and I'm going to make you pay."

The corners of Calico's mouth started to turn up slightly. He fought it but it was a losing battle as laughter started way down in his lungs and exploded out of him in a gusher as he took in the sight of Sal Fazio before him. Calico held his arm, pain lancing through it from the convulsions of laughter racking his body, and almost doubled over with hilarity. Around him the shocked expressions of the other policemen began to give way to amusement as Calico's laughter became a contagious virus of giggling.

"Oh, Sal," said Calico through the tears of laughter streaming down his face and then bursting into another fit of giggles which left him so weak he had to lean back against one of the patrol units. "If you could see yourself."

"Laugh all you want, but I've got you. That injury to your arm proves you weren't on duty last night and that car you pulled in here with is not the one you were assigned."

Calico made an effort to straighten up, but laughter got the better of him again. Tina came over and elbowed him in the ribs which settled him down some.

"Sal, Sal," he said. "You're right I didn't work the field last night. I was driving to Vegas and back. Had a hell of a good time."

"Then you admit it. You all heard him admit it," Fazio said to everyone gathered around. "Neglect of duty, misappropriation of city property, giving false and misleading statements to a supervisor. I've got you, you bastard. Your pension is history."

"Not quite, Sal. You see it was okay for me to go to Vegas last night."

"What the hell do you mean?"

"Well, you see, I went down to the pension board earlier this week and put my papers in. I became officially retired after yesterday's morning watch shift. Even though I turned up for Saturday night in time to start Sunday's morning watch shift, I was already retired. Coupled with the fact the black and white I've been driving all night belongs not to the city but to my good buddy Wild John, who bought it at the police auction, I haven't even misappropriated city property as you so eloquently put it."

"What?" Fazio looked about to fall apart.

Calico shrugged his shoulders. "Sorry, Sal. You lose." A cheer rose up from the crowd of coppers.

"What about your partner?" Fazio screamed.

"I was kidnapped," said Tina calmly. "But, hey, if you think you've got me, then go ahead and take your best shot. I have broad shoulders, I can handle the heat."

Another voice cut through the cheering. "Hey! A two-eleven silent just went off at the liquor store Victory and Fulton," said Ray Perkins who was standing close enough to one of the police units to hear the call come out over the radio. Immediately the parking lot was filled with action as everyone on duty jumped into their units and laid rubber in the direction of the robbery-in-progress call.

EIGHTEEN

EPILOGUE

THERE WAS DEFINITELY a black hole inside of him, a void where the star, his existence for thirty years, had finally burned out. A vast space of nothingness which he had no idea how to fill. Calico knew retirement would be different, but he hadn't realized how hard leaving the job would hit him. Knowing it was foolish didn't help the fact he suddenly felt like an outsider, no longer privy to the brotherhood of the badge. He felt guilty other cops were going to work without him, as if he were letting down the side. He also felt irrationally hurt that the police department could continue smoothly without him. It seemed the last thirty years of laying his life on the line, kicking ass and taking names, patching up broken lives, broken marriages, broken children, and broken dreams, had had no more effect than an aspirin on a brain hemorrhage.

There was a slight drizzling mist around the marina at King Harbor which shrouded the moored, creaking boats, both pleasure crafts and working rigs. The night was what Calico's father would have called black-smith's black, the moon and stars obscured by heavy clouds, the yellow glow of streetlights holding back as if fearful to venture into the darkness.

283

It was two A.M. on Tuesday morning. A time when Calico would normally be cruising the streets looking for drunk drivers pulling away from closing bars. His body hadn't adjusted yet to straight hours so he couldn't sleep, and instead found himself wandering around through the silence of the marina where he and his son would shortly be starting a new phase of life. The melancholiness which had overcome him would pass, he knew, but for a while he would cling to it as the last tie to the world he had left behind.

He wandered aimlessly across the deserted parking lot of Beach Bum Burt's, an island motif restaurant-bar, with a roll-back roof, where he had often spent his off evenings awash in teriyaki steak, Heineken beer, and kamikazes. There was a rumor the restaurant was to be sold, and if true, it would be another part of his life to put behind him. If he hung around long enough perhaps he would get used to change.

On the other hand, he thought, as a slim figure stepped out of the mist in front of him and struck a menacing pose in the diffused streetlights, the more things changed, the more they remained the same.

Even though he had discarded the sling, Calico's right arm was still virtually useless, hanging by his side like a dead steer. His ribs still hurt from old Number 98 and his knees weren't what they used to be. Over-all, though, he wasn't too worried by the apparition, he was in as good a shape as he ever was. A huge sniff of the night air filled his nostrils with the prison stench of King Carradine.

"Cali-co," said the wraith from the mist, drawing the name out into two long syllables filled with black soul. "Gots a message to be delivering from the King."

There was still an off-duty backup gun strapped to his ankle above his Nike high tops, but Calico knew the gun might as well be on the moon for all the chance he was going to get to pull up the leg of his tight, stovepipe Levis and get to it. He took several deep breaths, measuring the distance between himself and his assailant, before moving sideways slowly toward the marina railing which ran around the parking lot to stop drunks from dropping into the water.

"Start your gums flappin', boy. I'm waiting." As he spoke, his tone and inflection designed to bait, Calico took another sidestep toward the railing.

Jack Ketch snatched the nunchaku from around his waist and with blurring speed whipped the chain-joined pipes around his head and shoulders in a blazing display of ability. "Ain't nobody's boy, muthafucka."

"You must be lying 'cause your lips be moving." Calico continued to bait, his voice a perfect imitation of Jack Ketch's street jive. He took three more steps and ducked under the railing to balance on the two feet of concrete left before the land dropped off into the water of the harbor.

Ketch moved in after his target, whistling the nunchaku through the air and then crashing the free end down twice on the railing, once on either side of Calico, before allowing it to bounce back to its at-rest position, one pipe in his right hand the other trapped and nestled in the holsterlike sheath formed by his right armpit.

"The King says the Hangman gots to take you down, Cali-co."

Without bending over, Calico reached down and pulled his pants leg up to reveal his backup gun. He kept his eyes on Ketch, praying for an opportunity to bend over and grab the gun now it was in the clear.

"They warned me you is a bad mutha-fucka. But we both be carrying hardware, honkie, and I can damn sure get to mine a lot faster than you can get to that rat killer." Ketch smiled widely, displaying his ivories which had been filed to razor sharpness by a dentist inmate so Ketch could tear easily into human flesh during a knock-down drag-out fight. One of his front teeth sported a diamond inset. Standing with casual ease, he pulled back the front of his open Levi jacket to reveal the grips of the gun nestled at his waist.

The water and safety were behind him, but Calico knew that wasn't the route he wanted to take unless absolutely necessary. He'd goaded Carradine into sending an assassin after him and somehow he had to use Ketch to keep Carradine behind prison walls.

"You goin' down, Cali-co. The King says you gots to die."

"You forgot to say 'once upon a time,' boy."

"What you talking about, fool?"

"That's the way all fairy tales start."

Ketch whipped the nunchaku out again, shooting it out in front of him, grazing Calico's head, and then flicking it back under his arm. Ketch giggled strangely, the sound echoing in the night. "You be the only fairy I see, muthafucka."

Calico did not watch the dead eyes in Ketch's face for his clue to the next move. Instead, he concentrated on the muscles along either side of the black assassin's neck which would telegraph the next attack. When it came, Calico rolled with all the speed he could muster under the safety railing and crashed into Ketch's legs like a gutterball which had somehow miraculously jumped back onto the alley to pick up a difficult five–nine spare. Ketch went down sharply but slithered away like a serpent before Calico could get a grip on him.

Grabbing for the gun at his ankle, Calico felt the stinging blow of the nunchaku as it smashed across his hand, numbing it and sending lightning bolts of jarring pain to his brain. His two-inch skittered away and dropped into the murky harbor waters. He tried to roll after it, but the nunchaku hit him again, this time across the shoulders. Ketch was playing with him, enjoying the beating he was delivering, and Calico knew it.

The killer's giggling was building to a fever pitch, an insane hyena about to devour a helpless prey. Calico was on his knees cradling his bad arm and hand. Ketch stood over him, the nunchaku dangling from his right hand.

"Kiss you ass good-bye muthafucka."

Ketch's right hand brought the nunchaku up above his head where he began to twirl it in anticipation of crashing it down on Calico's head with skull-crashing force. The yell of physical power, which exploded from the killer's lungs, turned suddenly to a scream of pain when a lance of flame flashed across the parking lot preceding the crack of the bullet which turned Ketch's elbow to mush. The killer involuntarily spun to his left and dropped to the ground when another bullet tore into the back of his left knee and blew bits of bone out of his kneecap.

Moving with reserves of strength he didn't know he had, Calico leaped on his attacker and drove his good right hand into Ketch's chest, over the heart. It was a stunning blow which gave Calico time to drag the gun out of Ketch's waistband. He then rolled away from the killer and climbed unsteadily to his feet.

"You took your fucking time," he said in a shaky voice to Wild John who had sprinted across the parking lot with his gun in hand. "You were supposed to be watching my back."

"Hey, come on, I was taking a leak. I obviously can't leave you alone for a minute without you getting yourself into trouble. Looks like your bait was good enough to catch your first fish, though," he said, prodding Ketch with his booted foot. "Little on the small side, isn't he? Perhaps we'll have to throw him back."

"What you talking about? I'm bleeding to death, man. Call me an ambulance."

"Okay, you're a fucking ambulance," said Calico, making Wild John laugh. "I think my partner is right. We should just throw you back for being under the size limit. Throw you right back into the prison hole you came from. Right back where King Carradine can work you over for screwing up." Calico put his foot on Ketch's shattered knee and applied pressure. "You, of course, won't be in any shape to fight back." Ketch screamed and Calico backed off slightly. "You'll just have to lay there and take it as Carradine arranges for every con in the stir to poke you in the ass before he gets real serious."

"What do you want from me?"

Wild John laughed quietly again. "He might be small, but he ain't dumb."

Calico bent down on one knee and put his face up close to Ketch's. "I want Carradine. And you're going to give him to me."

"Are you crazy?" Ketch jumped with surprise.

With deliberation, Calico took Ketch's gun and pointed it at the ground alongside Ketch's head. He pulled the trigger. Even Wild John jumped, but not nearly as far as Ketch did. The badly injured black man screamed as the pain in his shattered joints from his thrashing about flared to match the pain in his ear and the burning along the side of his face.

Calico drove the barrel of the gun viciously into Ketch's good left knee, his finger whitening perceptibly. "You'll give me Carradine or, so help me God, I'll make it easier for him to screw you over than it is now. You might have commanded respect as a 'smoke' in the joint, but how much respect do you think a cripple who can't even wipe his own ass is going to get?"

"What do you want me to do?"

"John . . ." Calico said to his old partner who bent over and handed him a pocket tape recorder. "Now, while John here goes and calls an ambulance, you and I are going to have a little on the record chat which you're going to repeat for the parole board when Carradine's case comes up on Wednesday."

"He'll kill me."

"It's him or me, man. If I kill you it ends for you here tonight. If you testify against Carradine, I've already arranged with the D.A. to give you immunity. You'll still be on the outside. You'll have a chance to run. A chance to try and bury yourself deep enough Carradine won't be able to reach you. It won't be much of a chance, but any chance is better than none."

"What if I later deny what's on the tape."

"Then you go back inside and a copy of the tape will end up played over the prison P.A. system."

Calico watched Ketch's eyes and knew he had won. "Call an ambulance, John. We're in business here."

Nevada's Clark County jail was being good to Morgan Wales.

"Come on, my old son, put the money up or walk away. The point is seven. I've rolled three in a row. I'm willing to bet I can do it again the hard way."

The pile of valuables on the floor of the jail corridor was a curious mixture of paper money, coins, cigarettes, dirty magazines, and the odd homemade weapon or two. Wales held the twin ivories in his left hand and shook them vigorously under the noses of the cons assembled around him. "What's it going to be?"

More jailhouse tarrif was added to the pile and Wales smiled like a barracuda, changed hands with the dice, and slung them casually against the jail wall. Without waiting to look (he had read the result as the dice had rolled off his fingers), he began to gather his booty. The crowd around him groaned as the dice came up in his favor for the fourth time in a row.

"Thank you very much, gentlemen. Next time you get a little action going, don't forget to give me a call." He scooped up the dice and gave them to the con who had been running the game. "Ta, mate." He walked away as casually as he had thrown the dice.

Back in his cell he took a tattered envelope and lay on his bunk to reread, for the thousandth time, the letter inside it. He received the letter right after he had been bound over for trial and it had done much to relieve the gloom of prison life, giving him a new challenge.

The letter was in a strong, bold hand written on stationery from one of London's top hotels but was postmarked in Paris.

> Dear Uncle Morgan,
> I'm sorry to hear about your troubles, but from what I understand you made the right decision. I on the other hand have been more fortunate with my business practices. Those flying lessons I scrimped and saved for a few years ago finally paid dividends helping me to pull a million-dollar-plus contract out of the desert. I have been able to return to home base a winner and am planning to invest my profits wisely so there will be enough to take care of the family.

I'm not sure yet when I can arrange to be
in your area again, but it will be in the near
future, so don't be surprised if I drop by for
an unannounced visit. Until then I have
asked the family solicitor to come by and see
what can be done to help you out.

Cordially,
Your nephew,
Brixton

Morgan smiled and his heart began to pound thinking of the possibilities for Merric's unannounced visit.
The cocky little bastard had escaped clean with a cool
million, but wasn't going to forget his obligations.
He'd been examining the extent of his temporary
home with an eye toward escape ever since Merric's
letter had arrived. There was absolutely no doubt in
his mind it was possible, in fact it should be a doddle.
It was after the escape was accomplished, though, that
excited him. He'd made a few mistakes the first time
he'd tried to take down the Citadel. Next time . . .

Thursday brought with it a perfect morning. It was
Indian-summer warm without a trace of mist, smog,
haze, or rain. The water outside of King Harbor
winked and twinkled as if the stars from the night sky
had sunk into it.

A warm breeze wrapped around Tina's exposed legs
as she walked confidently down the dock toward Calico's boat wearing a simple yellow sundress and san-
dals. A wide-brimmed straw hat, with a flowing yellow
ribbon to match her dress, was in her left hand, and a
huge picnic hamper in her right. Ren saw her first as
she approached and called out to his father who came
out onto the deck of the boat to greet her.

"Permission to come aboard, Captain?" she said

cheekily, holding up her hat to shade her eyes as she looked up at Calico.

Calico wore only a pair of once-white stone-washed jeans, the hair on his chest a thick gray mat mixed with sweat and grime. "You weren't supposed to come until tomorrow. I wanted everything to be finished."

"I couldn't wait," said Tina. "Anyway, it looks like the paint is dry," she continued, pointing to the letters which spelled out the boat's new name, THIEFTAKER, freshly applied to the stern. "So it's time for the christening." She put the picnic hamper on the ground and opened the top to expose several bottles of champagne, a pile of sandwiches, cold beer, and other goodies.

"Permission granted," said Ren over his father's objections when he caught sight of the contents of the basket.

Calico grumbled under his breath but smiled happily when he helped Tina on board and she gave him a huge kiss for his efforts. His face colored when Ren laughed at him, and then became even redder when Tina laughed at his blushing. "No respect for elders around here," he said.

"How did it go yesterday?" Tina asked him.

"Carradine's parole was denied and the D.A. is bringing charges against him for conspiracy to commit murder."

"What's happening with Ketch?"

"D.A. gave him immunity and has put him in protective custody until the preliminary hearing on the new charges against Carradine. After that he's on his own. How did it go with you?" he ended, knowing Tina had gone before a police disciplinary Board of Rights for participating in the Vegas run.

"Seeing as the majority of the supervisors sitting on the board had won money on the run, it wasn't too bad. They gave me a ten-day suspension and a harsh verbal admonishment for the sake of appearances. Then after the board was adjourned, two of the captains asked if I'd be interested in transferring to their divisions and another one asked me out."

"The dirty old man," Calico said, making Tina laugh and give him another hug and kiss. "So, you have ten days off?"

"Yep."

"Fancy a spot of fishing?"

"Only if we cook it before we eat it. I hate sushi."

Ren broke into the exchange to pass out the three champagne glasses Tina had brought with her filled to the brim with Korbel Brut. "How about a toast?" he asked his father.

Calico looked around at Ren, a son any man would be proud to claim, and then at Tina, the beautiful woman who was his lover. He took in the graceful artistry of the marina, the fineness of the day, and the solidness of the boat under his feet. He reflected briefly on the fulfillment of the thirty-year career behind him and the appeal of the future in front of him. He smiled, and with great satisfaction, he held up his glass of champagne and declared, "Life is hard and then you die."

Special thanks to the following people for their inspiration, patience, and support during the writing of this manuscript: Det. I Kenneth Belt, Det. III Edward Pikor, Det. II Sandra Hendricks, Plm. III Harry Hollywood, Det. III Stanley Miller, Det. II Karol Chouinard, and my partner in crime Bob Kenney.

ABOUT THE AUTHOR

Paul Bishop was born in England in 1954. He immigrated to America with his parents in 1962 after spending several years in Vancouver, Canada. He is a ten-year veteran of the Los Angeles Police Department and has worked such varied assignments as uniform patrol, juvenile investigations, sex crimes, vice, robbery, and auto theft. He is currently assigned to the detective squad in West Valley division. He categorically denies ever making an on-duty run such as the one described in this novel and will continue to do so until the statute of limitations has expired.